Praise for
The Sacred Seal,
BOOK ONE IN THE GOODFELLOW CHRONICLES

"...a fantastical journey..."—*The Globe and Mail*

"...an imaginative, action-packed narrative.... Children who love reading will adore this book."
—*The United Church Observer*

"...J. C. Mills has crafted an intriguing fantasy...an engaging adventure.... Altogether a delightful read-aloud."
—Martha Scott, Canadian Children's Book Centre

"A new, young hero is about to emerge in children's literature, from the imagination of author J. C. Mills."
—*Books for Everyone*

"Certain books keep our attention to the point that we have difficulty putting them down. But these are books intended for adults. It comes, therefore, as a surprise when a children's novel has the same don't-put-me-aside impact on an adult reader.... *The Sacred Seal*...is one of those books."—*Lancette*

***

Chosen as one of the "Best Books for the Fall" by CBC Radio "This Morning" Children's Book Panel, November 2001

THE GOODFELLOW CHRONICLES

BOOK TWO

THE MESSENGERS

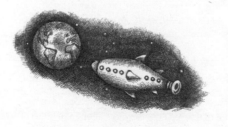

J. C. MILLS

KEY PORTER BOOKS

National Library of Canada Cataloguing in Publication Data

Mills, Judith
The messengers / J.C. Mills.

(The Goodfellow chronicles ; bk. 2)
ISBN 1-55263-551-1

I. Title. II. Series: Mills, Judith. Goodfellw chronicles ; bk. 2.

PS8576.1571M47 2003   jC813'.54   C2002-905159-2
P27

THE CANADA COUNCIL | LE CONSEIL DES ARTS
FOR THE ARTS | DU CANADA
SINCE 1957 | DEPUIS 1957

ONTARIO ARTS COUNCIL
CONSEIL DES ARTS DE L'ONTARIO

The publisher gratefully acknowledges the support of the Canada Council for the Arts and the Ontario Arts Council for its publishing program.

We acknowledge the financial support of the Government of Canada through the Book Publishing Industry Development Program (BPIDP) for our publishing activities.

Key Porter Books Limited
70 The Esplanade
Toronto, Ontario
Canada M5E 1R2

www.keyporter.com

Design: Peter Maher
Electronic formatting: Jean Lightfoot Peters

Printed and bound in Canada

03 04 05 06 5 4 3 2

*To the memory of my
grandparents*

"We have a guardian because we serve a
great cause, and shall have that guardian as long as
we serve that cause faithfully."

WINSTON CHURCHILL

CONTENTS

1

THE JOURNEY OF A MILLION MILES BEGINS WITH A SINGLE STEP

Kicking his feet against a tangled ball of bedsheets, Sam awoke for a few seconds before slowly slipping back to sleep. The strange dream returned then, just as it had every morning for the past week and a half. In the first moments of dawn, as his mind drifted in that filmy place somewhere between the real world and the realm of dreams, Sam heard someone call his name.

The voice was familiar: it was kind and friendly, and from the very first time he had heard it, Sam was certain it belonged to Edgar Goodfellow. Pulled into the dream again, Sam began what had now become an exhausting ritual. Rushing through a maze of dimly lit passages, he followed his friend's voice, stumbling over piles of jagged rocks and boulders that tore through the thin cotton of his pajamas and scraped painfully against his legs. Up and down trails that seemed to twist and turn back on themselves, Sam pursued Edgar each and every morning, until, breathless and bleeding, he would turn one final corner. There, the misty vision of his small friend, waving his arms wildly, beckoned to Sam with words he could never quite understand. And in this dream, as in every dream that had come before, the vision and the voice grew steadily fainter, disappearing altogether as Edgar suddenly vanished into thin air with a tiny burst of blinding light and a puff of red dust.

Hurled back into the real world, Sam stared into the darkness of his room, frustrated that he was still no closer to understanding Edgar's mysterious message. Lifting his head from a pillow that was damp with perspiration, Sam glanced over at the lighted dial of his bedside clock. Only twenty more minutes before the alarm would ring. Once again, it was going to be hard to stay awake during class. It was Tuesday, too, and after the way he had fumbled his clarinet fingering last week, Mr. Crandall was bound to call on him in music class. He'd have to practice on the bus. Sam longed for just a few moments of dreamless rest. He turned his pillow over to the drier side and pressed his pale, freckled cheek against it. He groaned when his wandering hand suddenly found a large tuft of "bed hair" that was standing straight up at the top of his head.

On the rooftop of Sam's old New England house, directly above his bedroom, a great heron weather vane spun in the wind. The bird pirouetted gracefully against a backdrop of blue-black clouds, its long beak pointing skyward. The long metal pole that held the heron aloft squeaked and squealed like Mr. Crandall's violin, and the bird's great copper wings rattled loudly with every gust of wind. Sam shuddered. He tried poking his fingers into his ears to deaden the noise, and when that didn't work, he grabbed the edge of his blanket, pulled it up over his head and rolled on his side. Oddly, the out-of-tune squeaking only seemed to grow louder. Sam wrestled his blanket back down and listened carefully. Something brushed against his nose. Sam quickly ran his hand across his face, colliding with a pointy object just in front of him. A flowery smell, like the purple soap his mother kept in the guest bathroom, hung thick in the air.

As carefully and quietly as he could, Sam stretched his arm toward the lamp on his night table, illuminating the room with a single tug on the dangling chain. Emitting a startled squeak, a small black mouse that had been perched at the top edge of the blanket leapt into the air with such force that the tiny letter it had been busily waving in front of Sam's nose flew from its paw. The letter sailed gracefully for a second or two before coming to rest at the edge of Sam's pillow.

"Rollo?" mumbled Sam. "What are you doing? I was half-asleep, you know. Couldn't you wait till I got up?"

The black mouse hung his head dejectedly for a moment, then pointed a tiny, still trembling paw toward the red sticker that was clinging precariously to one corner of the envelope. Sam reached for the magnifying glass he always kept near and began to read.

"Extra Special Express. For Immediate Delivery. Under No Circumstance Delay." Sam peered over the top of his magnifying glass. "Sorry, Rollo," he said apologetically.

Sam turned the tiny letter over and over in his hand as he inspected it with his magnifier. The postmark read "Wiltshire, England," and he was quite sure the handwriting was Mr. Goodfellow's. It had been a year and a half since Mr. Goodfellow and his nephew Edgar had left on their mission,

and almost six months since Sam had received any correspondence. Last spring, not long after his eleventh birthday, a letter from Mr. Goodfellow had arrived by express mouse courier telling Sam that the Governing Council had accepted Sam's decision to preserve his friendship with The Sage. There had been nothing much since then, just a very short postcard in the fall. *"A disappointing summer,"* it read. *"No new leads. Will just have to wait out another winter. Edgar sends his best. J.G."* Six long months of waiting had filled Sam with feelings of worry and longing, feelings that had grown only stronger with his recurring dreams.

Although Sam should have been overjoyed to be holding such a small letter in his hands again, he couldn't help but sense that something wasn't quite right. And it wasn't just the strong scent of flowers that didn't fit. Tearing open the folded edge, Sam had a sudden and overwhelming feeling that something was terribly wrong.

As Sam struggled to remove the little pages, memories of his first night in New England flooded back. He had been in the depths of despair then, thousands of miles from the home he loved and the backyard bug paradise he had built, trapped in a dusty old house that promised little more in the way of excitement than a few cobwebs and the odd rodent or two. But Sam hadn't bargained on bumping into the mouse-suited Jolly Goodfellow, a distinguished member of The Sage—tiny, secretive creatures who provide unseen inspiration to gifted people in their pursuit of knowledge and achievement. Disguised as mice in order to move freely about the world, The Sage had been whispering words of wisdom and encouragement into human ears for centuries, especially in times of doubt, despair and frustration. They formed a bond with their human assignments, a bond known as The Sacred Seal.

On the night in question, Mr. Goodfellow's communication networks had been down. Making matters even worse, Professor Cedric Hawthorne, his new assignment and the previous owner of Sam's house, had mysteriously vanished. With no other options open to him, Mr. Goodfellow had turned to Sam for help. Their fateful encounter had been a turning point in Sam's life. Mr. Goodfellow's stories of adventure with his young nephew Edgar had lifted Sam from his despair. These tales and his own meeting with Edgar had taught Sam that life was often full of strange twists and turns and some very curious coincidences. When it was revealed that he was to have shared a Sacred Seal with Edgar, Sam was required to make a difficult decision about his future. Putting his own dreams aside for now, and the secret guidance that only a Sage could provide, Sam chose to keep the love and friendship of his new companions, and join them in their quest to solve an ever-expanding puzzle.

While Edgar and Mr. Goodfellow searched for the missing professor in England, Sam watched over the Hawthorne scroll, an ancient and mysterious relic that provided the key to Professor Hawthorne's research. It was an important task: Sam knew that there were others who sought the power of the scroll for their own ends. The deviously ambitious Professor Avery Mandrake and The Fen (evil creatures who appeal to the darker side of humanity in an attempt to disrupt the work of The Sage) were never far from Sam's thoughts.

Now, holding the letter he had waited so long to receive, Sam found himself overcome with dread. He unfolded the first page and cautiously started reading. The handwriting was quite different from that on the envelope and harder to decipher. It had a lot more flair than Mr. Goodfellow's carefully executed style, with boldly drawn characters, wandering dots and wayward crosses.

Dear Sam,

    I do believe I may have you to thank, in part, for the most wonderful surprise that arrived at my door several weeks ago. At this time in my life, I could never have imagined that such joy could be mine—to finally see Jolly again after all these years! I am so deeply grateful for all the precious days that have followed since then. Jolly has told me so much about you, your companionship and courage particularly, that I feel I know you already. And now, I must ask a great favor, Sam. I know that you are young in years, but Jolly has great faith in you, and I believe you may be our last hope. Since Jolly has taken you into his confidence already, I feel that I can speak quite openly. As you know, he has been working on the Hawthorne assignment and attempting to solve the mystery behind Professor Hawthorne's disappearance. In the past few weeks, with Edgar's help, Jolly has been sifting through clues in an effort to pinpoint the professor's whereabouts. I am terribly sorry to be passing on such distressing news, Sam, but just two days ago, on the night of April 2, both Edgar and Jolly vanished without a trace. It is almost too painful for me to write about, but I must be strong now for their sake. I am enclosing a letter that Jolly was in the process of writing at the time of his disappearance, as he intended to ask for your help with something. I hope that whatever he has written makes some kind of sense to you. Jolly and Edgar's fate may very well be in your hands now. Please be brave, dear Sam. And good luck. I will be thinking of you and praying for Jolly and Edgar's safe return.

    With love and gratitude,

    Beatrice Elderberry

Shocked and dismayed at the contents of the letter from Mr. Goodfellow's old flame, Sam fumbled around with the envelope again, finally extracting two more pieces of paper that were lodged inside. The handwriting on these pages was much more familiar.

Dear Sam,

Hello again, my boy! Please forgive my tardiness. I realize that it has been quite some time since our last correspondence. I must tell you that there have been some rather wonderful developments in my personal life, but I will write to you about this at a later date. Suffice it to say that I finally took the advice that you and Edgar offered concerning an affair of the heart, and my only regret is that I waited so long.

Right now, though, I am going to get straight to another point. Needless to say, Edgar and I have been up to our mouse ears in work, but regrettably the whereabouts of Professor Hawthorne still elude us. With my computer up and running again, I was finally able to request for assistance, but it proved to be fruitless. I uncovered little more than what I already knew—that the bulk of the Hawthorne files disappeared with my dear brother Filbert, 120 years ago. This whole affair, it would seem, has been cloaked in rumor and conjecture since Dr. Elijah Hawthorne's death around the same time. If our current Professor Hawthorne has indeed resurrected the work of his great-grandfather concerning the scroll, it is imperative that we locate him as soon as possible. I know that he must be in need of a great deal of guidance. We are already aware that the scroll exerts a strange power and that it is some-how connected to the enigma of crop circles. I cannot help but feel that this connection is of paramount importance to all of us. And if, as I suspect, Professor Mandrake and The Fen have been tipped to this possibility, too, then there is no time to lose. We do not know what might happen if the scroll falls into fiendish hands.

This brings me to a rather important point. Despite our extensive searching, I still feel that the professor may have hidden his journal in your house or perhaps at the university. He is from the old school—a methodical keeper of notes, always writing everything down by hand and insisting on keeping copies as backup. Please, Sam, search for the notes again. Edgar or I would come to assist you if we could, but time is of the essence now and I fear we may miss our golden opportunity here. If you do need help, your friend Fletcher may prove to be an invaluable assistant. Seek him out, Sam. Follow your heart and it will never steer you wrong.

I must be off now! I will finish the letter later this evening and send it to you tomorrow. Beatrice has been kind enough to order an express mouse courier for first thing in the morning. There was an extraordinary number of crop circle sightings not too far from here last night. This is very welcome news after the long wait over winter, and Edgar and I are about to leave to investigate. The circles, after all, are what must have drawn Professor Hawthorne here in the first place. We have had several visions of Filbert, too. Edgar is desperate to uncover the truth behind his father's disappearance and the meaning behind these recurring apparitions, and I have pledged to him that we will not abandon our search on this front either.

One last interesting side note before I dash. As you know, many strange tales circulated after Dr. Elijah

Hawthorne's death all those years ago. I have been piecing the more interesting aspects of these stories together. Along with the rumors about the ancient scroll that had fallen into his hands, there was talk of an odd obsession he had acquired for magnets. This was confirmed by a number of eyewitnesses to the doctor's bizarre behavior in his final years, as he began collecting as many of them as he could get his hands on. At one time, the old Hawthorne place was supposedly filled to the rafters with magnets. Elijah was also prone to taking unscheduled trips to odd places at the oddest times, with suitcases full of the things. According to his last housekeeper, he had become more or less nocturnal, too, sleeping well into the afternoon so that he might remain awake through the night, often spending a good portion of it outdoors. These strange habits finally took their toll on him during a trip to the British Isles. It was particularly cold and rainy in the spring of 1882, and Elijah returned home to America with a severe case of pneumonia. The poor soul passed away not long after that. The story goes that before he died, he insisted on being sur-rounded by his magnets, believing, he was heard to mutter through his delirium, that they possessed supernatural powers of some kind. What all of this had to do with his research remains a mystery, I'm afraid.

I must sign off now, my boy! I am being paged from the front hall. Edgar is already whining about the uncomfort-able bulges in his mouse feet, and Beatrice is insisting we take a flask of tea and some sandwiches with us (I don't mind telling you that I am hoping for watercress and a bit of old cheddar). I must say, Sam, this little cottage of hers by the sea is as captivating as she always dreamed it would be. Beatrice definitely had the right idea all along.

Spending one's golden years in such a peaceful spot would be idyllic indeed.

And then the writing just stopped. There was no good-bye, no fond farewell, no "best regards" or "stiff upper lip," just a line or two of empty paper at the bottom of the page: blank, white and cold. Sam dropped the magnifying glass on the bed. At first, he could only stare across the room, his mind in turmoil. What had happened to Mr. Goodfellow? Where could he and Edgar be? First, Professor Hawthorne had disappeared, and now they had, too. If they had suffered the same fate as Edgar's father, they might be lost forever. Sam couldn't help wondering how Hazel, Edgar's mother, would take the sad news. Losing her young son again so soon after their joyous reunion was bound to come as a great blow. Sam began to tremble from his head to his toes. His heart pounded and his hands shook. He rolled out of bed and paced back and forth across his room, trying desperately to think of what he should do next. The alarm clock sounded. Sam switched it off, then threw himself backward onto his bed with a loud groan, launching Rollo, currently engaged in his morning grooming routine, into the air. The rest of the house was beginning to stir, too. The bedroom door suddenly swung open and a brown boxer dog trotted in from the hallway, leaping onto the bed just in time to catch the now descending mouse in his open muzzle.

"Figaro! Drop him!" said Sam sternly. "We don't have time for games right now. I'm thinking."

He glanced over his shoulder. "Sorry, Rollo."

The dog obediently obliged and Rollo was ejected back onto the bed, his once beautifully coifed coat frosted now with a soggy mix of kibble crumbs and dog drool. Rollo slid down the side of Sam's bed and scurried across the floor toward the mouse hole along the far wall, shaking long strands of slime from his coat and loudly protesting with a barrage of indignant squeaks. This, after all, was not the first time that Figaro had to be reminded to be a little less playful. Were it not for the fact that the dog's mother, Brunhilda, had been instrumental in saving the life of Rollo's friend Edgar Goodfellow, the little black gypsy mouse would have been much less forgiving. Figaro, Rollo concluded, as he slipped behind the wall and into the more civilized company of the house mice, had a great deal to learn.

Meanwhile, Figaro had settled himself down into the folds of Sam's blanket. He rested his soft chin on top of two white-tipped paws and sighed. Sam rolled over and pressed his face into Figaro's warm neck, where the scent was sweet and leathery.

"They're gone, Figgy," Sam whispered sadly. "Edgar and Mr. Goodfellow. Just like the professor."

Figaro let out another loud sigh, as if in sympathy. Sam patted the soft, crinkled crown of his head and remembered the night Brunhilda's puppies had been delivered. Thanks to Mr. Goodfellow's heroic efforts, and his expert application of mouth-to-muzzle resuscitation, the frail and tiny runt of the litter had managed to pull through. And *that* had been Figaro. Figaro's miraculous survival on the same night that Sam, The Sage and Brunhilda had banished The Fen from his house was a testament to hope that Sam was not about to forget. The words that Mr. Goodfellow had spoken that night returned to Sam over and over again, too. "Animals are pure spirits, Sam," he had said. "Wise and old, they return to the earth many, many times and in a host of different forms: fish or birds, monkeys or mice. And because they are inherently good, The Fen can't help but fear and loathe them. It is our duty to protect them, and they, in turn, have vowed to do the same for us. Whenever you hold one of those puppies in your arms, remember that it may, in fact, be a spirit that is many thousands of years old."

The very first time he had cradled the squiggling Figaro in his arms, Sam knew that the two of them belonged together. Figaro stood out from the other puppies, not just because of his slightly smaller size, but for the unique color of his coat. Unlike the chocolate-brown pelts of his siblings, Figaro's coat was tinged with flame orange. The black stripes running down each side of his body gave him the look of a small Bengal tiger, a creature that Sam like to imagine as one of Figaro's previous incarnations. Sam begged and pleaded with his parents for days, refusing to give up until they agreed, at the very least, to a trial adoption. After her disastrous "doggy-infested" dinner party (where Brunhilda had mangled the main course before retiring to the middle of the master bed to give birth), Sam's mother should have been impossible to convince. The joy and longing on her son's face, however, was sufficient to win her over. Armed with an assortment of antihistamine pills, nasal sprays and a crate full of tissues, Sam's very allergic father had finally relented, too. Eight weeks later, when he was old enough to leave Brunhilda's side, little "Figgy" came to live in the Middleton house. Over the next couple of months, Sam and the puppy established an unbreakable bond. Sam cautiously introduced him to the house mice that inhabited the space behind his bedroom wall, and to Rollo, too, loyal friend to Edgar Goodfellow, and Sam's messenger. There had been a few incidents involving exuberant play, but fortunately no one had been seriously injured. A thousand-year-old spirit or not, Figaro was still just an excitable young dog who would require a great deal of training and guidance for some time to come.

Absently stroking Figaro's velvety coat as he lay beside him on the bed, Sam closed his eyes and thought about Mr. Goodfellow's letter. He could search the house again, without too much trouble. All of his family's possessions had been installed by the end of their first month there, but the Hawthorne house was enormous and most of the rooms remained only partially furnished. As an added bonus, a large section of the downstairs had been cleared to make room for the art gallery that Sam's parents ran. Trevor and Peggy Middleton were toiling day and night in an effort to mount a major exhibition. The invitations for *A Brush with History: Folk Art in the Age of Revolution* had already been mailed out, and the couple were visibly stressed, uncertain that they would be ready for their opening reception. It was, in fact, the perfect time for Sam to engage in a full-scale house hunt. He would be able to investigate all the rooms to his heart's content, without so much as a question or a comment.

Searching again through Professor Hawthorne's office at the university, however, was a prospect that Sam didn't relish at all. It wasn't as if the thought hadn't already crossed his mind. Sam had considered it more than once since Mr. Goodfellow and Edgar had left, but the whole thing had been a near disaster the first time around, even with Mr. Goodfellow's able assistance. Should he really attempt it again? There would be no crowded reception to provide cover this time. Taking his friend Fletcher (a faculty member's son) along might help, but it would still be a risky business. And if they happened to bump into that dreadful Professor Mandrake again, or his equally hideous son, Basil—well, he didn't even want to think about that!

Sam wished with all his heart that this overwhelming task had not fallen to him. He turned on his side next to Figaro and curled up into a tight little ball. The tip of his nose touched the corner of the tiny letter, close enough to smell its sweet, flowery fragrance of lavender again, Beatrice Elderberry's trademark scent. A feeling of profound responsibility suddenly coursed through him. Beatrice was counting on him. She had had faith enough to ask for his help, and he was not about to let her down. The fate of Edgar and Mr. Goodfellow might very well be in *his* hands now, just as she had suggested, and he wouldn't let them down either. Edgar Goodfellow wouldn't have cowered, even in the face of the gravest danger imaginable, and neither would he.

Sam took a deep breath. It was time to think clearly and carefully about everything in Mr. Goodfellow's letter, especially the part about seeking help and following your heart. "Courage in danger," Sam recalled him saying, "is half the battle." The fog that had been swirling through Sam's mind suddenly began to lift, and he knew exactly what he had to do next.

With Figaro trotting faithfully at his side, Sam made his way down the stairs, past his parents and through to the kitchen. He picked up the telephone to call his best friend, comrade and confidant, Fletcher Jaffrey. When Sam heard Fletcher's voice at the other end of the line, he wondered, just for a second, what his friend would think if he knew he was about to be dragged into one of the most intriguing mysteries in the history of humankind. Sam couldn't afford to worry too much, though. His tiny friends across the sea were in trouble, and he was ready to move heaven and earth to help them.

2

A Bully Is
Always a Coward

Sam would never have dreamed of visiting Fletcher's without taking Figaro along. It gave the dog an opportunity to visit with Brunhilda and his three siblings: Luciano, Placido and José. Finding a suitable home for the trio of inseparable brothers had proven impossible. Several families, eager to adopt any *one* of the handsome puppies, had been frightened off by the odd condition of multiple adoption. Whenever Sam (and Figaro) rang the doorbell, all three would rush headlong into the hallway, their stubby tails a-wiggle, barking out a doggy aria. A tangle of twelve powerful legs lunged at the front door, sweeping up whatever other objects happened to be in the hallway and hurling them in every direction. It had become a routine, in fact, for Sam to spend his first few minutes at Fletcher's house helping the family tidy up their foyer.

This time, the upended items included several soda bottles and a stack of old science journals destined for recycling, as well as an assortment of household knickknacks that the Jaffreys were donating to charity. As they tidied up, Sam and Fletcher reclaimed an old wooden tennis racket.

Racket in hand, Fletcher led Sam toward the sanctuary of his room, away from the swarm of barking dogs and the powerful voice of Fletcher's mother, Leonora, rehearsing in the study for an early-morning audition the following day. A prestigious Boston opera company had launched a search for a new Valkyrie, and Leonora was determined to answer the call. The frantic voice of Fletcher's father, Sanjid, busily cooking curry in the kitchen and, at the moment, on a desperate search for *garam masala*, joined in. Fletcher's older sister, India, was lying demurely along the length of the living room sofa with a large bag of gingerbread cookies by her side. She glanced up from her latest historical romance novel just in time to smile at Sam. This habit was becoming a little too regular for Fletcher's liking, for it always made Sam blush. Those old-fashioned love stories were nothing but a menace, Fletcher concluded. Contrary to his suspicions, though, India's mind was not always fixated on romance. She may have been oblivious to many things, including the continuous tumult in her own house, but she had picked up the unmistakable scent of intrigue in the air. Oddly, it smelled of lavender (her favorite), and it was coming from Sam's direction.

Fletcher was excited to be aiding in a mission that might reveal some clues as to Professor Hawthorne's whereabouts. He lived in hope of uncovering some sort of unsavory link between the activities of Avery and Basil Mandrake and the professor's mysterious disappearance. After a brief ceasefire, young Basil Mandrake was once again engaged in a campaign of cruel and humiliating tricks aimed almost exclusively at Fletcher, and Fletcher had had just about enough.

As they closed the door to Fletcher's room, Sam reminded himself to be very careful about the information he shared.

The two friends had discussed Sam's suspicions about Professor Hawthorne's fate at great length, and the Hawthorne scroll had appeared in the annals of local folklore for decades. However, any mention of Edgar or Mr. Goodfellow, or the existence of The Sage, was strictly off limits. The mysterious power behind the scroll was to be closely guarded, too. As far as Fletcher was concerned, Professor Hawthorne, a highly respected member of the university faculty and a friend of his father's, had vanished under strange circumstances. He had been doing research on an ancient scroll that had been in his family for years. Whatever Professor Hawthorne had discovered had piqued the interest of his unscrupulous colleague, Professor Mandrake. Mandrake, no doubt, was determined to claim the academic glory for himself, and was likely prepared to go to any lengths to do so. To Fletcher, it was a classic case of good guy versus bad. Knowledge of the eternal battle of Sage against Fen weighed heavily on Sam's shoulders, though, and there were times when he longed to confide in Fletcher, especially now that Mr. Goodfellow and Edgar were lost. But Sam would not endanger his friend's future or compromise the dreams that meant so much to him. Sam had traded his own dreams away with no regret, receiving in return what he believed to be a much greater treasure. But Sam knew that it might not be that simple for Fletcher. Perhaps his friend's destiny lay elsewhere.

Sam reached into his pocket and pulled out a crinkled piece of the *Boston Herald*. Ever since Fletcher had revealed his secret desire to be the first person on Mars, Sam had been on the lookout for interesting stories.

"Did you see this one, Fletch?" Sam laid the ragged piece of paper on the bed and ran his hand across it a couple of times to flatten it before reading the headline out loud.

"FURTHER EVIDENCE MARS ONCE DELUGED BY WATER: EARTH'S GREAT FLOOD MAY HAVE BEEN PART OF SOLAR SYSTEM–WIDE CATASTROPHE, SOME SCIENTISTS SUGGEST." Sam looked up. "Neat, huh?"

Fletcher had already begun to read the rest of the article with great interest. Sam championed Fletcher's cause, taking every opportunity to provide encouragement. He had even started a scrapbook for him a few months before, and Fletcher had continued it, collecting all the current news items about Mars he could find and carefully pasting them in.

"Thanks, Sam," said Fletcher, as he pulled the oversized scrapbook from under his bed. "I guess I must have missed that one."

He reached for the pair of scissors and small bottle of white glue that were sitting at the edge of his desk and turned to the next empty page in his book. After carefully trimming the clipping, he placed a tiny, identically-sized droplet of glue at each corner, turned it over with care and positioned it directly in the middle of the page. Then, with precisely calculated pressure, Fletcher pushed a finger into each of those corners, making absolutely sure that not a smidgen of glue slipped out from underneath. Sam was in awe. He had a reputation himself for being methodical, even fussy, when it came to his hobbies, but compared to Fletcher he was an amateur. Fletcher had a tendency to worry about small items, to consider the minutest of details and to question the logic behind almost everything. This made him slightly annoying at times (even to Sam), but probably invaluable to NASA. Sam knew that they would never have to worry about Fletcher Jaffrey leaving some spaceship hatch open, or pressing the wrong button and accidentally jettisoning a piece of critical machinery. In fact, Fletcher was already working on some of the finer details of the trip. Lately, the long duration of the flight to Mars had been causing him some concern. The astronauts would have to carry enormous amounts of food just to get there and back. They might actually have to consider growing and processing their own food on board the spacecraft. Apart from the complicated logistics involved, Fletcher fretted that such an extended time in space would probably have a considerable effect on the health and morale of the crew.

Sam had been thinking about it, too, and had even tried to offer some help.

"You know, Fletcher, I've been thinking about this long-Mars-trip thing. Maybe they could put you into suspended animation, or something, just until they get you there."

Fletcher looked up from his scrapbook and sighed. Snoring and drooling really wasn't how he'd imagined his triumphant arrival on Mars.

Sam was warming up. "That's it, Fletcher! It'll be great! You won't have to worry about a thing while you're sleeping. They'll have the technology for that kind of stuff by then."

"I'm not so sure, Sam. I haven't read anything about any major breakthroughs yet..."

"No, it's true," interrupted Sam. "There's this guy from MIT working on a secret project for the Space Agency. It has something to do with cryogenics—you know, freezing people, and..."

"How would you know?"

"What?"

"If it's a *secret* project, how could *you* know about it?"

"Um...well..." Sam hesitated. "Ah, come on, Fletch! Think about it. There's got to be *some* guy, *somewhere*, working on that stuff, right?"

Still mumbling, Sam jumped up from the edge of the bed and lunged for the old tennis racket lying on the bedroom floor, leaving a rather confused Fletcher in his wake. Boy, that was a close call, Sam thought to himself, as he spun the racket in the air. He would have to remember to be more careful in the future. Mr. Goodfellow had shared that cryogenics information with him in the strictest confidence. Hoping that Fletcher was sufficiently distracted now with all of the twirling, Sam decided to change the subject.

"Great article, isn't it?"

"Huh?"

"If Mars had a global flood like they're saying now, there could be all kinds of neat things buried underground, right? Gems, minerals, maybe even fossils! It's going to be really great to finally go there and find out. Right, Fletch?"

The old wooden racket slipped from Sam's hand and clattered to the floor. Sam pondered it for a moment or two, its paint chipped and peeling, its days of carefree play seemingly gone forever. With the first glimmer of a great idea in his mind, Sam picked it up again, looked at Fletcher, and smiled.

Fletcher's father had been trying for years to encourage his children to participate in the classes offered by the university's athletic program. So when Fletcher (and Sam) suddenly displayed an interest in attending tennis lessons, Sanjid Jaffrey was overjoyed. He was more than happy to help out, too, offering to drive the boys there in the morning and pick them up after lunch. Their plot was hatched.

It was raining when Sam and Fletcher arrived for their first lesson. In addition to their sports bags and tennis rackets, they also carried two flashlights, a handful of assorted tools (in the event that lock picking was required) and, in Fletcher's case, a miniature camera he had received two birthdays ago from his Auntie Nellie. It was one of those gifts he had never gotten around to using, and, despite Sam's assurances that it probably wouldn't be needed, Fletcher insisted that this might be the perfect opportunity to try it out.

After Fletcher's father had dropped them off at the front door, the boys made their way to the gigantic sports bubble at the back of the gymnasium. The Saturday morning tennis lessons had attracted a large crowd of youngsters. Not long after they had entered the dome, Sam felt Fletcher elbow him in the side. He looked up to see Basil Mandrake standing at center court. Sam grimaced. Grabbing Fletcher's arm, Sam scuttled into a corner, hoping that Basil had not noticed them. After everyone had taken turns lobbing balls around the courts, the instructor divided them into groups according to ability. Fletcher and Sam, and a handful of four- and five-year-olds, were relegated to the very back court near the propped-open door, where gusts of wind occasionally blew in cold rain. It soon became apparent that their college student coach intended to wander over to their little group only when the feeling moved him. He was much more interested in consulting with the attractive young woman who was providing instruction two courts over.

Fletcher was annoyed. As with everything he did, he was immediately swept up in the spirit of the game. Fletcher had a highly developed sense of fair play and a desire to champion the underdog (having been, on so many occasions, one himself) and this kind of brush-off stuck like a thorn in his side.

"I really think that we should write a letter about that guy to the head of the athletic department," Fletcher complained, in a voice loud enough to attract the attention of the players in the neighboring court.

"Fletcher," whispered Sam, under his breath, "could you keep it down?" He sidled closer to his friend, trying not to slip

33

in the puddles of rainwater that had started to collect. "We're not *really* here to learn tennis, remember...the mission?"

"Oh...right. Sorry. But still, I really don't think it's fair to..."

"Fletcher!"

Fletcher reluctantly agreed to make the best of things until the lesson was over. The younger children in the group were thrilled to be in the presence of two older boys, and by the end of the first half-hour, Fletcher (determined to make their introduction to tennis as positive as possible) had learned all of their names. It was Sam, though, that they took particular interest in, pleading with him to toss balls for them to hit. Sam had always had an ability to relate to younger kids. He probably would have had fun, too, if his thoughts had not been so firmly on the mission. Every couple of minutes, Sam would glance down to the courts at the far end of the dome, where Basil Mandrake, on his third season of lessons, was playing a much more aggressive game.

At the end of the lesson, while everyone was busy packing up their equipment, Sam and Fletcher slipped quietly through the open door at the back of the court. Basil, engaged in a heated discussion with his last opponent, was too preoccupied to notice.

Balancing their sports bags on top of their heads, Sam and Fletcher sprinted through the rain until they reached the main building. They bolted up the wide stone steps, through the front door and down the dark, deserted hallway to the staff offices, leaving a long trail of wet sneaker prints behind them. When they reached Professor Hawthorne's office, they found the door wide open and every piece of furniture removed. Someone had even attempted to scratch the professor's black-lettered name off the glass door panel. Sam shone his flashlight around to get a better look. The only thing left in the office was Professor Hawthorne's globe of the ancient world, lying now in two broken halves in the middle of the floor. It looked so forlorn there, all by itself, that Sam felt compelled to pick up the remains. There was a click and a bright flash.

"Fletcher! Stop that! You scared me half to death!"

"Sorry...I just thought you might want some evidence," whispered Fletcher, as he reluctantly shoved his miniature camera back into his pocket.

"What evidence, Fletcher? There's nothing here!"

"Well, Sam, that's kind of the point, isn't..."

"Shh!"

Just then, Sam noticed that the closet door was ajar and moving slightly. He pushed it open to find that it wasn't a closet at all. It led into the adjoining office where the hall light was shining on the door panel. The black letters were backward, but Sam could read them quite clearly: A. Mandrake, Department of Archaeology. Sitting on the floor behind the desk was a row of file boxes, all taped shut with long, jagged strips of masking tape. Holding his flashlight in front of him, Sam slowly walked in as Fletcher tiptoed behind. The pungent smell of mothballs was everywhere. Sam held his breath, carefully peeled the tape from the top of one of the boxes and looked inside.

"These are Professor Hawthorne's papers, Fletcher. Professor Mandrake's taken everything."

"Is it the stuff you're looking for?" whispered Fletcher.

"I don't think so. If it was, Mandrake wouldn't have left it out here like this."

Sam directed his flashlight to the top of Mandrake's desk. It was neat and tidy. A copy of a letter dated several weeks earlier sat at the top left corner, partially obscured by a heavy resin paperweight bearing the suspended remains of a huge, hairy tarantula. Fletcher gasped when the flashlight's beam swept over it. Even Sam swallowed hard.

The letter was addressed to the dean of the university: *"Sadly, I must write to inform you that I have been contacted by Professor Cedric Hawthorne. He will be unable to return to resume his academic duties and has instructed me to clear his office and take possession of his files. He has suffered an emotional breakdown and will be in recovery for some time.*

Yours most sincerely,

Avery Mandrake."

Fletcher had been reading over Sam's shoulder.

"Poor Professor Hawthorne," he whispered.

Sam let out a sigh of frustration.

"Don't you get it, Fletcher! Mandrake's lying! Professor Hawthorne wouldn't hand over years and years of research materials to that, that...snake! And I don't think he's ill, either."

"How do you know that, Sam?"

"I just do, that's all."

This was awful, thought Sam. What was he going to do? There were no new leads, no clues at all apart from the fact that Mandrake was up to something rotten. But how was he going to help the Goodfellows now? The whole mission had been a miserable failure. As he and Fletcher made their way back to the main entrance, Sam felt terrible.

"Thanks for your help, anyway, Fletcher."

"Don't worry, Sam. Something else will probably turn up."

Fletcher, who had found that these forays into the world of espionage made him a little hungry, was looking forward to his lunch. But it was almost time for his father to pick them up, so they made their way back into the sports dome and waited inside the entrance. Fletcher read the notice board, while Sam played absently with the broken pieces of globe he had brought with him. A big, grubby finger suddenly appeared from behind and poked at one of them. Sam spun around.

"That's where I'm going on my summer holiday," said Basil Mandrake smugly. "My father's taking me on an archaeological dig, right there." He pointed in the general vicinity of Central America. "See?"

He pushed a bit too hard the second time and the piece of globe fell from Sam's hand, hitting the floor with a thud. It rolled toward Fletcher, who bent down to pick it up. This sight was too much for Basil to resist. He started to lift his big, booted foot toward Fletcher's backside. Suddenly, Sam sprang forward, grabbed the collar of Basil's jacket and reeled him back. Outside, a car honked its horn. Fletcher's father, smiling and waving through the half-open window, had pulled up in the rain right beside the front door. Basil loosened himself from Sam's grip and straightened his jacket collar.

"I'll be seeing you again, Middleton," he sneered, as he started to turn away. He looked toward the globe. "You really shouldn't be picking things up that don't belong to you."

"Boy! A lesson in manners from Basil Mandrake. That's rich!" laughed Fletcher.

"Come on, Fletch," whispered Sam as he tugged at his friend's sleeve. "Let's get out of here."

3

TIME REVEALS ALL
THINGS

Sam didn't go to school the next Monday. He had caught a bit of a cold, most likely from his sprint through the rain at the university. He lay in bed and looked around his room, recalling the first few days he'd spent here, camping out on the hard wooden floor in his sleeping bag. The dark wood paneling was covered now in a warm terra cotta wallpaper that complemented the sienna brown carpet. Sam had also acquired some posters for his closet door, including a huge black and white photo of the Empire State Building, complete with dangling King Kong, and a colorful scene of hang-gliders over Maui. Sam had placed several other items of interest throughout his room, including a seven-foot-high inflatable Godzilla, a hanging mobile of the sun and planets, and a Chilean rainstick. Professor Hawthorne's broken bookcase, nicely repaired by Sam's father, was still there, overflowing now with an ever-expanding collection of books and computer manuals. The old book that the professor had left behind, *The Complete Short Stories of H. G. Wells*, was still there, too, sticking out an inch or two from the other books as if it were hoping to attract some attention. Sam had glanced at it many times, sincerely intending to read it, but something had always interrupted. Today, however, he had all the time in the world. Perhaps an old-fashioned science fiction story would be an entertaining distraction. Sam really needed one right now. The university search had been a failure, and a quick survey of the house the previous night had not turned up anything new either.

When Sam hopped out of bed and crouched in front of the old bookcase, a feeling of sadness swept over him. This was exactly where he had been the night he had seen Mr. Goodfellow for the first time: a little brown mouse (or so Sam had thought) studying a floorplan of the Hawthorne house in the glow of his miniature flashlight. Sam sighed as he reached up to the top shelf, grabbing Professor Hawthorne's book and pulling it from its place. He opened the book and turned to the table of contents. He ran his finger down the lengthy selection of short stories, quickly moving past "The Time Machine," "The Empire of the Ants" and "The Sea Raiders." At "The Valley of Spiders," Sam suddenly stopped reading and shuddered. No, definitely not *that* one, he thought, remembering the resin-encased tarantula on Mandrake's desk.

When he returned to a section entitled *Tales of Space and Time*, Sam found one piece that really intrigued him: "A Story of the Days to Come." He stood up and walked toward his bed, flipping through the pages until he found the right one. He had only made it about halfway across his room when several pieces of paper slipped out of the book, floating slowly to the floor.

Sam dropped to his knees and gathered them together, his eyes quickly scanning each one. Handwriting covered both sides. The pages had been marked at the top with the words "C. Hawthorne—research notes." It was one in particular, though, that caused Sam's heart to beat a little faster. Every second line or so, interspersed between the professor's hastily written scrawls, was a series of hand-drawn symbols. Sam had seen these strange lines and circles once before, shimmering on the surface of the mysterious scroll, the scroll that now lay in the empty space behind his bedroom wall, under the watchful eyes of twenty mice. These were the same symbols that had sent Mr. Goodfellow and Edgar off to southern England, the hub of crop circle activity. The same strange lines and circles were appearing with increasing regularity in fields of barley and wheat, and Mr. Goodfellow was certain that Professor Hawthorne had gone there. Sam held the papers tightly in his hands. He had found the notes!

The rest of the pages held a few scribbled maps and a schedule of sorts with place names, dates and times. Scrawled at the very top of one page was a long and intricate line of mathematical figures and below that a heading: "Crop Circle Sightings." When Sam examined the dates and locations of these incidents a little more closely, he found that one of them coincided with the general time that Professor Hawthorne had vanished. Another, on the night of April 2, occurred at the same time and place of Edgar and Mr. Goodfellow's disappearance, according to the letter he had received from Beatrice. There were many other sightings listed before that, some dating back to the previous century, all with check marks beside them. Most intriguing, however, was the last half of the list; its predicted precise times and locations in the future. Sam shivered. Professor Hawthorne, it would appear, had stumbled onto a mathematical formula that accurately predicted the times and locations of crop circle formations.

One of the pieces of paper, with the words "Magnet Configuration" printed across the top, had a very detailed sketch of a circle composed of differently shaped objects. The arrangement of these objects needed to be absolutely precise, the professor emphasized in the notes, in order to achieve the desired effect. Anything less than this would result in an inability to interact with the "Crop Circle Energy Vortex" and, as Professor Hawthorne had boldly underlined, "Failure to Transport." A theory on the significance of this and how it all related to the disappearances of Professor Hawthorne, Mr. Goodfellow and Edgar slowly began to grow in Sam's mind. He had a feeling, too, that this was the information that Professor Avery Mandrake had been searching for.

The knowledge that he might be holding the key to Professor Hawthorne's, Mr. Goodfellow's and Edgar's whereabouts boosted Sam's hopes.

Sam telephoned Fletcher's house as soon as he knew his friend would be home from school.

"I've found them, Fletch! The professor's scroll notes!"

"Don't move, Sam. I'll be right over!"

Sam had read each of the pieces of paper over and over again by the time Fletcher arrived.

"They were here all along, in my room, Fletcher. All this time! Right in the professor's old book, and I never knew! Isn't that incredible!"

"What do you think it all means?" asked Fletcher, turning the pages over in his hands with a look of puzzlement on his face.

"I guess Professor Hawthorne was studying the symbols on the scroll, just like his great-grandfather Elijah had done," said Sam. "First he discovered a connection to crop circles. Then, he figured out some kind of weird formula that predicts where and when the circles will appear. It probably has something to do with him disappearing, too, Fletch, and I think that's where the whole magnet thing comes in. Maybe he found a way to use magnetic power to tap into an energy field that leads someplace else. His great-grandfather must have been making the same connection when he died. Remember all of the old stories people told about the magnets he collected and carted around? Everyone that knew him said he was nuts about the things. Maybe he had a reason to be!"

Sam pushed the "Magnet Configuration" paper toward his friend. Fletcher looked at it intently, especially at the sketch detailing the specific size and arrangement of magnets. Fletcher stared for an even longer time at the line written in Professor Hawthorne's scribbled hand, at the very center of the circle of magnets.

"Does that say what I think it does?" said Fletcher, pointing a little nervously.

"Yeah, I think so," said Sam. "You mean the 'Transportation Zone' part, right?"

Fletcher nodded and swallowed hard. He was beginning to feel just a little worried. What had started out as an adventure to locate a missing professor and the important academic find that he was protecting from an unscrupulous colleague was beginning to take on a much more ominous tone.

"There's something really weird about that scroll, isn't there, Sam? I mean, it's not just some priceless old Egyptian or Aztec thing, is it?"

"No, Fletcher. I think it might be a little more than that."

Fletcher slowly glanced around Sam's room.

"It's in here, isn't it Sam? The scroll, I mean."

"Ahh, come on Fletcher. You said you never wanted to know where it was hidden, remember? You begged me not to tell you. You said it'd be safer if only one of us knew where it was, right?"

"Yeah, I remember. But it's in here anyway, Sam. You don't have to tell me. I just know."

Sam and Fletcher sat together for a long time after that, quietly contemplating the significance of Professor Hawthorne's notes. Figaro trotted into the room with a rawhide chew bone clenched in his teeth and jumped up on the bed between them. He always turned up at his master's side whenever Sam found himself in a moment of trouble or faced with a seemingly insurmountable problem.

"What are you going to do, Sam?" asked Fletcher.

"I'm not really sure yet. All I know is that Professor Hawthorne probably needs help and I've got his scroll. People are starting to believe Mandrake's lies about him, too."

Sam looked down at the papers spread across his bed and absently began to move each piece around as if it were part of a much larger puzzle.

"Promise you won't laugh or anything, Fletch," sighed Sam. "I know that this may sound totally crazy, but ever since I found the professor's notes this morning, I haven't been able to think about anything else. I've just *got* to get to Wiltshire."

"Wiltshire?" asked Fletcher, incredulously. "The one in England, right? You must be joking!"

Sam looked at his friend in exasperation.

"Yeah, Fletcher! England! Haven't you been paying attention? Crop circles? Look at the professor's list, Fletch! His formula is predicting loads of circle formations in the next few months, and most of them are in Wiltshire. If you were Professor Hawthorne and you'd figured out all of this stuff, wouldn't *you* go there?"

"Hey! Wait a minute, Sam! I *have too* been paying attention! It's just *really* weird, that's all."

"What's weird?"

"My Auntie Nellie. You know, the one who sends me all the neat presents." Fletcher whipped the miniature camera out of his pocket and dangled it in front of Sam's face.

"Your Auntie Nellie's weird?"

"No! Well, maybe just a little. But what's *really, really* weird is that she lives in Wiltshire and what's even weirder is that India and I are supposed to visit her this summer. My dad has some big science conference in London and he and my mum have to go to a lot of receptions and stuffy dinners."

"Fletcher! Are you kidding? Why didn't you tell me you were going?"

"I don't know," Fletcher shrugged defensively. "I forgot, I guess. We've been over there lots of times before and it is kind of boring, you know. I'd rather stay at home. It's no big deal, Sam."

"No big deal!" Sam put his head in his hands.

"Maybe I could do something for you while I'm over there," suggested Fletcher.

"No...thanks, Fletcher. *I* have to find a way to go. I can't really explain why right now, but it's got to be me."

"Well...I guess we could ask my mum and dad if you could come."

Sam looked up in disbelief.

"You're kidding again, right?"

"No, really Sam. They won't mind. They'll think it's good for me to have a friend along. Parents are like that, you know."

"They are?" asked Sam hopefully.

The truth was, Sanjid and Leonora Jaffrey were not your average parents by any means, and Sam sincerely doubted that his own would be as understanding and accommodating when the time came. But Trevor and Peggy Middleton were not as horrified at the prospect of their son's overseas summer holiday as Sam had feared. To Sam's utter astonishment, his travel plans were made quite easily and within a week all was in place. Less than two months later, however, just before summer break finally rolled around, these arrangements completely crumbled. The best-laid plans of the Jaffrey family, like almost everything else they turned their hands to, always seemed to go awry.

For two whole weeks, the Jaffrey household struggled with disaster. A computer meltdown at the university had resulted in the loss of Professor Jaffrey's class marks. And Leonora had been called at the last moment to fill in for an ailing star in a traveling adaptation of *Aida*. It was to be a monumental production, arranged by one of the East Coast's most innovative young musical directors, complete with a cast of thousands, a spectacular Egyptian stage set, a caravan of camels and an entire herd of elephants. It was a dream come true for Fletcher's mother. The family agreed that she couldn't possibly turn it down. After all, such a magnificent opportunity might never come her way again.

At one point, the entire trip was about to be called off. Sam was heartsick. After waiting so long for the chance to search for his missing friends, he couldn't imagine that he might not be going at all. He had even sent a letter to Beatrice, via Rollo and the express mouse courier service, to tell her he was coming and that he had discovered some intriguing leads. He couldn't bear to write again and disappoint her now.

But when it became apparent that it was too late to turn the airline tickets in for a full refund, the Jaffrey family put a whole new set of arrangements into play, sweeping Sam's stunned parents into their plans.

The Middletons would just have to go instead, they explained. The hotel reservations had already been made, and Auntie Nellie was anxious for the children to visit. The Jaffreys were unwilling to take no for an answer, and Trevor and Peggy Middleton actually began to look forward to their trip, thrilled at this sudden opportunity to visit the auction houses and art galleries of London. In return, they would deliver Sanjid Jaffrey's latest research paper to the organizers of the Commonwealth Science Conference in London.

Just a few days after these alternate plans had been finalized, Sam found himself on an airplane bound for England, his knapsack at his feet, loaded with an assortment of magnets. He had decided to carry the professor's very precious notes as close to him as possible. They were folded into a neat little square, secure within the zippered inside pocket of his old fishing vest, where he could check on their condition whenever he needed to.

It had been difficult for Sam to say good-bye to Figaro even for just two weeks, but it was a great consolation that he was leaving him in the very able hands of Fletcher's father and an entire troop of boxer dog companions.

By the time the limousine arrived to take Sam, his parents and the two Jaffrey children to the airport, Figaro had already established himself at the house, running alongside Luciano, Placido and José, in the role of the fourth musketeer. Brunhilda happily watched the antics of her sons from the comfort of the living room sofa (now that India and her books had vacated the spot). The Jaffreys' two elder boxers, Gilbert and Sullivan, had decided, after assessing the situation, to retreat to the sanctuary of the music room for a rawhide chew and a good snooze, like a couple of old bachelor uncles.

Sam's last sight of Figaro was through the big bay window at the front of the Jaffrey house. Fletcher's father, his wooden spoon still dripping with the remnants of the curried egg brunch he had just prepared for the departing travelers, was waving a fond farewell at the airline limousine, while four young dogs circled him like a pack of hungry hyenas.

4

ONE STEP AT A TIME

Sam glanced through the small oval window across the aisle where the moonlight was illuminating the silver wing of the aircraft. They were traveling through the night, but Sam was far too excited to sleep. Fletcher, a book about black holes lying open on the tray in front of him, had drifted off to sleep. Sam's parents, in the seats directly in front of them, had finally talked themselves out and fallen asleep, too. Through the window next to India, Sam could see the thin orange streaks of dawn, the same dawn that was now slowly breaking across the English countryside as they sped toward it. People would be stirring in their homes soon, thought Sam. Fletcher's Auntie Nellie would be making herself a pot of tea, he imagined, excited at the prospect of welcoming three young visitors. And not all that far away, in a little cottage by the sea, Beatrice Elderberry (brewing a much smaller pot), might be standing by her open window. She would be breathing in the fresh sea air and watching the light of a new day as it danced on the tips of the waves, praying that it would not be too long before she welcomed Edgar and Jolly home.

Upon their arrival in England, Sam, Fletcher, India and Sam's parents spent their first day in London making the usual round of tourist sights: Big Ben, Buckingham Palace, The Tower and Westminster Abbey. On the second day, after a head-spinning introduction to every other historical sight of note, the three children, somewhat relieved, boarded a westbound train for their visit to Auntie Nellie's. A couple of hours later, after he, Fletcher and India had arrived at a train station in the beautiful rolling hills of the ancient kingdom of Wessex, Sam found himself fending off one of Auntie Nellie's customary greetings. A tiny, stout woman with a shock of curly white hair, she bolted onto the platform and charged them all like a rogue elephant, bellowing a loud "Halloooo!" as she made her approach. It wasn't an easy task, cramming three children and all of their baggage (including a suitcase devoted entirely to India's books) into her Mini, but Auntie Nellie attacked the problem with gusto. Since her husband had passed away ten years earlier, Auntie Nellie had lived all alone in a big stone farmhouse in the heart of the country. A busy, bustling person, she thrived on company and was particularly thrilled whenever friends and relatives accepted her invitations to visit. It gave her someone to look after again.

"Come on now, pets! Everyone in!" Auntie Nellie shrilled across the train station parking lot. She lashed one bag that wouldn't quite fit into the boot of her car onto its roof with a length of old and soggy rope.

Sam was sure he could see the little red car tipping to the left a bit, and when they all got inside and shut the doors there was a loud groan of metal against rubber as the extra weight suddenly shifted onto the Mini's very small wheels.

After settling into the driver's seat and donning her headscarf, Auntie Nellie turned the key in the ignition.

Sputtering several times before it turned over, the Mini's engine finally revved with an encouraging burst of power, then immediately lurched forward. Sam felt the sudden G-force sensation of his head pressing back into the worn leather of the rear seat as Auntie Nellie raced up the hill, manipulating the gears of the little car with the intensity of Mario Andretti on his final round at the Indy 500. The others, familiar with Auntie Nellie's driving style, had remembered at the last minute to brace themselves. India, in the passenger seat next to her aunt, pushed both of her arms firmly against the dashboard. Fletcher, grabbing onto the armrest of the door beside him, was able to use his free hand to catch Sam, in peril of being launched forward now as Auntie Nellie switched gears again.

"Sorry about that, Sam!" Auntie Nellie shouted over the squeal of the tires. "Should have thought to warn you, pet. It's the only way to navigate this wretched hill, I'm afraid."

She turned around then to smile at Sam, just as an unsuspecting sheep wandered onto the road. Turning back, she artfully careened around it with another squeal of the tires, never missing a beat as the sheep stood blinking its startled eyes and bleating.

"It won't be so bumpy, poppet, once we're up on the main road," she assured Sam.

That part was true enough, although Auntie Nellie showed no signs of slowing. And so Sam, who had never been to England before and was looking forward to seeing the sights, saw most of the Wiltshire countryside pass by in a blur, full of herds of barely identifiable farm animals.

Auntie Nellie's bright paisley headscarf billowed out through the open car window as they sped along, and she insisted on giving a running commentary about each and

51

every farm they passed. This information consisted mostly of personal histories of the local families along with tidbits of gossip that were making the rounds. Since Sam could only catch every second word that Auntie Nellie was shouting over the high-pitched whine of the car's engine and the rattle of the bag that was slowly working itself loose on the roof, he decided to catch a few winks.

When Sam awoke, feeling groggy and even more exhausted than before, Fletcher was leaning over him, shaking him roughly by the shoulders.

"Sam, come on, already! Wake up! We're here, okay?"

Sam struggled to pull himself into the light of day. He had had the dream again, and this time it had been even more vivid and real than before.

Although the car had come to a stop, and the incessant noise of the engine had been quelled, the vehicle continued to teeter back and forth, tipping even more to the left than it had on departure. Still in their seats, everyone glanced up in the direction of a loud scraping noise. The piece of excess baggage, suddenly freed from its bondage, slipped slowly to the edge of the roof before plummeting to the ground with a thud.

"Perfect timing...as always!" Auntie Nellie shouted as she swung the car door open and jumped out to retrieve the bag. "Bring your other things with you, pets!" she called out as she raced ahead, her nose searching the air. "I'll have to run! I'm afraid I may have left the cat's lunch on the cooker again."

Sam, weighed down with his luggage and still not fully awake, staggered behind Fletcher and India toward Auntie Nellie's front door.

"Hey, Sam," said Fletcher, as they climbed the three stone steps. "Who's Edgar?"

"Edgar?" said Sam, feeling the hairs on the back of his neck begin to tingle.

"You kept saying that same name over and over again, back in the car, while you were sleeping."

"Uh...he's...um, just an old friend, Fletcher. A *really* old friend, actually," Sam blurted out, as they walked into the front hallway. Sam sighed. This was all he needed. Talking in his sleep had just become one more thing to worry about.

They entered the farmhouse to the overwhelming aroma of burnt fish. India immediately planted herself in a chair in the front sitting room, her large suitcase of books by her side. Had it not been necessary to get up every now and then to eat and sleep, India would have been content to stay there all week. Despite the fact that it was the beginning of summer, Auntie Nellie had started a coal fire that morning to ward off the dampness her North American guests always complained about. So, warm and cozy, India curled herself up into a ball, just like the farm cat that had already claimed a spot on her lap. Jemima was always pleased to see the little red Mini pull up with visitors inside and luggage strapped to its roof, especially if those visitors spoke in a funny way. It meant that the fire would be kept burning for the next few days. Jemima had been named after Jemima Puddleduck from the Beatrix Potter books. Such an odd choice, everyone would comment at first, until the cat yawned and spread one of its huge marmalade paws toward the warmth of the fire, revealing the transparent folds of webbed skin that stretched between each of its toes.

While India and Jemima became reacquainted, Sam and Fletcher retreated to one of the upstairs bedrooms, loaded down with all of their stuff. They chose the room that had been outfitted with wooden bunk beds. Sam and Fletcher spent their first half-hour in Auntie Nellie's house arguing about who should get the top bunk, until it dawned on them that they could take turns. They spent their second half-hour arguing about who should be allowed to sleep on top first. When this problem was finally resolved with several rounds of Hangman, they began preparing for their mission, consulting maps of the local area and Professor Hawthorne's notes.

Auntie Nellie, happy just to have other people around her again, didn't seem to notice that everyone had disappeared almost as soon as they had arrived. She set to in the kitchen, happily cooking and baking, and chattering away to no one in particular as she did.

According to the crop circle timetable, there would be a formation on the third night of their stay, in a farmer's field about ten miles to the east. Fletcher was concerned about transportation, but Sam wasn't worried. On the crazed car ride in from the train station, he had noticed a fair-sized fleet of farm tractors and wagons making its way along the roads. He remembered how Edgar and Mr. Goodfellow had made use of this mode of transportation during their adventures in the past, and he trusted that he and Fletcher would be able to use it, too.

The boys devoted the rest of that afternoon and evening to planning and plotting, with the exception of dinner and the rousing game of charades that Auntie Nellie insisted they all play. It was her favorite game, but one that required a few more players than herself and a marmalade farm cat. She had been looking forward to it for weeks. Sam and Fletcher didn't mind playing all that much, except when it came to India's turn. Since it was impossible to guess any of her obscure literary choices, they were in over their heads every time. It wasn't even worth the effort. Auntie Nellie, however, an avid reader of obscure books herself, had no problem at all, squealing with delight as she solved every clue.

The boys discovered right away that Auntie Nellie not only adhered to the farm community's "early to bed" rule but was an extremely sound sleeper, too. On their first morning in the house, she slept quite peacefully through her alarm clock, which buzzed for at least twenty minutes before India went into her room to turn it off.

Sam and Fletcher realized that Auntie Nellie's sleeping habits would give them much more time in which to carry out their plans. Believing India to be completely oblivious to the rest of humanity as she explored her worlds of romance, the boys did not even consider her in their calculations. Had Mr. Goodfellow been present, he might have suggested to Sam that he would be well advised to take heed of an old proverb: "All are not asleep who have their eyes shut" (or, presumably, stuck in a book, either). Sam, however, had far too many other things to consider and little time to worry about anything but their impending mission.

By the middle of the second day, having discussed the professor's notes, maps and magnet instructions a dozen times since their arrival, Sam and Fletcher were eager for action. The weather had turned quite dreadful though: windy, cold and very wet. The English summer was upon them. Outdoor activities were definitely off. There was little to do now but wait and hope that the rain would clear up before the following day.

Auntie Nellie, rather delighted that everyone was trapped indoors, had swung herself into the production of an endless supply of traditional treats. There were hot scones with jam and clotted cream, Yorkshire puddings swimming in rich savory gravy, Cornish pasties and kippers, and Auntie Nellie's own special version of "bubble and squeak." Sam was grateful to discover that the last item tasted a whole lot better than it sounded. Auntie Nellie's passion for food preparation extended to its consumption. She was never satisfied until every morsel presented had been eaten. Sam, not used to such large quantities, was a little overwhelmed. He would have given just about anything for a couple of hungry boxer dogs under the table.

With the rain continuing to fall late into the afternoon, Fletcher searched the upstairs rooms for something to do, finding an old jigsaw puzzle with a picturesque scene of a Portuguese fishing village. Sam had never been all that fond of jigsaws and decided to explore the sitting room bookcase instead. Disappointed that the vast majority of Auntie Nellie's reading material was devoted to cooking, gardening and household hints, Sam retreated to his own chair with only a handful of books. These included a collection of partially solved crossword puzzles (with pen conveniently attached), a pamphlet on fly-fishing and a guide to local hiking trails (the accompanying maps, thought Sam, might be of some use later on). The last book was a concise English dictionary that looked as if it had survived both a raging fire and substantial water damage. Sam picked it out anyway. He had been meaning to look up a couple of words for awhile, and after tossing his other reading choices aside, he turned to these.

"F"..."felon"..."felt"...Sam ran his finger down the page. There it was: "fen." Sam read the definition: "A low-lying place, a marshy swamp, a bog, a quagmire." A vision of slimy, slippery, bubbling ooze came to Sam's mind. That sounded about right, he thought.

He turned now to "S." "Safety"..."saffron"..."saga" and "sage." He read the definition of the last word. "A person of wisdom, a philosopher, one sought for guidance." Perfect, thought Sam. Just as he had imagined.

Sam returned the grubby dictionary to its shelf and wiped the soot off his palms. Wondering what to do next, he peered out the window, where extra-large drops of rain were colliding against the little squares of leaded pane with considerable force. He popped his head into the dining room. Fletcher, a look of grim determination on his face, was sprawled across the table now, clutching small pieces of cardboard puzzle in both hands. Sam walked back to the sitting room and picked up the crossword book and its attached pen. He turned to a puzzle in the middle of the book and read the first clue, then the second and the third. None of them made any sense.

"What's with these things?" he muttered to himself. "Better start with an easier one first."

Sam turned to the puzzle at the front of the book and read another clue, but once again, he was stumped. These were the strangest crossword puzzles he had ever seen. He looked at the front cover.

"The World's Best Cryptic Crossword Puzzles," Sam read out loud. "What are *those*?"

Sam was about to retrieve the dictionary when India spoke up from her chair.

"Oh, I *love* those. They're the best kind."

Sam looked up in surprise. He hadn't realized that he had been talking out loud and he had certainly never expected that India would take the time to comment.

"What?"

"You know," India continued. "The clue could be a play on words, or a pun or an anagram," she continued. "It's easy, Sam. The word that you are looking for is hidden somewhere in the clue."

"Oh, I get it," said Sam. He wasn't really sure that he knew what she was talking about, but he nodded his head anyway.

He *was* sure, however, that this was the first time India had said his name in such a friendly way.

"Try again. They're really lots of fun, once you get the knack." Then she smiled at him.

Sam felt obliged now to attempt another one of the frustrating clues. India, after all, was trying to be kind. He read the first clue over again. Then the second one, but it was hopeless. He was pretty sure he knew what an anagram was, and an antonym and a synonym for that matter, but he just couldn't get the hang of *these* things at all. He supposed he should try and look busy though (India kept glancing up from her book every now and then). He turned to the inside back cover and began to doodle around its edges, drawing words and letters and mixing them all around. First he wrote *SAMUEL*. He looked at it for a while, then moved the "S" to the end. He had written *AMUELS*. It wasn't a word really, but if he switched the "L" with the "E" and added a "T" after them, he had *AMULETS*. That was definitely a word and he even knew the meaning. An amulet was an object, like a rabbit's foot or a charm or something that protected you from harm. He could probably use an amulet or two right now, he thought.

Sam doodled around a bit more, then wrote *SAGE*. He put the "S" at the end, like he'd done with *SAMUEL* and wrote *AGES*. Well, he thought, The Sage *did* live for ages, no doubt about that. This was rather an interesting new game and Sam was quite pleased with it. It was certainly more fun than the cryptic crosswords. Adding another element to it now, he wrote out the entire alphabet at the top of the page. Then he closed his eyes and counted to twenty-five (just like Mr. Goodfellow did when he combed his fur) as he moved the pen around and around. Whatever letter it landed on at the end of the count would be added into the word game. He landed first on an "L" and then, in the next round, on an "N." He was just about to add these letters to his last word when he heard Fletcher's voice calling from the dining room.

"Hey, Sam! Come on! The rain's finally stopped!"

Sam looked out the sitting room window. Little spots of blue sky were struggling to break through a thick layer of clouds. Sam pushed the puzzle book and pen under his chair again and walked into the hall.

"Finish your jigsaw yet, Fletcher?" asked Sam as he plucked a puzzle piece out of Fletcher's hair.

"No. Not yet." Fletcher shook himself like a wet dog, and two pieces that had been stuck to his sweater came loose and fell to the carpet. Sam bent down and picked them up.

"Hey, look, Fletch! If you put all these pieces together they almost make a whole sardine."

Fletcher seemed unimpressed. He had grown very tired of his fishing village jigsaw puzzle and didn't want to discuss it anymore.

"So what have you been doing, anyway?" he asked Sam with a sigh.

"Just looking at some books and doing crossword puzzles. India said the cryptic ones are really fun when you get used to them, but they were too hard for me and..."

"India! Are you kidding? She doesn't bother with anything when she's reading her silly books."

"Yes, she does," said Sam.

"No, she *doesn't*, Sam. Believe me. I've known her since she was three. Well... you know what I mean. Anyway, dynamite wouldn't blast her away from those books."

"But, she... oh, never mind," said Sam, as he trailed out the front door after Fletcher.

5

NEVER SAY DIE

Both boys fell into their bunks that night, utterly exhausted from two hours of exposure to the purified country air, and full to bursting with Auntie Nellie's culinary offerings. As tired as he was, Sam found it impossible to fall asleep, especially now that he had the added worry of his own "sleep-talking" to contend with. He lay in the top bunk (his turn tonight), tossing and fidgeting. Every now and then he would peer with envy over the raised edge of his bed to where Fletcher lay below, snoring contentedly.

Sam's eyes scoured the dark floor. He was hoping that Jemima would make a return visit. She had almost scared him to death the previous night, slinking under the covers and nestling into the crook of his arm. After he had recovered from his initial shock, though, he had found the warmth of her body and her gentle, rhythmic purrs comforting. And like cats often do, she had blissfully padded her paws back and forth against his chest: big, marmalade, webbed paws.

The need to sleep finally overcame him, and Sam began to drift off. He barely felt the soft crushing of the blanket on top of his bed. He didn't even open his tired eyes to look but gently reached out his hand and began to search through the folds of soft material for the marmalade cat.

"You're a good climber, Jemima," he murmured sleepily.

He moved his hand slowly down his side toward his knee.

"There you are," he sighed. "Nicc kitty."

His hand patted the tuft of fur that was Jemima's head. It was strange that she was not purring, though. Sam moved his hand along to stroke her back, but he hit another mound of blanket instead.

"Jemima?" he whispered nervously.

There was a strange silence.

"Um...I'm afraid not, dear," a soft voice finally answered. "Please don't be too alar—"

With an impassioned "Aaahh," Sam suddenly came to his senses and shot out of bed, hitting his head on the ceiling above the bunk. He fell back down onto the mattress with a thump, rubbing the top of his head.

"Oh, please try to calm down now," said the voice. "I've just had a dreadful time trying to get your young friend back to sleep down there. I did everything possible to convince him that I was just a dream."

They both listened as the sounds of Fletcher's loud snores drifted up toward them.

"Well, that's a relief, at least," the voice declared. "I'm terribly sorry, but the marmalade cat in the garden assured me that you were slumbering in the bottom portion of the bed."

"Not tonight," said Sam breathlessly. "I was there *last* night. We're taking turns."

Sam squinted into the darkness at the little blob of fur by his knee. When he leaned forward, the familiar scent of lavender wafted into his nostrils.

"Beatrice Elderberry?" he whispered very slowly.

"Indeed," the soft voice replied.

"Wow!" he cried. "I can't believe it's really you!"

"It really is, Sam. And please, dear, do try to keep it down."

"How did you find me?" Sam whispered excitedly. "The farm cat network...or...or...a super express mouse courier message or something?"

"No. It was the local telephone directory, actually," Beatrice replied.

"Oh," said Sam, sounding a little disappointed.

"Well, you did mention your friend Fletcher's aunt in your letter, Sam, remember? I couldn't stay at home doing nothing, you see. So I popped a few things in my carpetbag and came as soon as I knew you'd be here."

Beatrice reached into her mouse suit just then and pulled out a frilly, embroidered handkerchief. She unfolded it very carefully with the tips of her slender claws. She was just as Sam had imagined she would be. Her warm, brown eyes, framed within a face that was somewhat wrinkled after 900 years, still glowed vibrantly with life. Black hair, streaked with silver, had slipped out from under her mouse cap where it mingled with the sleek, chestnut-colored fur of her immaculately groomed mouse suit.

Her voice trembling slightly, Beatrice began to dab at her eyes with a corner of the hanky. "I just can't stop thinking about Jolly and Edgar. They are in my thoughts every moment."

"Same as me," said Sam. "In my dreams, too."

Beatrice nodded her head and placed one of her delicate paws on Sam's knee.

"I've come to help in any way that I can, if it's alright with you, Sam. When you wrote about finding Professor Hawthorne's scroll notes and said that you were hoping to try something out with the crop circles, I decided that it was high time I came out of retirement, especially if Jolly and Edgar needed me. What do you say?"

"Wow," Sam replied quietly. "That would be great! If the professor's notes are right, there's going to be a crop circle coming up tomorrow night, not too far from here."

Sam twisted sideways and peered over the edge of the bunk.

"What about Fletcher, though?" he asked. "He's supposed to be helping me."

"He's your friend, isn't he, Sam? And from what Jolly has told me, a very good one, too. I'll just keep out of sight. You may need his help. It's always a comfort, I find, to have someone you care about to confide in," said Beatrice. "With some obvious omissions, of course."

Sam nodded. "That's the problem. I just found out that I talk in my sleep."

"Oh, dear, I see," said Beatrice. "I suppose that's why you were tossing and turning this evening. Reluctant to drift off, I imagine?"

Sam nodded again.

"Well, Sam, since I'm here now, I'll promise to give you a nudge if you start up, alright?"

By this time, Beatrice had recovered enough from her emotional thoughts of Mr. Goodfellow and Edgar to return the slightly damp hanky to her suit again. As she did, she pulled out a small flashlight from the same inside pocket, switched it on and aimed it upward.

"I hope you don't mind, Sam," she said, moving the beam through the air as she moved closer to him, "but I do so want to see your face clearly. I've had an image of you in my mind for the longest time..."

"No...it's okay, I guess," said Sam, a little embarrassed. A tiny stream of light hit his cheek first, then slowly moved across the rest of his face. Beatrice was right next to his shoulder now.

"Just as I had imagined," she remarked with satisfaction, "or, should I say, as Jolly described you to me. Lovely thick hair, a pleasant mouth, strong chin, and your eyes..." Beatrice's voice grew softer. "It's true," she whispered. "They have the same light in them as dear Edgar's. It's quite remarkable."

"It's probably The Sacred Seal thing," offered Sam. "Edgar and I were supposed to..."

"Oh, I know *all* about that, Sam. No, that's not it. Anyway, as you must know, the Seal had to be adjusted somewhat between the two of you. It caused the Governing Council no end of confusion, I've heard tell." Beatrice tilted her head from side to side as she moved the flashlight across Sam's face. "No. There's definitely more to it, I think. Something else, Sam; something special. A yet-to-be-revealed destiny for you perhaps, and Edgar, too. Jolly was right."

"Mr. Goodfellow said that?" asked Sam. "What does it..."

There was a disturbance in the bunk beneath them just then: a rustle, a thump, a sleepy moan from Fletcher and a muffled caterwaul. Jemima, the hairs on the back of her marmalade coat standing on end, suddenly leapt to the top bunk, trying to make her grand entrance with the grace and agility of a jungle cat. Hoping to salvage as much of her dignity as possible, she immediately nested on the blanket by Sam's elbow and set about licking her great webbed paws, as if nothing untoward had happened at all.

"There you are, my dear," Beatrice called over to her. "The boys have taken to switching spots, apparently," she added with empathy.

Jemima looked up from her washing and let out a plaintive mew.

"Cats do so hate to be surprised like that," Beatrice whispered to Sam. "Most embarrassing for them." She shone her flashlight down the blanket. "She seems to be having trouble with something." Beatrice climbed across the blanket toward the cat. "I'll see if I can't be of some assistance."

Jemima, during her sudden, frenzied leap, had snagged one of her claws, causing it to split down one side, and was now trying desperately to pull the hanging bit off.

"I have the perfect thing for that," Beatrice announced. "It's in my carpetbag over there. I'll just be a tick."

Beatrice crawled down to the end of Sam's bunk where she had left her luggage. She opened up the carpetbag, thrust her furry arm through the top and began to search.

"Ahh, there it is!" she cried, removing a very small object (even by Sage standards).

Beatrice made her way back across the hills and valleys of woolly blanket to Jemima's side and knelt beside her with the flashlight.

"Give me your paw, dear. I'll have that nasty piece of claw off in no time."

Jemima obliged, resting her paw carefully on Beatrice's lap. Beatrice grasped the split claw tightly in one paw as she fiddled with the shiny silver thing she was holding in the other.

"Let's see. Where's that file part now?"

Sam pulled out his ever-present magnifying glass and moved in for a closer look.

"Wow! That's the neatest Swiss Army Knife I've ever seen. I didn't think they could make them that small, though."

"They don't, Sam. This little tool is something quite different. It's amazing what they have managed to fit into it."

Beatrice turned it over in her paw and began to pull out each gadget, one by one.

"There's the standard-issue stainless steel knife to begin with, of course," she explained, "and a pair of scissors, for whisker trimming. Next there's the toothpick, corkscrew and grappling hook, plus the pup tent, collapsible cot, rainwater collector, fire extinguisher, foghorn, inflatable raft with bilge pump," Beatrice took a quick breath, "three types of flares, two oars, a compass, waterproof matches, and a knife and fork. Last but not least, and thankfully the very implement I've been looking for, the claw file. And all of this, I might add, in an attractive, watertight case." Beatrice took another big breath as she folded everything back in but the last item. "These knives are as rare as hen's teeth," she said, as she carefully examined Jemima's claw. "It's an age-old tradition, you know, that the knives must never be bought or sold. They can only be given as a special gift, usually as a token of great friendship or admiration and only by a member of the very elite group whose name adorns the side. See?"

Beatrice lifted the tiny knife up high for Sam to examine.

"Scandinavian Sea Mice," he read through his magnifier.

Beatrice pointed her claw underneath. "They have a lovely coat of arms, don't they? Mouse rampant with seaweed clusters."

"*Fidelis Mare Maris Mus Muris,*" Sam read from a thin line just below the red crest.

"Who are *they*?" he asked.

"A most unique band of creatures, Sam." Beatrice began to file away at the bottom of Jemima's broken claw, giving the cat's webbed paw a comforting pat. "You know all about them, don't you, my dear?"

Jemima purred.

"You see, Sam," Beatrice explained, "all animals endowed in this manner share a special kinship."

"So they're mice with webbed feet, huh?" asked Sam.

"On first glance, perhaps. But Scandinavian Sea Mice are really much more than that. Each one is a member of a highly skilled force. It's an ancient association steeped in tradition. Training in the deepest Norwegian fjords, Sea Mice, with their extraordinary lung capacity and the ability to swim great distances, are frequently called upon to perform acts of bravery. Many off-course seabirds, beached or injured whales and dolphins have depended on the Sea Mice and their code of honor. They are elusive creatures and much about them is veiled in secrecy, but make no mistake, Sam, they are fiercely loyal to their code. When called upon, they will sacrifice everything to secure the rescue and protection of any creature in peril."

"Wow," said Sam, staring solemnly at the knife.

"There now, Jemima," Beatrice suddenly announced, struggling to lift the cat's heavy paw from her lap. "I think we're done. Give that a try."

Jemima stood up and circled around a few times before happily settling back down to resume her bath. Beatrice rubbed her own fur-covered legs for a moment before standing up and stretching her arms high above her head. "It's getting a little more difficult to perform these emergency field repairs," Beatrice complained. "I'm not quite as agile as I used to be, I'm afraid."

Sam was too busy examining the Scandinavian Sea Mouse Knife with his magnifying glass to look up.

"No, Sam!" Beatrice lunged across the blanket with furry arms outstretched. "Not the raft, dear! Please! It's an absolute nightmare to get back in once it's been inflated."

Sam quickly dropped the tiny rip cord he had been about to pull with his fingernail.

"Sorry to startle you," Beatrice apologized, trying to catch her breath. "I can still recall a scene of utter chaos when twenty or so of those things had to be deflated in stormy seas and stuffed back into their knifes in a matter of seconds. It was quite terrifying. They're actually not used all that much anymore, I understand. Only when absolutely necessary."

"Really?" asked Sam, more than a little intrigued by the thought of such a bizarre operation.

Beatrice smiled and patted his hand.

"Well, enough of my silly stories," she said. Looking at the twinkle in Sam's eye, Beatrice knew that this was not going to be the end of it.

Sam continued to examine the knife with reverence.

"I guess that having this means it was given to you by an actual Scandinavian Sea Mouse. And for some special reason, too, right?"

"Well, yes, dear, that *is* true, but it was a very long time ago and..." Beatrice paused. Sam was looking at her with one eyebrow raised.

"You know, Sam," Beatrice remarked, wagging her claw at him, "Jolly warned me about you and your insatiable appetite for stories, and usually in the middle of the night, I've been told!"

"I'm not sleepy," Sam declared.

"Young people with appetites for stories seldom are, I've found," Beatrice sighed. "You're not going to let this drop, are you?"

"No," said Sam with determination and a smile.

"Blasted inflatable rafts!" Beatrice whispered under her breath. "Very well then. But before I get into the rafts, you must allow me one small indulgence: a little bit of background information. Agreed?"

"Sure," said Sam, "I'd like that."

Beatrice called across the blanket. "Jemima, dear? Could you move a little more this way? Thank you."

Beatrice nestled down into the soft fur that ran along the cat's side, which had been conveniently moved closer to Sam's right ear.

"Just a minute!"

Jumping up, Beatrice made her way down the bed to where her carpetbag lay. She quickly removed a gold-hinged, red velvet glasses case, which she carried back with her. She once again made herself comfortable in the soft hollow of Jemima's side.

"Are you going to read something?" asked Sam.

"No, dear...no," said Beatrice, a little distracted.

She opened up the red case to reveal not reading glasses, but two plump, chestnut-colored cigars, each about the size of half a matchstick, lying side by side on white satin lining. Beatrice took one out, lifted it toward her nose, closed her eyes and inhaled its smell.

"I gave these up years ago, Sam, as Jolly was *very* pleased to hear. Dreadfully unhealthy habit, of course, but their aroma always reminds me so much of dear Mr. Churchill that I couldn't bear to part with these last two. They are the only souvenirs I have kept, along with the Sea Mouse Knife, of the most memorable years of my life," Beatrice sighed. "It seems so odd, Sam. Just a few months ago, I was telling Jolly this very same story because we had been apart during all those years, and here I am, telling it to you now, and he's gone again."

Beatrice took out her hanky and gave her nose a discreet wipe.

"You really never heard from him for all that time?" asked Sam.

"Sadly, no. When we returned to England late in 1936 after our summer together in America, I immediately became engrossed in my new assignment. Jolly and I lost touch rather quickly, I'm afraid. In fact, I had no idea for quite some time that Edgar, bless his heart, had disappeared. Poor Jolly! What he must have gone through. First his brother Filbert, then his young nephew. How I wish he had thought to get in touch with me. Perhaps we could have been a comfort to each other. But that's Jolly, isn't it? Always so independent."

"I know that Mr. Goodfellow spent a lot of time searching for Edgar right after that, but what about you?" asked Sam.

"Well, it had always been a wish of mine that one day I might be able to inspire something especially meaningful, perhaps guide someone special on to greatness. Most of my assignments up until then had been successful, but small. You know, I think it may actually have been my admiration for Jolly's wonderful career that spurred me on. I had gotten wind of something in the air in Europe, even before my American trip. That's why I was so anxious to return home. I was hoping that something might be offered to me, and I was determined not to lose the opportunity."

"It was just before the Second World War, right?" asked Sam.

"Yes, it was, dear."

"And the assignment was this Churchill guy? Winston Churchill, right?"

"Indeed, Sam," said Beatrice, delighted that a boy of his age was familiar with a man she had so admired.

Beatrice turned the cigar over in her paw.

"Mr. Churchill was a man of unusual attributes and remarkable courage. His was called the 'voice in the wilderness,' you know, in the years leading up to war. He warned that Hitler could neither be trusted nor appeased, but by the time others finally began to heed his words, it was too late."

There was a look of great sadness in Beatrice's eyes as she recalled the road to war.

"The Fen had been very busy in those last few years, I'm afraid, whispering their dark and evil words into many willing ears. By the end of the decade, Europe was on the brink of an inevitable conflict and the world was about to change forever. Mr. Churchill's guidance up until then had been provided by a very, very old and wise Sage by the name of Rudyard Elderberry."

"Another Elderberry?"

"My great-uncle. He had begun to grow quite frail with advancing years. If the world was heading into a time of great trial, as we Sage had begun to believe it was, then it would be too daunting a task for Great-Uncle Rudyard to carry on."

"The Sacred Seal was passed to you?"

"Eventually, Sam, but not without some dissent. It was the main topic of discussion at several meetings of the Governing Council, causing them no end of trouble and leaving them with a difficult decision to make. There were other Elderberrys who wanted to continue Great-Uncle Rudyard's very special work and they were probably much more deserving of the honor than I. I hadn't distinguished myself with anything particularly memorable, after all."

"So how did you end up with it?"

"Well, it was Jolly, actually. In an indirect sort of way."

"Mr. Goodfellow! How? You guys never even saw each other for years."

"But I had taken heed of all of Jolly's advice during our summer together. He'd had years of experience dealing with the darker forces, and encountered them enough times in his life to develop an intuition about their presence. It had proven to be his salvation on many occasions."

"I remember that in Mr. Goodfellow's stories! He taught it to Edgar. He called it the 'ominous presence' or something," said Sam.

Beatrice nodded her head. "It was very important for a Sage of Jolly's caliber to become attuned to these sensitivities, and he was particularly good at it. During our time together at Sparrow Ranch, Jolly insisted that I learn the things I might need to protect myself. Even though I had come dangerously close to eternity at the hands of The Fen that summer, I continued to argue that my missions would be of little interest to them. But Jolly won out in the end, and I finally agreed to take him up on his offer. I often wondered, years later, if Jolly had had an intuition of sorts—that one day I would find myself faced with an assignment of such proportion that I would be in need of every bit of his insight and wisdom. And, indeed, it was the intuitive skills I had honed at Jolly's side that convinced the Governing Council that I should be the successor to the great Rudyard Elderberry. They sensed that the job I was about to inherit would be fraught with danger and intrigue, and their suspicions were confirmed just a few years later when war broke out and the world was plunged into darkness. It was a tremendous responsibility to inspire a man who would inspire so many others in those perilous times, and one that I sincerely hoped I would be able to live up to."

Beatrice looked intently at Sam.

"Speaking of Jolly like this puts me in mind of one of his favorite proverbs. It goes like this. Search all things..." she began.

"Hold fast that which is true," Sam finished for her.

Her eyebrows raised, Beatrice continued. "Take heed of many..."

"The advice of few," Sam finished again.

"And always..."

"Paddle your own canoe."

Beatrice squealed with delight and clapped her paws.

"How absolutely wonderful, dear! You must have learned that at Jolly's knee. Wouldn't he be pleased to know that *you* have taken heed of some of his lessons, too? Dear, sweet Jolly," she murmured, reaching for her hanky. "I've always treasured those lines, too. They remind me so much of Mr. Churchill."

Beatrice settled back even further into Jemima's soft fur, holding the cigar up to her nose again.

"This does bring back such memories, Sam—the aroma of a fine cigar and the comfort of feline companionship. Those were two things in particular that got both of us through some very difficult days."

Jemima purred in response.

"Mr. Churchill was a great admirer of cats, you know. There was always one or two about, first at the Admiralty House, then later at 10 Downing Street, the many family residences before and after that, and always at the country home in Kent. Such lovely creatures, too."

Jemima mewed.

"No, dear, there wasn't a Jemima, but you will be interested to know that Mr. Churchill had a particular fondness for marmalade cats. Let me see if I can remember their names."

Beatrice lifted up both paws and started to count on her claws.

"There was Smokey, then Nelson, and three Jocks over the years, Tango and one named Cat. Great-Uncle Rudyard spoke fondly of Mickey, too, a resident tabby at the country home some years earlier, to whom he grew quite attached." Beatrice held her last two claws in the air. "I'm sure I must have left *someone* out."

Beatrice drummed all of her claws on her knees now and stared into space.

"Rufus I and Rufus II were the dogs..." she slowly recalled, "so, perhaps that *was* everyone after all, apart from the house mice, of course. Such delightful hosts they were, too! Even during wartime, they never failed to set a nice table. I was constantly amazed that they could accomplish so much with just a bit of ingenuity and a sample or two from the kitchen. Mr. Churchill was partial to good food, and Mrs. Landemare, the family cook, was a genius in the kitchen. I imagine that Jolly would have been in his element there. And young Edgar, too, no doubt!"

Beatrice suddenly glanced up at Sam.

"I'm sorry, dear," she apologized. "I believe I have drifted off topic."

"That's okay."

Beatrice could see by the expression on Sam's face that the burden of responsibility he felt for the welfare of Jolly and Edgar had become a heavy load. She picked up the little cigar that was resting on her knee, held it up and shook it in front of him.

"Sam. Never give in, never give in, never, never, never, never—in nothing, great or small..."

Sam looked up.

"Did Mr. Churchill say that?"

"In 1941, to a group of schoolboys at Harrow not much older than yourself, at a time when the fate of the world hung most precariously in the balance. He was so masterful with words, a man of such poetic thought and rare insight that I was quite often in awe of him. He remained steadfast through it all, Sam: the fall of Europe, the anxious hours at Dunkirk, the bombing of London. From his moments of greatest despair and struggle, when I felt the need to lift his spirits, to whisper a word of advice or encouragement, he would rise up and answer the next challenge with courage and determination. His speeches were like great, stirring songs that people everywhere would sing over and over to themselves, and the fact that I could add a note or two, every now and then, was a monumental honor."

Brown eyes twinkling, Beatrice looked up at Sam.

"Those last two never nevers were mine, you know," she whispered.

Beatrice ran the little chestnut-colored cigar under her nose one last time. She took a final sniff and then returned it to its white satin bed.

"I grew very fond of Mr. Churchill over the years. I stayed with him always, through the declining years of his career and his life. I was offered many other fascinating assignments after my wartime success, but I passed on them all. We built the brick walls in his garden together, and painted the Isles of Scotland and the countryside of his beloved Kent in morning sun and evening shadow. And when he was gone, I decided to retire. Nothing I could do, I thought, could ever compare with those years. Try as I might, I would never be able to make myself more useful or find someone who would need me as much. At least not until now, perhaps." Beatrice patted the red velvet case affectionately. "And that, in a nutshell, was..."

Sam opened his mouth to speak.

"It's the inflatable rafts, isn't it?" Beatrice said, reading his thoughts.

"Well..." Sam began.

"I was working my way up to that part, I assure you, Sam. I just need to reshuffle myself."

Beatrice twisted herself around then and, with both paws, gently patted Jemima's fur like it was the cover of an old, beloved chair.

"There, that's much better," she announced, turning back to Sam.

"Whenever people find themselves in moments of great fear and despair, Sam, it is sometimes the simplest things that keep the heart from giving in: a kindness observed, a gesture of friendship, a word of hope, an expression of love, even a small pleasure indulged. Now, like many other people trying to keep their chins up, Mr. Churchill had a few little indulgences that he allowed himself in those bleak and desolate war years. There were his beloved pets, as I've mentioned, his trademark cigars, of course, his garden, his poetry, his painting and, from time to time, a single glass of the finest French champagne, a commodity that became increasingly difficult to obtain when France was occupied by hostile forces. For a country under siege, hope can be found in even the tiniest glimmer of resolve and defiance. In this particular tale, Sam, that hope came disguised as a case of French champagne, smuggled out of the Pol Roger vineyards at Epernay, spirited across the English Channel and deposited on the doorstep of 10 Downing Street in the middle of the night, to be discovered the next morning by Mr. Churchill's aide as if it had fallen from the sky above."

Beatrice smiled at Sam, whose expression had suddenly lightened in anticipation.

"I had been hearing, through the grapevine," she continued, "about a courageous band of French mice who were giving the occupying army a taste of what rodent resistance was all about. This little group of heroes had, in fact, become legendary among their British brethren, disrupting important meetings of the high command, infesting food supply depots and overrunning officers' quarters, all at great personal risk. Word had come through to us from them about a contingent of the human French Resistance that had infiltrated a convoy of enemy soldiers and confiscated a code-breaking machine. Before being captured, the resistance fighters had hidden the device at a local vineyard, where it remained for a number of days with no means of safely transporting it to England. If this critical piece of equipment, used to decipher enemy messages, could be dropped into the hands of the Allied command, it might shorten the war by many months. Armed with a loosely conceived plan to conceal the device in a shipment of local champagne, I contacted the French mice by underground courier and awaited a reply. They could transport the goods through the countryside and as far as the French coast, they confirmed by return mouse, but hauling a crate of champagne across the frequently perilous waters of the English Channel would require a specialized force and a good dose of luck.

"Scandinavian Sea Mice!" whispered Sam.

"Indeed," Beatrice replied. "I have to admit, though, it *was* a most unusual request for a group of highly trained marine operatives, but they accepted the mission with a particularly fervent dedication. After the occupation of Norway, the waters of their homeland fjords had begun to swarm with flotillas of enemy submarines, constantly disrupting their own movements and maneuvers. They were eager to engage in any kind of work that would boost the war effort and support the cause of freedom. The fact that the transportation of the crate would be occurring under the very noses of the enemy, with bottles bearing the royal coat of arms of Britain (which the French vineyard labels discreetly but defiantly displayed), was, I believe, the icing on the cake."

Sam shuffled closer to Beatrice as the tale unfolded.

"After I had secured everyone's cooperation, a plan of action was launched with the French mice that included a timetable of dates and rendezvous points. Throughout its journey across the country, the crate was transferred many times from one band of dedicated volunteers to the next, all performing their backbreaking work without complaint. Every contingent comprised a hundred mice or more, each one struggling valiantly under many times its own weight, with no other thought but the successful completion of the mission. I was kept informed every step of the way through the underground mouse network, including word of a near disaster in the Paris restaurant district. After stopping to rest and refresh themselves at the back of a busy bistro, one troop of enthusiastic participants resumed their mission, only to discover ten kilometers later that they were transporting a crate of rapidly ripening Camembert cheese instead! They rushed back to reclaim the precious code machine and champagne with all due haste, stuffing into their cheeks, of course, as much of their accidental cargo as possible before it spoiled."

Beatrice suddenly stopped speaking. She looked around the blanket, then at Sam.

"I'm afraid I've made myself a trifle peckish, dear. Any tid-bits about?"

Sam thought for a moment before he pushed an arm under his pillow and pulled out a half-eaten bag of potato crisps.

"Lovely," said Beatrice, reaching out her paw to take the large crisp that Sam was offering. "It's refreshing to know that young boys are still the same the world over."

"These are Fletcher's from last night," said Sam. "I think there are some cheese snacks under the pillow down there."

"Really?" Beatrice remarked, peering over the side of the bunk to where Fletcher lay peacefully sleeping. "More of what I had in mind, actually, but perhaps a bit too risky at the moment. These will do, I suppose," she concluded, nibbling on a crisp before she settled back into the story.

"After a journey of almost three days," Beatrice began, quickly swallowing the last mouthful, "the crate was finally delivered to the coast of northern France. The beaches were swarming with enemy forces. The last brave band of rodents, in constant danger of discovery, camouflaged the crate with thick clumps of wet sand and seagrass before carrying it down to the surf to await the next leg of its voyage."

"The Sea Mice, right?" asked Sam intently.

Beatrice nodded her head. "And what would become the trickiest part of the whole operation."

Sam stopped crunching his potato crisps and leaned forward, not wanting to miss a word.

"Waiting until dark, twenty-five Scandinavian Sea Mice, their pink paws and noses blackened with marsh mud, waded ashore. The tide had begun to turn about an hour before, and was creeping ever closer now to the solitary clump of sand and grass on the beach and the prize that lay beneath it. Foamy waves were soon lapping up against the crate's wooden sides, slowly dissolving the artfully applied camouflage, piece by small piece. The band of Sea Mice, armed only with their legendary knives, crawled toward their quarry, ever mindful that just a few feet away groups of enemy soldiers, carrying machine guns and floodlights, were patrolling the beach. At any moment they could have been discovered, shot for sport or trampled under the heel of a tall black boot. Or the unthinkable: captured and shipped off to some hideous experimental lab somewhere. They were, after all, an undiscovered species."

Sam swallowed hard.

"But Scandinavian Sea Mice, of course," Beatrice continued, "would never have allowed such thoughts to enter their minds. As the approaching tide slowly began to rock the crate back and forth, they scurried toward it, knowing exactly what each one of them had to do. Slipping their paws through the crate's wooden slats, the Sea Mice quickly opened their knives and pulled down hard on the dangling rip cords. Twenty-five yellow rafts suddenly and silently inflated, encircling the crate with a collar of air. When the next big wave rushed onto shore, the crate, with the Sea Mice guiding it along, was lifted high in the water, then slowly carried out to sea as the wave retreated. At first, it seemed as if everything was going according to plan, until..."

"Someone saw them!" Sam cried with concern.

"A patrolling soldier," Beatrice continued, "thinking he had spotted a piece of valuable booty from the debris of a torpedoed ship, threw his boots and jacket onto the sand and rushed into the water. Grabbing hold of one corner of the floating crate, he began to pull it back to shore, as twenty-five Sea Mice, holding their breaths just beneath the surface, madly paddled through the waves, trying desperately to gain the upper hand. When it was beginning to look as if their valiant efforts would be in vain, one of them lunged at the soldier's hand, sinking two sharp teeth deep into his flesh. With a cry of pain, the soldier fell back for a moment, then reached for the knife on his belt. Not knowing exactly what had happened, he flailed his arm back and forth through the water, eventually losing his grip on the crate and crawling back to the beach, his hand throbbing and covered in blood."

"Was the Sea Mouse okay?" asked Sam.

"Fortunately, he sustained only minor injuries," Beatrice assured Sam, "involving, I believe, a cut to his ear and a chipped tooth. A short time later, however, when the crate began to list heavily to one side, it was discovered that the soldier had managed to puncture several of the encircling rafts. From that moment on, the voyage across the channel became a race against time, made especially urgent by the arrival of dark storm clouds. It would take every ounce of Sea Mouse strength and skill to complete the mission now. For those of us waiting in the moonlight on a small stretch of sand near Dover, it became a nerve-wracking ordeal as the clock ticked well past the rendezvous time."

"*You* were there?"

"Indeed I was, Sam, with a large group of British mice who were to take the crate on the last few legs of its journey to London. Standing on the beach that night, though, I began to grow disconsolate, as the time slowly ticked away and there was no sign of our gallant Sea Mice or their cargo. Angry waves lashed against the rock pier that ran down one edge of the beach and far out into the ocean. An hour or so later, heavy rain began to pound violently on the surface of the sand, whipped up every few seconds by fierce gusts of wind that drove it against our bodies with stinging accuracy. Even the seagulls, quite accustomed to the foul coastal weather, had flown inland with reports of gale force winds and swelling seas. Visibility, they said, was next to nothing. Two hours had passed beyond the rendezvous time. Soon it would be three. Panicked by the discouraging mumblings among the mouse ranks, I decided to take matters into my own hands. Lashing a piece of discarded fishing line about my waist, and against the protests of my companions, I climbed up onto the seawall, then made my way down the long pier toward the ocean. Dodging the incoming waves as they rose up and dashed against the rocks at my paws, I could feel my claws slipping against strands of seaweed that the waves had churned up. By the time I reached the end of the pier, I had resorted to crawling on all fours, clinging onto the final few rocks at the edge of the sea with all of my strength. Making sure that my mouse friends at the other end of the fishing line had a good, tight hold of it, I let go of the rocks for just a second while I reached into my suit and pulled out my flashlight. I held the light as high as I could, directing its piercing beam into the dark sky above the surface of the water, hoping that somehow it could act as a beacon for any souls who might be out there on the raging sea."

Beatrice paused for a moment to rest and catch her breath. Sam could tell that even though she enjoyed telling him her story, it was an exhausting and emotional memory.

"You know, Sam," Beatrice began again, "it's rather strange. The whole time this was happening, I couldn't get dear Edgar out of my mind. I think now it was because of the ordeal he must have gone through on those sea cliffs in northern California just a few years earlier, risking everything to save me from The Fen. It gave me great comfort and strength at the time and the determination not to falter."

"Well...what happened next?" asked Sam, a little impatiently.

"Nothing, actually, for what seemed like an eternity. But then, a single red flare rose into the night sky, then another, and another, followed by the absolutely wonderful sound of twenty-five portable foghorns drifting over the roar of the wind. Their Sea Mouse compasses had brought them as far as the coastline, but it was the beam of a single flashlight from

the shore that had found them in the storm and steered them to safety."

"And that's why you were given a Scandinavian Sea Mouse Knife, right?" asked Sam.

"For exemplary conduct, they said, in accordance with the Sea Mouse code of honor," Beatrice replied proudly. "It was a lovely ceremony, held right there on the beach, just after the rafts had been deflated and the crate safely deposited on shore. Sea Mice aren't known to waste time with these things, you know. The young fellow who was injured by the soldier received a citation right there, too. The highly coveted Purple Claw, as I recall. After that, the other mice picked up the crate and began their trip to London, while the Scandinavian Sea Mice slipped away to their next mission. I made a quick mental note at the time to send them a formal thank-you note when I returned home, as well as a new penny."

"A what?" asked Sam.

"A penny, dear. It's a very old tradition. When one receives a knife as a gift, you must return a penny to the giver to ensure that the relationship between friends will not be severed."

Sam nodded as Beatrice continued.

"There was only one mystery remaining: a missing life raft, solved upon my return to 10 Downing Street, when I discovered that it had somehow hooked onto a jagged piece of the wooden champagne crate and was now assuming its new role as a cat toy."

Beatrice took a long breath.

"And that, Sam, is just *one* little story in a very big war. I heard later that when the champagne crate was discovered on the steps of the prime minister's residence, a very delighted Mr. Churchill insisted that his staff share in his mysterious good fortune. I understand there was an even louder celebration of victory when the other bottles were removed from the crate to reveal the greater prize inside."

"That's really neat," Sam declared. "Do you think there's anyway *I'll* ever see a Scandinavian Sea Mouse?"

"It would be most unusual. I haven't seen one since the war, myself, Sam. They are like a sudden wind that ripples over the waves. Gone before you even knew it was there. But you never can tell, dear. You seem to have a knack for seeing and doing unusual things. In any event, I think it might be a good idea to get some sleep now. Jolly was always such a stickler about young people and their rest, I suppose I owe it to him to keep an eye on you, and make sure you look after yourself."

"But the crop circles," said Sam sleepily. "We never got around to talking about..."

"We'll have chance enough tomorrow to discuss the finer aspects of Professor Hawthorne's theories," Beatrice assured him.

Sam nodded his head and crawled under his blanket. He was too tired at the moment to offer much protest anyway. There was something important he should be telling Beatrice about the upcoming mission; something that had been preying on his mind since he had left home, but he was suddenly very sleepy. It could wait until tomorrow, he supposed, as he yawned and turned on his side.

6

A Friend in the Market
Is Worth Money in
the Pocket

Auntie Nellie was up with the birds the next morning and down to business, preparing a breakfast that could have satisfied the entire Scandinavian Sea Mice fleet and then some.

The smell of frying ham wafted up the stairs and down the hall to Sam and Fletcher's room, where it rose to the ceiling and settled under Sam's nose as he lay in the top bunk. He was racing once again through the corridors of stone and rock and red dust, following the sound of Edgar's voice, preparing to turn the last fateful corner before his friend vanished. But even in the foggy haze of half-sleep, Sam knew that this time something was different. There was a strange new sound now, like machinery, or an engine. Sam's mind was struggling to make sense of it when something wet touched his nose, and he awoke with a start. Jemima, her big, webbed, marmalade paws folded neatly in front of her, was nose to nose with him, staring straight into his eyes and purring like Auntie Nellie's motor car as the smell of ham curled in her nostrils.

"Is he awake yet, Jemima?"

Sam could hear Beatrice Elderberry's soft voice in the background. He lifted himself up on his elbows and rubbed the sleep out of his eyes.

"Ah, there you are!" she said. "Excellent timing, too. I believe Fletcher's auntie has just called up to announce that she is holding breakfast for you."

Beatrice was sitting on the blanket next to Sam, sorting through her carpetbag.

"Have a good sleep?"

Sam, unable to speak just yet, nodded his head slowly and yawned. Suddenly remembering Fletcher, he leaned over the side of his bunk. Unable to rouse his friend with several hearty thumps on the bottom of his bunk, Fletcher had already departed for the kitchen.

"No need to worry, Sam," Beatrice continued. "I gave you a shake every time you started to talk in your sleep. You were dreaming about Edgar again, weren't you, dear?"

Sam nodded once more, then asked with a croak, "Didn't *you* sleep at all?"

"No, but it's alright. I wasn't much of a sleeper to begin with, and I became accustomed to even less during my years with Mr. Churchill. He never slept for more than four hours a night, you know, and sometimes not even that. He used to take short little naps throughout the day. In fact, while you're downstairs having breakfast, I think I might just catch forty winks."

Sam slid over the side of the bunk and down the narrow wooden ladder. He dressed quickly, then climbed halfway back up the ladder and rested his chin on the edge of his mattress.

"I'll bring you something back," he offered.

"That would be lovely," said Beatrice, already comfortably nestled at Jemima's side. "A few bits of fruit or cheese would do. I'll leave it to you."

The marmalade cat mewed softly.

"And a piece of ham for Jemima. If it's not too much trouble, she says."

Like the dinners, breakfasts at Auntie Nellie's were remarkable in both content and volume. There were rashers of bacon and ham, long links of country sausage, fried eggs and stewed tomatoes, boiled potatoes with drizzled butter and the unbelievably delicious, but shamefully greasy, stack of fried bread, accompanied by three different types of HP sauce and two homemade chutneys. For a boy like Sam, who usually observed breakfast by nibbling a granola bar on the school bus, this was an overwhelming spectacle. And Auntie Nellie was already busily planning an outing to the town market to acquire even more supplies.

After he had eaten, Sam collected a nice selection of cheese crumbles, a quarter of a tea cake and a large gooseberry for Beatrice. Then, waiting until everyone was distracted, he reached across the table for Jemima's piece of ham, carefully folded everything into his napkin and excused himself.

Auntie Nellie had announced her intention to leave for the market within a half-hour, giving Beatrice just enough time to enjoy her breakfast and attend to herself and her wardrobe. If it had been the very particular Mr. Goodfellow, instead, thought Sam, they would have been hopelessly delayed, but Beatrice quickly freshened her face with a damp cloth and groomed her coat with a few short strokes of a comb. Sam donned his beige canvas fishing vest again, which he usually reserved for serious camping expeditions. Sam had determined that it would be ideal for this trip, too, with its rows of Velcroed pockets at the front and two large zippered compartments on the inside. He wished that he had thought to use it on the many occasions that Mr. Goodfellow had accompanied him and complained bitterly about the cramped quarters of his one-pocket shirt.

Accustomed to this sort of travel arrangement only with Mr. Goodfellow and Edgar, Sam found it strange, at first, to have a lady aboard. Beatrice chose to occupy the top pocket, front left, and Sam helped her inside. Concerned about her comfort, he insisted on checking her condition every few minutes or so until she finally grew impatient with him. The sound of tearing Velcro was beginning to give her a headache.

"You won't be able to go on like this in public, Sam. I'm quite alright. I have managed under far worse conditions, and I'm a lot tougher than I look, dear. If I need you, I'll give a nudge."

Sam shrugged and finished getting ready. There was one more thing he needed to do. Opening up his backpack, he took something out and transferred it to one of the vest's large inner pockets. Then, apologizing to Beatrice, he tore open his top left pocket and passed in the folded wad of paper containing Professor Hawthorne's notes. He was just about to say a last word when Fletcher rushed into the room to grab his baseball cap.

"Come on, Sam! Auntie Nellie's already got the car going. Better fasten your seatbelt real tight this time."

The trip to market was no less exciting than the one from the train station, but this time, Sam knew just what to expect. This particular route was obviously one that Auntie Nellie had taken a thousand times before. Turning her head to India or leaning over the back seat to chatter to the boys, Auntie Nellie seemed able to navigate every hairpin turn, maverick sheep or bump in the road without looking up. It was a relief to reach town, but even then, the excitement was far from over. Racing up and down the narrow, winding streets in a mad search for a parking spot, Auntie Nellie shouted with glee upon discovering a small space that had been left between two much larger cars. Waving off frantic protests from her passengers that it wasn't actually a *real* spot, Auntie Nellie proceeded to execute an amazing series of lurching maneuvers until she had squeezed the car in with barely enough room to pass a piece of paper between the bumpers.

India, Fletcher and Sam got out of the car as quickly as possible before anyone could associate it with them. They made arrangements to meet at the town clock in forty-five minutes, giving everyone lots of time to explore their own areas of interest. Auntie Nellie, clutching an armful of reusable shopping bags, immediately headed toward the food merchants, while India made a beeline for the bookstalls selling new and used books. Fletcher, who had been to market many times before, was anxious to show Sam the sights.

Market day in the picturesque little town always attracted huge crowds of locals and tourists alike. Open-air stalls, filled with a variety of items, lined the meandering streets of biscuit-colored, Cotswold-stone shops and buildings. There were tables brimming with curd tarts and sponge toffee, jam rolls and licorice sweets, sheets of old stamps and rolls of copper coins, bales of cloth, antique lead soldiers, toy trucks and tin flutes, gold watches, silver hair barrettes, polished horse brasses and fine leather bridles. Fingering the spending money that was burning a hole in his pocket, Fletcher couldn't resist purchasing a tin flute right away. He had wanted one ever since he had seen them a couple of holidays ago, but his parents, very wisely, had steered him elsewhere. Emitting high pitched squealing sounds that conveniently parted the crowd, Fletcher led Sam past the rest of the stalls to the end of a road where he remembered having an ice cream once. Along the way, they stopped to look at a table of antique toffee boxes when one in particular happened to catch Sam's eye. The asking price was a little out of Sam's range, but Fletcher, an old pro at market-stall haggling, stepped in and bargained the man down to a more affordable level. They continued on their way, Fletcher blowing his tin flute and Sam right behind him, clutching a newspaper-wrapped package containing a 1930s toffee box adorned with a painting of the RMS *Queen Mary* surrounded by a flotilla of tugboats.

What a strange coincidence finding a thing like that, here and now, thought Sam. He just *had* to get it for Edgar and Mr. Goodfellow, not so much to remind them of their voyage on the famous ship, but because he had a superstitious thought that buying it might guarantee him sufficient luck to find them.

Fletcher had been right about the ice cream vendor, and before long the two boys were enjoying their vanilla cornets, made all the more interesting, thought Sam, by the addition of a long stick of flaked chocolate shoved into the middle. There were many cultural differences here that Sam was really starting to appreciate.

With about twelve minutes remaining before their rendezvous with Auntie Nellie, Fletcher and Sam finished their ice creams and set out on the prowl for something else to eat, slowly making their way back through the crowd toward the old town clock. They stopped at a few confectioners' stalls along the way, settling, with Fletcher's insistence, on another treat that Sam had never tried before: a roll of paper-coated cardboard filled with sherbet powder. A thin black licorice straw was used to suck the flavored mixture out and when this procedure was complete, the licorice was devoured, too. When he had almost finished his treat, Sam tore open one corner of his vest front pocket and slipped a bit of licorice straw through the opening. There was a very muffled "Thank you" from inside.

There was one market stall that Sam and Fletcher wished they had noticed earlier. This area of the country, a veritable trove of ancient archaeological sites, had provided enterprising members of the local community with many souvenir opportunities, and the old couple running this stand had all the angles covered. The first table, the bread and butter of their business, held the usual assortment of items that tourists had come to expect. There were images of Stonehenge, Sillbury Hill and the Avebury Stone Circle on calendars and coins, tea towels and T-shirts, back-scratchers and ballpoint pens, posters and postcards. Sam and Fletcher turned instead to the stall's second table, which held an interesting display of artifacts for the more discerning collector. The little man left his wife to handle the busload of tourists that had just arrived and shuttled along to where Sam and Fletcher were studying the long rows of braided leather necklaces that hung from a wire stand. The boys passed over the crystal amulets and sarsen stone pendants, stopping to take a closer look at a group of dangling pewter charms, each one engraved with a different pattern of lines and circles: crop circles. Fletcher gave Sam a nudge. Sam reached out and took the last hanging charm between his fingers. At that very instant, the face of Edgar Goodfellow popped into his thoughts with such clarity that it caused Sam to step back in surprise.

93

"A fine choice, young sir," the old man remarked.

Two bright eyes peered out at Sam from a wrinkled, weather-beaten face. The man's wide smile revealed a single gold tooth in his top gum.

"An intricate pattern, that one. Interested in the circles are you, then?"

Sam nodded.

"Well, no better spot than right here, lad. Whole place is swarming with them, especially this season. More than I've ever seen, and I've lived in these parts for donkeys' years."

Hoping to make a sale, the old fellow pointed a finger toward the hanging charms.

"Made all of these up myself," he said proudly. "See that one you were holding? Made it just this spring. It was lambing time and I'd gone to help my brother on his farm. Stormy night it was, too, thunder and lightning all about. I was just a field away from the house when I saw these odd sparks flying in the air. By the time I got out of the car to take a look, they were gone. I felt so strange though, sort of faint and tingly all over, I barely made it to my brother's. Couldn't get out of bed the whole next day. Doctor figured I'd had a run in with a bit of lightning myself. If you ask me, it had something to do with the crop circle that was there in the morning. I've heard about other people having the same funny feelings 'round the circles when there hadn't been a storm for miles about."

The old man leaned toward Sam and Fletcher and whispered, "And I know what's doing it, too." He glanced over his shoulder. "The wife doesn't like me saying this; thinks it'll bring all kinds of trouble our way. But, it's the government, you know, as sure as I'm standing here. Top secret, MI 5 stuff. Army flying-machine tests. All that other nonsense about aliens and whirlwinds and hedgehogs running amuck is just a ruse." He waggled his finger. "People should know where their good tax money's going. Mark my words, one day it'll all come out."

The old man suddenly stopped talking and looked around. His wife was standing behind him with a stern look on her face.

"Well, young sirs," he quickly muttered, lifting the crop circle charm off its wire hanger, "shall I be wrapping this one up for you?"

"Umm..." Sam fumbled about in both of his pant pockets, scraping as much change together as he could and placing it on the table.

"Do you have any money left, Fletch?"

Fletcher turned his own pockets inside out, too, coming up with just a few more coins.

"Why don't you buy one of the other ones, Sam?" he whispered, "they're a little cheaper, you know."

"No, Fletcher. *That's* the one I want. Okay?"

Fletcher shrugged and looked down at the rather pathetic amount of money on the table.

"You're in luck," the old man suddenly announced. "Special sale, just today." He leaned forward and winked. "Just don't be letting anyone else in on it."

The old man wrapped the necklace in a piece of white tissue paper and popped it into a small brown bag. Before giving it to Sam, he reached under the table and brought out a thin paper book.

"I keep these for my special customers. It's just a local publication. An old chum of mine has a little printing business." He held the book up. *The Growing Crop Conspiracy: Your Tax Up in Flax*, by Stanley Ramsbottom, it said.

"That's me," said the old man, grinning as he pointed to the name under the title.

The sun slid from behind the clouds and glinted off his solitary gold tooth. He popped the book into the paper bag, too, and handed it to Sam.

"No charge for that," he said, looking about nervously. "Someone has to get the word out, you know."

"Thanks," said Sam. "By the way. That night in the spring, when you went to your brother's place, was it April 2?"

"Let me see," he replied, scratching his chin. "It was a week to the day after our wedding anniversary."

He rolled his eyes at his wife who was carefully wrapping up a pair of monolithic stone-shaped salt and pepper shakers for another customer.

"I wouldn't dare forget that date, I can tell you. So that would make it . . . why, yes, that would have been April 2! How could you have known that? There were dozens of sightings this spring."

"I think I must have seen a photograph of that one in a magazine or something," said Sam, suddenly looking down at his watch. "Hey! We'd better get going Fletcher. We're going to be late for your aunt."

Sam dashed off into the crowd, clutching the brown paper bag in his hand, with Fletcher at his heels.

"Boy!" said Fletcher as they neared the clock, "that old guy was a total nut, wasn't he?"

"Maybe," Sam responded, taking the book out of the bag. "But a nice old nut, and a helpful one, too. Look!" Sam put the book under Fletcher's nose. "He's put all these little maps in here, and drawings of the circles and the fields they were in. They're not half as messy as the professor's maps, Fletch. This could really help us!"

Sam pulled the little book away and shoved it back in the bag.

"Hey!" Fletcher protested.

"Shh! Here comes India. Act normal."

India, loaded down with used books, walked out of the crowd toward them. Waving at her, Fletcher turned to Sam and whispered, "How *did* you know about the April 2 circle, anyway?"

"It was one of the dates in the professor's notes, remember? In his crop circle prediction table," said Sam, sighing impatiently.

"I *remember* the table, Sam! I just don't get how you knew *that* was the date for the circle on the charm."

"Just a weird feeling, that's all," Sam replied, fingering the brown paper bag. He looked up with relief as India arrived.

"What's with you guys? You look goofy standing there, waving and grinning like a couple of chimps."

Fletcher made a face at her and reached into his pocket for the rest of the licorice and sherbet treat he had saved. Sam, stinging a bit from India's barb, felt a surge of embarrassment. He glanced at his reflection in the jewelry shop window across the street and discreetly grinned at himself, trying to determine if he really did look like a chimp. Scanning the passing crowd for signs of Auntie Nellie, India checked her own watch against the town clock they were standing under and tapped her feet.

"Where *is* she?"

India's preoccupation with her aunt's whereabouts was interrupted by the sounds of choking. As sherbet powder flew in every direction, India grabbed the stick of licorice that was dangling out of Fletcher's mouth, while Sam patted him furiously on the back.

"He must have swallowed the wrong way or something," said India. "Are you okay, Fletcher?"

"Ma—Ma—!" Fletcher coughed, raising his arm.

"What is it? What's he pointing at?" asked India, squinting against the sun. Sam gave Fletcher's back one last powerful blow.

"Ma—Ma—Mandrake!" Fletcher spewed the word out, along with a tiny piece of licorice straw.

Sam felt a cold shiver creep up his spine. He slowly looked in the direction that Fletcher was pointing, to the market stall they had just left. Professor Avery Mandrake, tall and imposing, stood over the little man with the gold tooth like a vulture about to feed, perusing a copy of the crop circle book through the glasses at the end of his long, pointy nose. Sam felt the blood drain from his cheeks, and a series of forceful nudges from inside his front left vest pocket.

"S-S-Sam!" Fletcher spluttered. "He's supposed to be on a dig in Central America, isn't he? What's he doing *here*?"

"I don't know, Fletcher," whispered Sam. "Maybe the same thing we are."

"Do you think he saw us?" There was a note of rising panic in Fletcher's voice.

"I really don't think I want to hang around to find out, Fletch. We'd better get out of here."

"What are you two so upset about?" asked India, a quizzical look on her face. "I know Mandrake's a creep and everything, but—"

Just then, Auntie Nellie rushed up to the three of them, her shopping bags full to the brim.

"Sorry I'm a bit late, pets!" she said breathlessly. "The butcher was just writing out a lovely recipe for coq au vin. Thought we'd experiment with a bit of continental cooking tonight."

Auntie Nellie stopped talking and dropped her bags,

then turned to look in the same direction the three children were staring.

"What's going on?" she asked, craning her neck to see. "I do hope it's not another one of those shoplifting episodes."

"See that really tall man standing over there?" said India, pointing through the crowd. "That's Professor Mandrake. He works at the same university as Dad."

"Really?" declared Auntie Nellie.

The prospect of another dinner guest brightened Auntie Nellie's whole day. She bent down and started gathering up the overflowing bags at her feet.

"What a delightful coincidence! I'm sure I can make the coq au vin stretch out for one more. We should make some inquiries at the local hotels and find out where he's staying. Perhaps we can invite him over for the evening."

"No!" screamed Sam and Fletcher together, with such conviction that Auntie Nellie clutched her groceries to her chest and took a step backward.

"Well, my goodness! I just thought that..."

"Dad and Professor Mandrake don't really get on that well," explained India. "There's been a few incidents, actually."

"Oh, dear. I see," said Auntie Nellie, visibly deflated as her distinguished-looking dinner prospect turned away from the market stall with a little book in his hand and vanished into the crowd.

"Perhaps not, then," she declared sadly, as she turned and walked away.

7

WHERE THERE IS A WILL
THERE IS A WAY

When they returned to the farmhouse, Auntie Nellie enlisted India and Fletcher's help in putting away the groceries. As a guest of the family, Sam was spared this menial chore. Taking advantage of a few moments alone, he raced upstairs to examine the contents of the brown paper bag and to consult with Beatrice. A lot had happened since they last spoke. He flopped onto the bottom bunk, which was to be his territory for the night, and tore open his top vest pocket. As Sam lifted Professor Hawthorne's scroll notes out, Beatrice came out, too, clinging to the last partially folded page.

"A fascinating read, Sam!" she remarked. Sam set her down on the blanket. She bent over and began to straighten her coat.

"It's just as Jolly explained to me," Beatrice said. "Professor Hawthorne has definitely made headway with his great-grandfather's research and his own study of the scroll. He's zeroing in on a most fascinating mystery. The crop circles, the scroll, everything's connected in some way. And that whole theory about the circle formations, the energy fields and the magnet interactions, too. It's worth a try, isn't it? That

Mandrake character, turning up here and now, though; I couldn't believe it!" Beatrice looked at Sam with concern. "A most disturbing turn of events. I don't know if he had a chance to tell you this, or if he even wanted to worry you, but Jolly was growing more and more convinced that Mandrake was being counseled by The Fen. When I heard his name mentioned at the market this morning, I was just thankful that the scroll is safe and sound, thousands of miles from here."

The room started to spin in front of Sam's eyes. He felt weak and sick to his stomach, as if he were about to faint. His heart beat faster and faster in his chest. The pounding was so intense, in fact, that Sam was certain that any second now his heart, or the thing that he had slipped into the big, inside zippered pocket of his fishing vest that morning, would burst right out. But Sam didn't faint, and his heart didn't explode either. That, he thought, as the bedroom continue to reel, would have been too easy. No, this was going to be difficult and painful—just like everything else lately. Sam closed his eyes tightly.

"I...I...brought the scroll with me," he said in a sad little voice that Beatrice could barely hear.

"You did what, dear?"

"Professor Hawthorne's scroll," said Sam, a little louder this time. He placed his hand over his chest. "It's here, in my fishing vest."

The silence from Beatrice's direction seemed to last forever.

Sam sat up and rested on his elbows. Beatrice, her paws clutched in front of her, her eyes wide and flashing white, opened her mouth to speak.

"Oops."

Sam let his head fall back down again and covered his face with his hands.

"I was going to tell you about it a couple of times," he lamented. "I meant to leave it at home with Rollo and the other mice, but I was so worried! The house was going to be empty the whole time we were away. Mandrake could have broken in and found it. I didn't know what to do! Just before we left, I ran back to my room and grabbed it. It seemed like the best thing to do at the time. But it's been making me nervous ever since, and that was before I found out about Mandrake!"

Sam rolled over and lay face down on his bunk.

"What about the crop circle that's coming tonight?" he mumbled through the thick blanket. "What am I going to do now, with Mandrake here?"

Beatrice sat next to him, trying to sort through her thoughts.

"You shall do what you intended to do all along, Sam, Mandrake or not," she announced. "You did nothing wrong by bringing the scroll with you. You acted as your heart directed you. You'll take the scroll with you tonight, and you shall take me along, too. I came to help you, and to search for Jolly and Edgar, and that's exactly what I intend to do."

"What about Fletcher?" asked Sam.

"What does your heart tell you?"

"That there's no way he's going to let me go to that field by myself, anyway."

"Then, it's settled. I might suggest, however, that you keep the location of the scroll to yourself for the moment. I'm not sure Fletcher would be able to handle that sort of classified information on top of Mandrake's sudden appearance. The poor boy almost choked to death back there."

Sam nodded his head.

"Now if you don't mind, I'm going to take a little time to prepare myself for this evening." Beatrice smiled at Sam before making her way to the carpetbag she had hidden behind the pillow. "Polish up the old Sea Mouse Knife, perhaps?"

Beatrice suddenly stopped and turned back.

"By the way, Sam, your purchase of the old toffee box was a most thoughtful gesture. I'm sure that Jolly and Edgar will feel very touched when they see it. I have some wonderful memories of that great ship, too, you know. During the war, Mr. Churchill and I sailed across the Atlantic many times on her, although he was known as Colonel Warden at sea. That was the code name he used to throw off enemy agents."

Beatrice smiled as another memory came back to her.

"I never told Jolly this, you know, but years later, the ship's mice were still speaking of him and Edgar in the most admirable tones. They obviously made quite an impression on the maiden voyage. It must have been a grand crossing, indeed."

Sam raised his eyebrows.

"Did Mr. Goodfellow tell you much about that trip?"

"Not specifically, dear. Why?"

"Oh...never mind," replied Sam, recalling Mr. Goodfellow's tales of one disastrous shipboard incident after another.

Beatrice, a look of mild confusion on her face, continued.

"The *Queen Mary* of wartime wasn't the same as the colorful ship on your toffee box, Sam. She had been painted gray from bow to stern, all her portholes blackened out, anti-aircraft guns mounted on her once elegant decks. They called her 'The Grey Ghost' then. She was the fastest ship afloat and the scourge of enemy submarines, relying on speed and coded orders to elude her pursuers. With an enemy bounty on her head, she served faithfully for almost six years, transporting tens of thousands of troops around the world. But, enough of these war stories! I really must get cracking, you know."

Beatrice gave a quick wave and returned to her carpetbag.

Sam sat on the edge of the bunk and looked down at his brown paper bag. He reached for it now and tipped it upside down. Mr. Ramsbottom's small book fell onto the blanket first, then the wad of white tissue paper. Sam unwrapped the package and gingerly held the leather necklace in his hands. When he ran his fingers over the pewter charm's circles and lines, Edgar's image flooded his thoughts again, bolder and clearer than ever before. Sam placed the charm around his neck, picked up the book beside him and headed downstairs to find Fletcher. They still had a few things to study before nightfall.

At about 9:00 that evening, after making sure that everyone was sufficiently stuffed with coq au vin, Auntie Nellie said goodnight and retired to her bed. Half an hour later, India, with Jemima for company, anchored herself in her own bedroom, thoroughly engrossed in her second reading of *Tales of the South Pacific*. The coast was clear.

Fletcher and Sam, with Beatrice traveling undercover, slipped out of the house and into the cold damp of the evening.

With a compass, two flashlights and an assortment of maps, Sam and Fletcher made their way down the long winding lane to the road. As Sam had predicted, a suitable mode of transportation soon presented itself. When a farm tractor chugged slowly past, the two boys silently scrambled up the grassy embankment and grabbed onto the back of the hay wagon that was trailing behind. Sam got a leg up first, then pulled the rest of his body on board by holding onto the wooden slats that formed the wagon's side. Fletcher, running on much shorter legs, was clearly having a harder time.

"Come on, Fletch! Just a little higher!" Sam whispered encouragingly, as Fletcher tried over and over again to lift his foot onto the back of the wagon.

"I—I—can't!" Fletcher panted, almost out of breath. "You'll...have to...go!"

"What! Are you nuts or something, Fletch? I'm not going without you! We're a team, remember?"

Bracing both of his feet against the wagon, Sam leaned down, slipped his fingers through the leather belt at Fletcher's waist and pulled. Fletcher's legs rose up into the air then hit the ground again, two or three times, before achieving a sustained liftoff. With a great groan and one last tug, Sam dragged his friend into the wagon beside him. They rolled onto their backs, gasping for air, until they had recovered enough to sit up and consider their next move.

About forty minutes later, after consulting the maps one more time, Sam pinpointed their location and prepared to jump. He eased himself off the back of the wagon and carefully touched the ground with the tips of his sneakers, slowing himself to a stop. Fletcher, though, flustered and uneasy after his boarding experience, decided to try another method, and proceeded to fling himself off the end of the wagon with reckless abandon.

"FLETCHER!" cried Sam, galloping after his friend who had rolled several feet along the road before tumbling down another embankment and landing in a water-filled ditch.

Damp and exhausted, they walked the rest of the way to what Sam believed was the right field. A cool wind had picked up and Fletcher, considerably soggier than Sam, began to shiver. With ten minutes or so to go before the circle was scheduled to form, Sam found a clump of bushes at the edge of the field to provide Fletcher with some shelter.

"It must be getting close to the time, Fletch. I think I'd better go out there, now. Maybe you should stay and wait for me here, okay?"

Fletcher, teeth chattering, nodded his head vigorously. He was happy to oblige, actually. It made perfect sense, after all. In every adventure story he'd ever read, there was always some guy who was expected to hold the fort or stay at base camp.

Pushing the knee-high wheat to one side, Sam walked into the field until he was standing at its approximate center. He strained his neck and looked back to the clump of bushes at the edge, where he could barely see the top of Fletcher's head. It was safe to open the top of his left front vest pocket again, and when he did, Beatrice popped up, clutching Professor Hawthorne's magnet configuration notes.

"Here you go, dear. I'll hold these for you, if it will help."

Sam reached into his fishing vest and unzipped one of the large inside pockets. A slew of magnets tumbled out and landed on the earth at his feet. Carefully following the professor's instructions, Sam arranged the magnets in a circle around him. He placed the largest one, shaped like a horseshoe, directly in front, with the closed end pointing away. He alternated the other magnets (some round, others long, thin and flat) in order of decreasing size, placing them at each side of his body in two sweeping arcs that joined behind his back. He stared at the pieces of crinkled paper in his hand, then at the magnet circle, until he was confident that his configuration matched the professor's exactly. The prediction sheet said that the circle would begin to form at 10:58, but according to Sam's watch, it was past that already. Had he set his watch incorrectly when they'd landed in London? Sam began to feel a little anxious. He didn't know, after all, what he was about to get himself into. Even if Professor Hawthorne *had* theorized a way to transport himself using the power of magnets and the energy fields unleashed during the formation of a crop circle, how could Sam be certain that the theory had proven successful? For all Sam knew, Professor Hawthorne could have been vaporized in the process, or electrocuted, or burnt to a crisp. If it hadn't been for the overriding sense that Edgar and Mr. Goodfellow had passed this way, too, Sam would never have attempted it. Edgar Goodfellow was alive *somewhere*. Sam could feel it.

The trembling that had started in Sam's feet inched its way up his legs. He closed his eyes, took a deep breath and recited Mr. Goodfellow's proverb.

"Courage in danger is half the battle."

"You know, Sam," said Beatrice, leaning out of his pocket, "this situation puts me in mind of something Mr. Churchill once said: 'Without courage, all other virtues lose their meaning.' He also said 'Never run away from anything. Never!'"

"He really liked that word, didn't he?" remarked Sam. "The 'never' one, I mean."

"Indeed, he did, and he used it, I always thought, with great aplomb," said Beatrice.

"Never run away, never run away, never run away," Sam chanted to himself, even as the waiting became almost unbearable. Sam stared at his watch again. Maybe he hadn't read the timetable properly. Maybe he was standing, with magnets at his feet, in the wrong field entirely. Something wasn't right. Sam jumped out of the circle and waded his way back through the wheat, shining his flashlight in front of him. He dropped to the ground at the edge of the field.

"Fletcher! What time does it say on your watch?"

Fletcher popped his head up and pressed the light-up button on his wristwatch.

"It's exactly 10:58. Hey, what was that?" he whispered.

A slow and steady humming was rising from the center of the field. Sam gasped and scrambled to his feet.

"Rats!" cried Sam, giving his own watch a hard slap. "We've come all this way, and now I'm going to miss it!"

Strange lights danced and flickered in the air above Sam's head. Discovering that his flashlight would no longer work, he stumbled through the dark on his way back to the ring of magnets. As he moved closer to the center of the field, the temperature plummeted and Sam felt his ears pop. He stepped into the middle of the magnets. A strong gust of wind blew bits of stray wheat about and the humming noise started to create a painful throbbing inside his head. When the sound had reached a deafening level and the glare from the lights had obscured his view of the field, Sam felt a rumbling at his feet. He looked down at the ground below, while Beatrice, her paws pressed tightly against her mouse ears, leaned out of his pocket and looked down, too. Hovering a few inches above the soil, the magnets began to rotate around them. They turned slowly at first and then with increasing velocity, finally transforming into a single band of brilliant, spinning light. Faster and faster they spun, radiating waves of heat that burrowed under Sam's leather-trimmed sneakers and right through his thick, woolly socks. Sam began to feel light-headed as the spinning circle of white-hot light rose from the ground and completely surrounded him. He put his hand next to Beatrice to warn her that he was about to tumble, then fell with a thump to his knees. Blackness closed in around him.

8

Forewarned Is
Forearmed

When Sam opened his eyes, he was curled up on his side. The magnets, in no particular order, were scattered around him in a thick red dust that covered the ground. There were no stars in the blackness above him now and, apart from a few stray strands that clung to his clothes, the crop of wheat had vanished, too. The damp air of the countryside had been replaced with a warm dewy mist that swirled about in small clouds just above the ground. There was a strange, unnatural feeling to the place, and, at first, Sam was not entirely sure that he had woken up at all. This was exactly where his dreams of Edgar had been taking him night after night.

Sam struggled to sit up, trying to shake the strange, heavy feeling from his head. He tore the thin strip of Velcro open at his chest pocket and peered inside for Beatrice. She was just beginning to stir, and Sam reached inside to give her a hand. He was about to inquire if she was feeling as strange as he was when he heard an approaching sound. Beatrice had heard it, too, and quickly slipped back down into the pocket.

When Sam looked up, the figure of a man was trotting toward him out of the mist. He was an elderly gentleman, small in stature, who looked somewhat like an inverted pear on top of two stocky legs. He had a round, pleasant face and shoulder-length white hair that had been loosely swept out of the way, behind his ears. He was covered, from head to toe, in a layer of the same red dust that surrounded Sam.

"Good heavens!" the old man cried. "Who are you?"

Sam tried to stand up. When he opened his mouth to speak, he could feel prickly pieces of wheat sticking to his lips. He brushed them aside with the back of his hand, sputtering a bit as he forced out the words.

"I'm Sam," he said with a deep croak. "Sam...Middleton."

The old man, trembling with excitement, helped him to his feet.

"Well, Sam Middleton, whoever you are, you're a sight for sore eyes! I just can't believe it! I was beginning to imagine I'd never see another living soul again! How on earth did you do it?" He looked straight into Sam's face. "Good heavens, you're just a boy!"

"Are you Professor Hawthorne?" asked Sam, still trying to stand.

"Good heavens, again! How did you know that?"

"I live in your house now," said Sam. "I hope you don't mind Professor, but...well...I searched through it and your office, too, and found your notes about the crop circles and the magnets, and...well, here I am, I guess!"

"Really? How extraordinary!" replied the professor, scratching his head for a moment before he suddenly slapped his forehead. "Those blasted notes! I thought I'd retrieved them all before I left, but I was in such a dreadful hurry that day, you know. The house and the office, you say?"

Sam nodded his head.

"Drat!" exclaimed Professor Hawthorne.

Sam wobbled a bit on his unsteady feet. The professor reached out his arm to support him.

"Don't worry, young man. These unusual feelings will pass. I felt drained and light-headed at first, too, and rather unwell. Then, after a short time, a strange exhilaration took over. It grows stronger, too, I'm delighted to report. Right at this moment, I've never felt better in my life! There must be some kind of healing and rejuvenating properties at work here, magnetic in nature, I suspect. It's my guess that this sticky red dust is the culprit. It gets everywhere, accumulating in layers all over one's body. It's a little disconcerting at first, but you adjust. It's actually quite useful, too. As well as making you feel on top of the world, it's immensely helpful in toning down that dreadful glow there. See?"

Sam looked down at himself for the first time. An aura of green pulsating light was emanating from his body. Professor Hawthorne picked up a handful of the dust and began to rub it into Sam's sleeve.

"That's how I pinpointed your location. You were glowing like a great, green searchlight! I'm inclined to believe that it's some sort of side effect from the massive energy flow created at entry. A curious phenomenon, indeed. Whatever the reason, it appears that the longer one stays here, the better one feels. That troublesome lumbago of mine has vanished completely."

The professor took a little jump into the air, clicking his heels together before lightly touching the ground.

"And, look here," he said, pointing to the dozens of long, white strands at the very top of his head. "My hair is starting to grow back, too, and I've been as bald as a bat's wing for thirty years! I'm going to have to start brushing again pretty soon." He picked up another handful of the red dust and rubbed it vigorously into his scalp.

113

"Wow!" said Sam, in a tone of admiration. "That's really neat."

The professor was clearly beside himself at the arrival of a companion. He chattered on and on as he helped Sam (who was feeling a bit better now) finish the job of dousing the green energy aura with generous applications of red dust. He then helped him retrieve his magnets and return them to his inner vest pocket.

With the strange feelings in his head beginning to fade, Sam took the opportunity to have a good look around. The professor was right. The red dust was everywhere. It covered the ground, sat in mounds on top of jagged, crystal-encrusted rocks and hung in little particles in the misty air. Sam was puzzled. They couldn't still be in the crop field, could they? There was nothing but blackness directly above him, yet the occasional light that floated past provided adequate illumination. From what he could see, the rest of the place was littered with outcroppings of stone and rock and huge boulders, forming tunnel-like pathways that meandered off in a dozen different directions. And, in the rose-tinged distance, as if he were peering through a filmy curtain, Sam could make out a series of undulating hills.

"Are we still in Wiltshire?" asked Sam, a little hesitantly.

"According to the timetable, we are...in a manner of speaking," said the professor rather vaguely as he consulted a crumpled piece of paper that he had pulled from his coat pocket. "Actually, I believe we're in another section of the field I originally entered. The whole experience of breaking through this netherworld renders one more or less invisible to the real one, with the occasional ability to appear as a somewhat ghostly specter. If I set my mind to it, I can project myself beyond the confines of this place for brief periods, but I remain trapped, always returning here in a moment or two. It happened quite by accident the first time, when I became passionately distraught over my predicament. The sudden surge of emotional power from my thoughts seemed to act as a catalyst. My subsequent attempts at projection have elicited some rather confused stares from passing farm folk and the odd cow. It has been an interesting experiment, but I have found, I'm afraid, that I have little control over it or anything else. The standard laws of physics don't seem to apply here at all. We are in a world within a world, still occupying, I believe, the space of the latest crop circle, but on another plane entirely, or another dimension, if you will. One minute I am here and then suddenly I'm hurtling through space to pop up in another circle in some field on the other side of the world. Unless they have begun importing kangaroos into the English countryside, I believe I was in Australia for a brief period of time just yesterday. Let me tell you, it takes quite a while to recover from one of those little trips. By the way," Professor Hawthorne inquired, with a hopeful look on his face, "you don't happen to have any tea bags on you, do you, young man?"

"No...sorry..." replied Sam, who had other things on his mind. "How did you figure out the formula for predicting the crop circles and the whole magnet thing, anyway?"

"It was in front of me all along, my boy. In a copy of *Mathematics Monthly*, sitting on top of a pile of other scientific journals bound for the recycling dump I believe. I picked it up quite accidentally one evening at the home of a friend of mine. It was not my area of expertise, of course, but later that night, unable to sleep, I turned to an article written about the great French mathematician Benôit Mandelbrot. Imagine my surprise and excitement when I discovered that his studies combining pure math and chaotic theory translated into a pattern that coincided with one of the symbols I was trying to decipher from the scroll. More astonishing was the fact that this design was turning up in crop fields, too. The pattern was even being referred to, by crop circle hunters, as the 'Mandelbrot Set.' With the information I had already taken from my great-grandfather Elijah's years of scroll study and Benôit Mandelbrot's mathematical calculations, developing the formula for crop circle prediction and the magnets was actually quite easy. It became possible for me to know in advance when and where a crop circle was going to pop up, enabling me to prepare..."

"The magnet ring, right?" asked Sam.

"Indeed! Our mode of transport into this place, my boy, and critical to the whole process. Great-grandfather knew it, too. The references were in the scroll, but his research was cut short, I'm afraid, by his untimely demise. I can't take that much credit, though. I really just finished off his work, with a little help from a mathematical equation for infinity. It was the missing clue. I've come to believe, since being in here, Sam, that the occurrence and utilization of magnetic energy is quite commonplace to whomever, or whatever, is behind this. Perhaps it's even a part of their physical makeup. A 'ticket to ride,' as it were. A bit more of a difficult excursion, though, for simple creatures such as ourselves. It's an odd thought, but if these crop circles *are*, as I'm beginning to believe, some sort of message to the world, then it is as if whomever is responsible for them is becoming a little impatient with mankind. More and more circles appear every year, in patterns that have been growing in their complexity and content. Perhaps this is an effort to be finally understood and heeded."

"Wow," declared Sam. "Like notes that someone left behind! Maybe they're messages from an ancient, advanced civilization, like Atlantis or something. Right, professor? That would be amazing!"

"A bit of a tame explanation, don't you think, Sam? What would you say if I told you it might be a place *considerably* further away than that?"

Professor Hawthorne slowly turned his head and looked straight at Sam, his eyes twinkling with mystery. Sam wasn't exactly sure what the professor meant, but he felt a sudden shudder of excitement run through his body. A slight fluttering in his vest pocket told him that Beatrice was listening, too. He thought about Fletcher, waiting at the edge of the field, and realized how much he wanted to share this with him.

"Have you tried getting out of here, Professor?" Sam asked.

Professor Hawthorne looked a bit uncomfortable.

"I was so excited to discover how to get in that I fear I may have let my scientific detachment lapse a bit." The professor smiled sheepishly. "I'm rather embarrassed to admit that I failed to think any further than that. I've since discovered, through trial and error, that getting out of one of these things is a little more complicated than getting in."

Sam's heart sank. "What! You mean you *really* don't know how to get out of here?" he cried.

Professor Hawthorne shrugged his shoulders awkwardly, then cheered up.

"Well, I do have a promising theory."

Sam sighed with frustration. If only the Governing Council had reactivated the Hawthorne case earlier, Mr. Goodfellow might have been able to provide critical guidance to the professor before the old fellow had lunged ahead with his experiments.

"Don't look so glum, my boy," said the professor. "I feel that I may be close to the solution. Perhaps it's the cumulative effects of the red dust in here or the enlightening atmosphere, but I do seem to have become much more focused lately. The first part of my hypothesis is based on the arrangement of magnets. These, I believe now, need to be reversed in exiting."

"Well, that makes sense, I guess," said Sam. "Haven't you tried it?"

"I would have, dear boy, if it were all that simple. There is a slight complication, however," the professor explained. "Crop circles, it would appear, have the ability to tap into and trap a variety of different energy sources, magnifying their power a hundredfold in the process. When a crop circle forms, there is a great surge of energy and the creation of a massive electrostatic field, as you would have noticed from the strange lights and humming sounds. Only at that very moment, using the exact combination and arrangement of magnets to create a sort of force field, can one be transported into this dimension. After the circle has been created by the effects of a swirling vortex, the power dies down considerably. Another source of energy, of the kinetic kind I believe, might facilitate transport out. This could be accomplished with something as simple as a very powerful push, executed in concert with the reversed magnets at the exact time that the electrostatic power surges again. But, alas, I have been alone here, with no way to test my theory."

Professor Hawthorne suddenly and quite deliberately stared at Sam with even greater interest.

"You say that you found my notes, young man...but of course you must have, to have been able to find your way here!"

"They were in the book that you left behind in the house," explained Sam. "When I got the chance to come to England this summer with my friend, I brought them with me. I followed the timetable and the magnet instructions, made the circle like you'd drawn, and at the right time, the lights in the field began to flicker and the humming started. At first I was cold, then when the magnets began to spin around, I felt really dizzy and hot all over, passed out for a while, I guess, then woke up here."

"Exactly as it was for me. Fascinating, isn't it, my boy? Now, if we can just find our way out."

Sam stared at the professor with growing panic.

"But you've been gone for over a year already! I can't do that! My friend's waiting for me. And what about my mum and dad? I have to be able to get out! Now!"

"Has it really been that long?" asked the professor with surprise. "My, it doesn't seem that way at all; a few days at the most. It's odd, you know, but I've not been hungry at all; not once. Lately, though, I've been having these strange cravings for a cup of tea. What an extraordinary place! You know, you can actually get quite used to it. It must be the rejuvenating aspect. I feel quite euphoric."

Sam was beginning to understand what the professor was talking about. A feeling of well-being was already starting to spread through his body. Determined not to let this strange world take hold of him, though, Sam made himself think of home. He had to keep the professor's mind on track, too. He looked around.

"Do these pathways actually lead anywhere, Professor?"

"Well, I'm not certain, but according to what I have been able to learn from the scroll so far, the crop circles are not only a message of some type but also a portal—a window into another world, perhaps, as well as a means of transport. The erratic behavior of these things, however, leads me to think that this is a travel system that requires a bit of fine-tuning, or at the very least someone who understands its complexities. To answer your question, Sam, I think that what we find ourselves in right now is quite simply an outer passageway. There's a central core to this place, too, you know—an inner chamber of sorts. It's mentioned in the scroll, but I have been unable to locate it yet. I believe that this area may be the real key to the mystery; a repository of information, in fact, that may explain the origin and purpose of the circles and the scroll. The references to this place in the scroll are unclear and very hard to decipher. Some parts of the scroll's surface, I believe, have been damaged; rubbed away perhaps with time and handling. I have learned a great deal in this place already, Sam, but if I had gone on my first instinct and brought the scroll with me instead of leaving it hidden in the house, I might be making greater leaps ahead. It is a decision that I have come to regret."

Sam, feeling a sudden sense of vindication, began to speak. "Professor, I..."

"You know, I must say, young man," interrupted the professor, "I am very relieved that it was you who found those sets of notes that I left behind, instead of..."

"I only found one set of notes, Professor," interrupted Sam. "In the house."

"But you said that you searched my office at the university, too."

"I did, but I didn't find anything. The first time I went there all your files had been messed up and the second time they were stacked in boxes in Professor Mandrake's office."

"That scoundrel!" cried the professor. "He's finally decided to strike, has he? I knew he would, one day." Professor Hawthorne's face grew flushed with anger. "You know Mandrake, then?" The name rolled off the professor's tongue in a very unpleasant way.

Sam nodded his head. His decided to put his happy

announcement about bringing the scroll aside for now. He cringed, swallowed hard, and blurted the next sentence out as fast as he could.

"He's here. I saw him at the market."

"Who? Mandrake?" cried the professor. "Here . . . in Wiltshire?"

Sam nodded again.

"But, how did he . . ." Professor Hawthorne suddenly turned pale. "There was an old globe, Sam! It was on the credenza behind my desk. Did you see it?"

"It was on the floor the second time I was there," murmured Sam. "It was broken in two."

Sam's heart sank and his knees turned to jelly. He just knew, by the look of absolute horror on Professor Hawthorne's face, that this was where the old fellow had hidden another set of his scroll notes.

"Heaven help us now!" Professor Hawthorne suddenly grabbed Sam's arm. "I've put us all in the soup by forgetting those blasted notes! Mandrake must have found them and now he's come to find me. He's made the crop circle connection, or rather helped himself to the connection that my great-grandfather Elijah toiled over all those years ago." Professor Hawthorne began to wring his hands anxiously. "Goodness knows that fool couldn't have done it himself. The man has the intellectual capacity of a squirrel. It's a mystery to me how he has been able to secure such a long string of academic posts. Those questionable family connections of his had something to do with it, I'll wager. He's nothing better than a cheat and a liar, and he's been the very bane of my life, I can tell you. The existence of the Hawthorne scroll has been a popular rumor around the university for years, and Mandrake's been hounding me about it for just as long."

Sam could feel Beatrice hammering at his chest from inside his pocket. He put his hand on his vest and felt the outline of the scroll tube just beneath the beige canvas material.

"What did you mean you've...um...put us all in the soup?" Sam asked nervously.

Professor Hawthorne had begun to pace.

"There's something more to the scroll, Sam. It's not just the written word that's significant, it's the properties of the scroll itself. Great-grandfather Elijah was adamant about this in his notes but had only just begun to conduct a series of experiments on the material. His suspicions have led me to the most startling piece of the puzzle yet. The scroll is of a most unusual composition, looking somewhat like thin metal, but possessing a strength and resiliency that is unique. This may explain how it has survived for all these years. I did manage to slice off a small sliver of it with a diamond-cutting device and pass it on to a chemist friend of mine for analysis. His preliminary tests were completed just before I left and the results were startling. It was one of the reasons that I felt it important to come here right away and hunt for the scroll's origin and meaning. Dating back tens of thousands of years, it could not have been created by any advanced human civilization that we are currently aware of. My friend is quite sure, too, that the scroll is of a substance hitherto unknown, and," Professor Hawthorne lowered his voice to a whisper, "most probably not even of this earth."

Icy goosebumps began to form all over Sam's arms and legs. He could barely whisper back a response.

"You mean, it's from another pla..."

"Indeed, my boy!" interrupted Professor Hawthorne. "And there's a great deal more to the story, too." The professor's eyes flashed with excitement as he began to pace even faster.

"Great-grandfather Elijah's research notes, which I

discovered in the walls of the old house along with the scroll, tell a fascinating story of the intrigue and betrayal that swirled around its discovery. Great-grandfather had a partner back then, a gentleman by the name of Hugo Trenchmount—a wealthy businessman with a keen interest in the antiquities. In exchange for providing money to fund Elijah's academic pursuits and his many trips abroad, Trenchmount would be allowed to keep the odd artifact for his own personal collection. This was a rather unseemly arrangement, but Elijah was desperate for financial support. When Elijah discovered the scroll in the possession of a black-market trader on one of his expeditions to the Middle East, Trenchmount came up with the money to buy it. Great-grandfather would be able to study and decipher the scroll, but it would be Trenchmount's to keep."

Elijah initially agreed, but after a few days of study, he began to realize the rarity of the relic and its great significance. It may have been the greatest archaeological find in history. A violent argument erupted between the two men. Regaining his academic scruples, Elijah argued that the scroll must be turned over to the Royal Historical Society so that all the world might see and study it. Trenchmount was enraged. Mesmerized by the scroll, he was determined to keep it for himself at any cost. He demanded that he be given what he had rightfully paid for, but Elijah would have none of it. The story goes that on a dark, moonless night—the night before Elijah was to have returned to England with the scroll—Hugo Trenchmount attacked my great-grandfather in his tent, hitting him over the head with his own elephant-tusk walking stick and leaving him for dead. Trenchmount fled with the scroll, but great-grandfather Elijah, of course, survived. I have heard it said that he was never quite the same after the tusking though, and..."

"But Trenchmount *couldn't* have taken the scroll!" interrupted Sam. "Your great-grandfather took it home and hid it in the house!"

"Indeed he did, my boy. But not the *same* scroll, and that is where the mystery takes another interesting turn. Unbeknownst to Trenchmount, Elijah had purchased an identical scroll from another black-market trader. That was the scroll he sheltered for years and eventually hid in your house. His relationship with Trenchmount was a rocky one at best and Elijah had never completely trusted him. He never told Trenchmount about the second scroll. Great-grandfather knew that if Trenchmount were to learn of its existence, there would be no stopping him. Trenchmount would be determined to possess both of them, and that prospect, as Elijah had determined from studying the one scroll that he had, might be catastrophic."

"So there are *two* scrolls, then?" asked Sam excitedly.

"Apparently there are, my boy. They had been separated at some time in their history but remained in the same area, falling into the hands of an assortment of tribespeople, adventurers and unscrupulous traders. After his attempted murder, Elijah was determined to protect the security of the one scroll in his possession. Turning it over to the Royal Historical Society would be far too risky now, so Elijah returned to his home, where he toiled alone for the next few years, trying desperately to make sense of the scroll's message. It was during this time that the legend of the Hawthorne scroll began to emerge, fueled by great-grandfather's odd behavior and his self-enforced solitude. He eventually translated some sections of the scroll, specifically the ones that related to the crop circle link and the ability to move between the real world and the one that we are in now. I have reason to believe that he was just about to attempt to transport himself when he became ill. He managed, before he died, to hide the scroll and his many years of research notes. When I fell upon them years later, I simply finished the job to which he had devoted his life. Had I not undertaken some renovations and uncovered the scroll and the notes behind the walls of the house, Elijah's knowledge would have remained hidden to this day."

"What happened to Hugo Trenchmount?" asked Sam. "And the other scroll?"

"It's a most fascinating story, Sam. After leaving the Middle East, Trenchmount apparently bounced around the world for years, never staying in one place for very long. Every now and then, great-grandfather Elijah would hear that he'd turned up at some academy or university somewhere, seeking information about hieroglyphics, runes, cuneiform writings and the like. In his later years, haunted perhaps by his attempts to murder Elijah, he turned to the bottle for solace and companionship. He was finally committed to a psychiatric hospital in Upstate New York, where he remained until his death in 1902. Great-grandfather never revealed to another living soul what had happened between him and Hugo Trenchmount, including the attempt on his life, save for what he wrote in his own private notes."

"But the other scroll!" cried Sam. "You haven't said what happened to it."

"Well, having no heirs of his own or a will of any kind, and committed to a home by his 'trusted' attorney, all of Trenchmount's possessions were sold at auction. The money received was put into a trust fund to pay for his years of care at the nursing home, all arranged and administered by the fund's trustee, one Benedict A. Mandrake, attorney-at-law."

"Mandrake!" cried Sam.

"Precisely. A great-great-uncle, in fact, and a childless bachelor who doted in his very old age on one young nephew in particular who showed great interest in the field of..."

"Archaeology!" interrupted Sam with a cry. "Avery Mandrake has the other scroll!"

"I can't prove it, my boy, but that has always been my belief," replied the professor. "And if Mandrake has managed to decipher even a small portion of it, then he is aware that our own Hawthorne scroll is much more than myth. Presumably, the two scrolls contain different information, although I believe that each one makes clear reference to the existence of the other. Everywhere I have turned over the years, Avery Mandrake has never been more than a step or two behind me. That hideous man has made a career out of following me around, dogging me from one academic institution to the next. He believes, I suppose, that because I am Elijah Hawthorne's only surviving relative, I must be in possession of the other scroll. It's a bit funny, really, but that's been true only for a couple of years. Up until then I was as much in the dark about the location of the legendary Hawthorne scroll as he was."

"I knew it!" cried Sam. "I knew all along that Mandrake was up to something! He came over to our house for dinner with that creepy kid of his, Basil. I could tell he just wanted to poke around the house, but Fletcher and I wouldn't let him!"

"Fletcher? You don't mean young Fletcher Jaffrey, do you?" asked Professor Hawthorne with interest.

"That's right! I almost forgot. You know Professor Jaffrey from the university don't you? Fletcher's my best friend. In fact, that's who I came to England with. He's here tonight, waiting at the edge of the field right now. He's very trustworthy and..."

"Indeed he is, Sam, as is his father. Sanjid Jaffrey is not only a dedicated scientist but a man of the utmost integrity, too."

Sam felt another outbreak of goosebumps.

"The chemist friend that you gave the sliver of scroll to. It's Professor Jaffrey, isn't it?"

"Indeed, Sam. I trust his judgment without reservation. I can see that you feel the same way about your young friend."

Sam nodded and sighed, wondering if he would ever see Fletcher again.

Sensing Sam's concern, Professor Hawthorne gave him a pat on the shoulder.

"It was a very courageous thing to do, Sam, coming here to look for me like this. We'll find a way out of here somehow, my boy, I promise you that. We'll have to anyway, won't we? If Avery Mandrake has indeed found the other set of notes, he'll know where and how to find me. I was hoping that it would not come to a confrontation yet. I had planned to finish great-grandfather Elijah's transportation experiment, discover what I had to here and head back home to toss Mandrake another slew of red herrings. Things haven't really worked out as well as I had hoped, though. But if I could somehow find my way to the core of this place then perhaps all would not be lost."

A slight stirring in Sam's vest pocket suddenly distracted him from the professor's conversation. Beatrice! How he wished he could talk to her. Ever since they had entered this other world, he had felt the overwhelming presence of Edgar. If he and Mr. Goodfellow had indeed found their way here, how could he even begin to search for them without attracting Professor Hawthorne's attention? Sam gently pushed the tip of his baby finger into his pocket where Beatrice gave it a comforting squeeze.

"Well, if Avery Mandrake wants a confrontation then that is what he will have!" Professor Hawthorne suddenly shouted, jolting Sam back to attention. "There's nothing that man would like better than to get his slippery fingers on both the scrolls, and heaven help us if he does! The two scrolls together may provide the key to great power and knowledge for anyone who cracks their code. In the possession of a character like Mandrake, they could be quite dangerous. All we can be thankful for right now, Sam, especially with Mandrake turning up, is that I had the foresight to leave the scroll hidden in the walls of your house, safe and secure, at least for now."

Sam clutched his vest.

"What is it?" the professor asked with concern. "You look positively petrified, dear boy!"

Sam opened his mouth, but the words wouldn't come right away.

"Scroll...in vest," he finally managed to spit out.

The professor's eyes flew wide open.

"You've found the scroll, too? It's here?" he gasped.

Sam, somewhat relieved that he had finally confessed, sat down on a large rock, put his head between his knees and took several deep breaths.

"I'm *really* sorry," he mumbled.

"Goodness, you have been busy, haven't you?"

Professor Hawthorne, trembling all over, slumped down on another rock and sat quietly for a few moments. Sam, feeling as if the world was about to end, put his head in his hands.

"It's alright," said the professor, patting Sam on his shoulder. "In fact, this may turn out to be a great boon to me, Sam. It will give me the opportunity to do some critical fieldwork with the scroll. There are a few things I *must* look at again, in light of what I have seen here..."

The professor stopped speaking in mid-sentence, pointed his nose into the air like a bloodhound on the trail and sniffed.

"Mothballs, if I'm not mistaken," he declared. "These many months of incarceration have sharpened my senses. It's an unpleasantly familiar stench, too. Where *have* I smelt that before?"

A look of concern slowly crept across the professor's face.

"You don't think someone could have followed you here, tonight, do you, my boy? I didn't think too much of it at the time, but when you passed through the circle, I did feel a much larger energy ripple than someone of your size would be able to produce."

Sam, completely unnerved by the professor's mothball announcement, stammered a reply.

"Uh, I . . . I don't know. I'm not sure, really. Maybe Fletcher saw something."

Mothballs! That could only mean one, awful thing! Sam shuddered. He thought about Fletcher, all alone, at the edge of the field. Had he put his friend in danger *and* led Mandrake to Professor Hawthorne, himself, Beatrice and anyone else who might be trapped in the circle? A cold sweat trickled along Sam's arms and all the way down his back.

9

HE IS RICH ENOUGH WHO
HAS TRUE FRIENDS

The professor jumped up from the rock he was sitting on. "Stay here, Sam. I think I had better have a quick look around. I'll be right back."

As soon as Professor Hawthorne had disappeared into the swirling clouds of mist, Beatrice popped out of Sam's vest pocket. She had a stern look in her eyes.

"Now listen to me, young man. I know exactly what you're thinking, but you mustn't blame yourself. I happen to know that both you *and* Jolly searched Professor Hawthorne's office. You should not feel solely responsible. If Mandrake did indeed find the notes in the globe, then he's probably figured out the same things that you did. The magnets, the timetable, everything. If anyone is to blame, it should be Cedric Hawthorne for being such an old fusspot about leaving backup notes everywhere. I really don't know what that man was thinking! I know he's a brilliant eccentric, but one set of notes in a safety deposit box would have been quite sufficient, I'm sure. You know, he's exactly like..." Beatrice interrupted her speech just long enough to reach into her furry suit. Dabbing at her eyes with the tip of her lavender-scented hanky, she finished her sentence with a whisper.

"Jolly."

Sam knew that Beatrice was probably right, but he couldn't help but feel a little responsible anyway. If he had had the nerve to search Professor Hawthorne's office sooner, he might have been able to beat Mandrake to the globe and the hidden notes. And on top of all that, if anything had happened to Fletcher, he would never forgive himself.

There was a sudden rustling noise at Sam's feet.

"Yes, Sam, what is it?"

Sam looked into his pocket, where Beatrice was tidying herself up. Pushing the last few wayward strands of silver-streaked hair back under her mouse cap, she glanced up at him with a quizzical expression.

"That wasn't you, dear . . . was it?"

Sam slowly shook his head.

"Psst . . . pssst! Sam . . . over here!"

With Beatrice grasping the edge of his pocket, Sam stood up, then suddenly dropped to his knees, groping feverishly through the thick bands of mist that floated just above the ground. About ten inches or so in front of him, his hand forcefully collided with a small, fur-covered object. There was a muffled thud, accompanied by an indignant yelp.

"I beg your pardon!"

Sam recognized the voice immediately.

"Mr. Goodfellow! Is that you? Are you okay?" Sam could barely contain himself. He scooped his old friend into his hands, stood up and began jumping up and down with excitement.

"Sam! So it is you, after all! I thought I recognized your shape under that slightly faded green glow. Still, I can hardly believe it! How on earth did you know to find us here and how did you..."

"I found the professor's crop circle notes!" Sam began excitedly. "Beatrice wrote and told me that you and Edgar had disappeared and sent me your letter, too, so Fletcher and I searched the offices again at the university, but we couldn't find anything. I found them later in a book at home. Remember that H. G. Wells one that Professor Hawthorne left in the old bookcase?" Sam took a deep breath. "Well, I was sick at home from school one day and something told me to look at it, I guess, and so I followed the professor's instructions and..." Sam was forced to pause for a breath again, and Mr. Goodfellow grasped the opportunity to jump in.

"Sam, my boy, please slow down! Although I understand your excitement completely, you must refrain from moving about so erratically. Those size-seven sneakers of yours could be lethal weapons in a thick fog like this. There are others of us here, you know."

"And over here, too, Jolly."

Mr. Goodfellow looked up in surprise at Sam's vest pocket, from which Beatrice Elderberry's voice was drifting down. He stood up, balancing as best he could in the cradle of Sam's hands. He quickly brushed himself down with his paws and straightened his mask. At the same time, he gave his protruding mouse teeth a forceful push upward. He had recently been experimenting with a new adhesive compound, and sincerely hoped that there would be no embarrassing dislodgment, especially now.

"Beatrice! Good heavens, my dear! I never expected to see you *both* here. It's wonderful that you have chosen to come to our aid, but I can't help but question the wisdom of such a decision. To place yourselves in possible peril like this..."

133

"Really, Jolly!" interrupted Beatrice. There was an air of annoyance in her voice now. "I may be a retired old girl, but I haven't lost my touch completely, you know. I was quite a capable operative in my day, as you well know, and I wasn't about to let Sam face whatever might lie ahead all alone."

"Yes, you're quite right, my dear," said Mr. Goodfellow, feeling duly admonished and a little deflated, too. A familiar thought ran through his mind. It was always the same, wasn't it? Just when things seemed to be going well with Beatrice, he'd go and put his foot in his mouth again. He tried for a rebound.

"Well, Sam, we should thank providence that you've had Beatrice along to provide guidance."

"Yeah, it's just like having somebody's mother around all the time," said Sam.

Beatrice's expression soured even more.

"But in a really nice way," Sam offered quickly.

"The distinction is much appreciated, dear." Beatrice beamed at him. "I've grown quite fond of this young man, Jolly. He is so like young Edgar, isn't he?" She leaned out of the vest pocket a little further, squinting her eyes to see past the fog at Sam's feet.

"Which reminds me, Jolly..."

"Yes, Edgar's with me, of course. Safe and sound, too. Or as much as one can be, I suppose, trapped as we have been. At any rate, our time here has been rather an emotional journey, as you will soon discover."

Mr. Goodfellow gestured for Sam to set him back on the ground.

"The lad was right on my tail just a minute ago. I imagine he must have lost me momentarily in the mist."

Mr. Goodfellow cupped his paws to his mask and hollered.

"EDGAR! Are you still there? Follow the sound of my voice, my boy, and bring that wonderful surprise with you!"

Sam knelt down on the ground and gently lifted Beatrice out of his pocket. As he set her down beside Mr. Goodfellow, Edgar appeared through the curtain of fog. There was another mouse-suited figure by his side. It removed its mask and mouse cap and stepped forward. Beatrice let out a shrill cry and lifted her paws to her cheeks.

"I don't believe it! Filbert Goodfellow! After all these years!" Beatrice dropped the frilly hanky she was clutching and rushed forward to embrace him. "It's nothing short of a miracle!"

Holding him by both of his arms, Beatrice stepped back to get a better look.

"My, you're looking well, Filbert."

"Indeed," he replied. "Not bad after 120 years."

"It's remarkable. You look just as you did on your graduation day, right down to that distinguished goatee you were trying to grow on your chin all that spring."

Beatrice removed one of her mouse paws and ran her fingers through Filbert's thick, wavy hair.

"And how, my dear, did you ever manage that? Please forgive my bluntness, but you were, after all, as bald as a billiard ball when I last saw you."

"It's the strange nature of this place," replied Filbert, smiling as he rubbed his head defensively. "You never were one to mince words, were you, Beatrice?"

"I'm sorry, Filbert, really I am. But this has all come as such a great shock."

"Well, you can just imagine how shocked Edgar and I were when Filbert suddenly appeared," Mr. Goodfellow interjected. "After we made our grand entrance into the circle, Filbert found us almost immediately."

"The green aura?" asked Sam.

"Yes, quite a light show at first, isn't it?" said Filbert. "I see that you've already discovered the benefits of the red dust in dousing its effects."

"Yes, from Professor Hawthorne," replied Sam.

"So you've met him then, my boy?" asked Mr. Goodfellow, rubbing his paws together. "A nice old gentleman, isn't he? A little eccentric, perhaps, and a trifle fussy, too, but he comes with a heart of gold. He must have been overjoyed to encounter another human. Filbert, of course, has been keeping a watchful eye on him since his arrival."

"The poor old soul has been frantically piecing together his research, trying to solve the riddle of these circle formations and, most importantly, find a way out," explained Filbert, as he pushed one of his paws inside his suit. "It has been hugely frustrating for me, finding myself unable to pass along any inspirational thoughts or nuggets of wisdom. Until Jolly arrived, I was unaware that I was no longer the active Sage for the Hawthorne dynasty."

Filbert pulled a wad of papers out of his mouse suit.

"I have been patiently hanging onto these files for more than 120 years, from my days with Elijah Hawthorne. Now, with Jolly's able assistance, Elijah's great-grandson has begun to develop some interesting theories about our crop circle world here and its connection to the Hawthorne scroll."

"Now that we have the files *and* our professor, Sam," interjected Mr. Goodfellow, "and the professor has his Sage, we're hoping to be back on track in no time."

Everything was happening so quickly. Sam's head started to spin again, and he felt frightened and confused. He couldn't shake the thought that, in his enthusiasm to help, he may, instead, have sealed everyone's fate. There were many things he should explain to the Goodfellows, if he only knew where to start. Sam took a deep breath. It was as good a time as any.

"If the professor was right about Mandrake coming through, too, then..."

"Mandrake's here?!" cried Mr. Goodfellow. "Good gracious, my boy! How do you know?"

Sam winced.

"He's here, in Wiltshire," said Sam. "I saw him myself. And, well, the professor wasn't sure, but he thought he felt a bigger kind of disturbance than there should have been when I came through the circle."

"Indeed," declared Mr. Goodfellow, glancing over at his brother. "I believe we commented on a large power surge at the time, didn't we, Filbert?"

Filbert nodded.

"And the professor thinks that Mandrake *may* have found another set of his research notes," Sam continued nervously.

"Then it would just have been a matter of time before he got in here, Sam!"

"I know! I know!" Sam wailed. He put his head in his hands. "It's all my fault, Mr. Goodfellow!"

"What on earth are you talking about, my boy?"

"I should have done a better job searching Professor Hawthorne's office, then Mandrake wouldn't have found the notes in that old globe."

Mr. Goodfellow shook his head vehemently.

"Nonsense, Sam! You may be too upset to recall this right now, but you and I searched the professor's office together, so we *both* must have overlooked the professor's hiding place. You see? It's no more your fault than it is mine!"

"Well, actually," said Sam, looking a trifle less upset, "Beatrice did say something like that, too."

"Did she now?" asked Mr. Goodfellow, lifting his eyebrows. He cleared his throat noisily and glanced in Beatrice's direction, but she pretended she hadn't heard.

"There's something else we've found out, too, Mr. Goodfellow," Sam continued. "Worse than anything you could ever imagine." He paused and took another deep breath. "Professor Hawthorne told me there's another scroll and Mandrake has it, and even *worse...*"

"It's alright, Sam," Mr. Goodfellow interrupted. "Filbert has already filled us in on all the details. He was Elijah Hawthorne's Sage, don't forget, and privy to everything that went on in those times. Truth be told, I've actually been worrying about how to break the news to *you*, my boy. It's come as a bit of a relief to me that you already know. It does mean, though, that we are probably dealing with a much more dangerous adversary than we first thought. The type of individual, I'm sure, who has already attracted the attention of even more formidable evildoers."

Sam swallowed hard and shuddered. Just thinking about The Fen started his temples throbbing. He took little comfort in knowing that the cruel and vengeful Shrike Fen had been conveniently ingested by Fletcher's dog, Brunhilda. Sam had no doubt that there were many equally formidable Fen anxious to take Shrike's place and avenge his death.

"Avery Mandrake is a desperate man, Sam," Mr. Goodfellow continued, "and one, I suspect, who will stop at nothing to gain possession of both scrolls. We'll have to make sure that never happens."

Sam put his head in his hands.

"Come on now, lad. Chin up!" said Mr. Goodfellow.

"No, you don't understand!" cried Sam. "I've been trying to tell you! I brought the scroll with me! To protect it." He pulled his vest open so that Mr. Goodfellow could see the outline of the scroll tube inside the pocket. "It's in here!"

Mr. Goodfellow began to cringe in horror, but the overwhelming look of sorrow and regret on Sam's face caused him to straighten up and recover his composure.

"Well, that may complicate things a *little* bit, I suppose, but it's nothing we won't be able to handle," Mr. Goodfellow announced, with as much enthusiasm as he could muster. He looked over at Edgar and Filbert, who were both standing with their mouths open.

Sam prayed that Mr. Goodfellow was right. In his distress, Sam turned to Edgar for reassurance. He was standing at his father's side, staring up at him with a look of complete admiration. Now, Edgar looked away from his beloved father and up at his friend. Their eyes locked in quiet understanding.

"Dad was with me all those times, and with Uncle Jolly, too," whispered Edgar, though Sam had not even asked the question. "He was at the sea cliffs when The Fen captured Beatrice, and time and again during those years that Shrike Fen vowed to hunt me down and avenge his brother's death. He was in your house, too, Sam, on the night they had us in their clutches. Remember? He was drifting in a passage somewhere between this world and the one outside. He wasn't an illusion or a dream, as we had imagined."

"He could see you, Edgar? While you were growing up?" asked Sam.

Edgar wiped his eyes with the back of his paw and nodded.

"From time to time, he could. Can you imagine, Sam, how awful it must have been for him, trying to make me understand that he was still here and that he loved me? All that time was lost."

"But you always felt him there, didn't you?" replied Sam. "Your dad got you through all that stuff, Edgar, and helped you to keep going. Maybe he led you to Mr. Goodfellow and me, too, and even brought us all here. Not everything can be explained by that fate thing, you know. I think your dad helped out, too."

"Maybe, Sam," said Edgar, nodding his head.

"I dreamed of this place lots of times, even before we came to England," Sam continued. "It was the same dream every time. You called my name. I think you must have been trying to tell me where you were."

"Wow! I *had* been thinking about you, Sam! The whole time! Even though I was happy that we'd found my dad again, we were still trapped, and you had been left all by yourself with the scroll. I knew that you must have been worried sick. I thought if I concentrated and tried really hard to let you know we were alright, it might work."

Mr. Goodfellow had been standing off to the side, quietly listening to their conversation.

"The Sacred Seal is a formidable force, even in its common manifestation, but you two lads share something no Sage or human has ever encountered. The true power of your new bond and the extent to which it will affect both of your lives is something that has yet to be discovered."

"I've been meaning to ask you, Mr. Goodfellow," asked Sam. "Without the professor's instructions, the magnet diagram or timetable, how were you able to get in here, anyway?"

"Quite by accident, really," explained Mr. Goodfellow. "Edgar and I knew from the stories about Elijah Hawthorne that magnetic energy was the most likely key, but we didn't know anything about the number of magnets, their arrangement or the nature of the energy force behind them. Whether the ones we brought with us would have provided an adequate energy supply did not matter in the end. Edgar quite handily took care of that."

"What do you mean?" asked Sam.

"Well, as you will recall from my stories of our summer together in '36, Edgar has an ability to attract the forces of nature directly to him. On the night in question, while we were continuing our search for Professor Hawthorne, there was a sizeable electrical storm. With just one very accurate bolt from above, Edgar and I—with the supply of magnets we had brought with us acting as a conductor of sorts—found ourselves catapulted into a crop circle that was just beginning to form. It appeared to be the one missing ingredient. Edgar's unique *gift*, unpredictable as it may be, really came through for us that night. It was quite an impressive ball of fire, too, I might add, wasn't it Edgar?"

Edgar nodded in agreement, then gracefully twirled himself around. The backside of his black and brown spotted suit had even more blotches than Sam remembered. Directly in the middle of one, he could see clear through to Edgar's underpants.

"I believe that Edgar's garment may be salvageable, but mine is probably beyond repair," said Mr. Goodfellow. "I'm afraid I have no spare ones, either. We were whisked into the circle with such speed that I had no time to grab my traveling trunk. I really don't know what possessed me to take it into the field that night, anyway. Habit, I suppose. I should have left it in Beatrice's care instead. I imagine it's still sitting in that farmer's field where I left it. I do hope the crows have been kind enough to leave it alone. There is a lifetime of wonderful memories in that trunk, and some really nice suits, too."

He turned slightly to show Sam the back of his furry coat. The uppermost section, from Mr. Goodfellow's waist right up to his shoulder, had been burnt clean off, and the blue-checked shirt beneath was hanging in sooty tatters. Poking out at each side, directly at shoulder-blade level, were the bony protrusions that Sam had first seen on the night of the Fen attack at his house. Even though he had seen them before, Sam was no less fascinated now.

"What do you say, Beatrice?" Mr. Goodfellow called to her. "Could you possibly work your magic on this old suit of mine?"

"I'm no miracle worker when it comes to sewing, Jolly, and I really think you give my domestic skills much more credit than they deserve. But, as you know, I've never been able to resist a challenge."

Beatrice pulled her handbag out from under her suit and began to root through it, eventually extracting a small sewing kit. She then directed Mr. Goodfellow to remove the remains of his coat. Sam, with Mr. Goodfellow, Filbert and Edgar trailing behind, retreated to a nearby rock to sit and wait. Everyone seemed to lose himself in his own thoughts for the next few minutes, until Filbert walked forward and tapped Sam on his leg.

"You know, Sam, I haven't really had the opportunity to tell you how grateful I am for the friendship and loyalty that you have shown to both Jolly and Edgar. Jolly has told me about the difficult choices you had to confront and the sacrifices you made in regard to your Seal with Edgar. I know it can't have been easy for you, Sam, but it has meant everything to Edgar."

"It's meant everything to me, too," said Sam quietly.

Filbert nodded his head and gave Sam's foot a pat.

"It hasn't been easy for you, either, has it?" asked Sam. "Wanting to reach out and talk to Edgar the whole time he was growing up."

"I tried to help him as much as I could. I only wish I could have done more," said Filbert, with an air of melancholy in his voice.

"Are you kidding! You saved him lots of times and me, too, once," said Sam. "Thanks."

"Don't mention it," said Filbert. "And don't ever regret your decision either, Sam. I've had 120 years in here to ponder what's most important in the real world, don't forget."

"How *did* you end up in here, anyway?" asked Sam. "I guessed it was some experiment of Elijah Hawthorne's or something."

"It was, Sam. Elijah was a brilliant scientist. Although he died before he fully understood the significance of the scroll, I believe he was close. He had actually determined the proper configuration of magnets, as his great-grandson discovered years later in his research notes. The magnets Elijah was using, though, were not quite powerful enough to propel him through. They were, however, more than strong enough for me. On one very cold and rainy night, the same night, I have since discovered, Elijah fell ill with pneumonia, I was transported here by accident and have remained ever since. The poor professor wandered home, after another apparent failure, to die alone a few weeks later, unaware that he had actually succeeded by sending me."

"What was it really like?" asked Sam. "Being in here for 120 years, I mean."

"Well, by virtue of the strange nature of this place, 120 years didn't really seem as long as it sounds," Filbert replied. "Perhaps more like a *really* long weekend."

"No kidding! Really?" said Sam. "Is it true that you never get hungry in here?"

Filbert nodded his head.

"Boy, I don't think your brother or Edgar are going to like it much in here; especially Edgar. He likes to eat too much!"

"I have noticed that," Filbert remarked. "Oddly enough, though—and I don't know if it's the excitement of seeing everyone again or just 120 years finally catching up with me—I could eat a little something right about now."

Sam thought for a moment, then tore open one of the small pockets at the front of his fishing vest and reached his hand inside. He pulled out a square of golden-colored sponge toffee, a little fuzzy around the edges, but edible nevertheless. Filbert appeared intrigued, so Sam started to pick away at the pieces of vest lint that had stuck to it.

Beatrice arrived from her sewing corner just then to announce that Mr. Goodfellow's suit was ready. She reached into her own suit and pulled out her Scandinavian Sea Mouse Knife. She reached up and handed it to Sam. With his magnifying glass to assist him, Sam proceeded to make a fairly good job of cleaning up the toffee for Filbert with the tiny, stainless steel blade, making sure he didn't accidentally inflate a raft while he was at it.

"We shall not weaken or tire... Give us the tools and we will finish the job," said Beatrice, with satisfaction.

"Churchill again, right?" asked Sam.

"But of course, dear."

Mr. Goodfellow looked up and chuckled.

"I see you've been telling your war stories again, Beatrice. They never seem to fade in the retelling over the years, do they?"

"Indeed, Jolly," she replied smiling. "There are many things, I find, that don't fade over the years."

Mr. Goodfellow felt his cheeks growing a little warm. He quickly reached for the suit that was draped over Beatrice's arm.

Although the new garment fell somewhat short of her usual

standards. Beatrice felt she had done all that was possible to salvage it, considering the materials available. Perhaps if she'd had her proper sewing supplies with her, she lamented, or a patch or two of spare fur pieces, the results would have been a little more professional. Mr. Goodfellow, however, would have none of her modesty. He swept the suit into the air with a flourish and held it up for everyone else to see.

"A masterpiece, my dear. Truly a work of genius."

The others nodded in agreement, but Beatrice, still clinging to the bottom edge of one suit leg, did not want to let go until she had fully explained the extent of the repairs. Mr. Goodfellow wrestled it from her grip, however, and began slipping it on.

"Shh!" Filbert suddenly raised a paw to his lips. "There's someone coming! Listen!"

The sound of footsteps echoed in the foggy air.

10

A Picture Is Worth a
Thousand Words

Sam looked about nervously. "Professor? Professor
Hawthorne?" he called out in a whisper. "Is that you?"
"I sincerely hope it is him," said Mr. Goodfellow, who
was having more than a little trouble struggling into the rest
of his repaired suit. "The other possibility doesn't bear thinking about right now."

Mr. Goodfellow quickly zipped up the front of his suit and
raced after the other Sage, who were scattering now for cover.

"No, Mr. Goodfellow! Wait!" Sam whispered after him,
opening up his fishing vest to reveal the inner pockets. "We'll
end up losing each other again."

"You're quite right, my boy." He turned in the other direction and waved his paws over his head. "I say, everyone back
over here to Sam!"

As Sam knelt down and leaned over, Beatrice, Edgar and
Filbert climbed into one of Sam's large inner vest pockets. Mr.
Goodfellow stayed back and held onto Sam's sleeve for a
moment. There was a look of grave concern on his face.

"This may be more serious than we imagined, Sam. There is suddenly a most disturbing presence here and I fear it is growing stronger by the second. I suspect from the look I just saw on Beatrice's face that she has felt it, too."

"The Fen!" cried Sam.

"I'm afraid so, my boy. Take great care!"

Professor Hawthorne, trotting as fast as his stocky legs would carry him, loomed out of the mist.

"Sam! Quickly! It is as I feared! Mandrake has broken through! I'd recognize that horrible green shape of his a mile away! And I've just remembered where I encountered that dreadful mothball aroma before. Mandrake's office! The place was always littered with them. He was obsessive about protecting his papers from pests, convinced that moths and rodents had conspired to nibble them up, or some such nonsense."

Mr. Goodfellow had barely enough time to leap into Sam's pocket before Professor Hawthorne grabbed Sam's arm and pulled him to his feet.

"There's no time to rest, dear boy. We'll have to keep one step ahead of him. Thankfully, I've been here longer than he has; long enough to learn a few tricks, at least."

Professor Hawthorne waved his hand about, gesturing toward the inside of Sam's vest.

"I'll take a look at the scroll while we're on the move, too. There's a series of swirls and dots at one spot that may be important. I spent days locked in my study trying to decipher those blasted things. Perhaps another look will jog the brain cells."

Sam ran directly behind the professor, struggling to keep up with him as he changed direction over and over again.

"It's rather like finding oneself in a maze, isn't it?" remarked the professor.

Professor Hawthorne looked up from the scroll every few moments. He had removed it from its casing and unrolled it in front of him. The scroll tube was wedged securely under his armpit. Sam felt a sudden flurry of movement in his vest pocket. The Goodfellows and Beatrice, deafened, he imagined, by their proximity to the exposed scroll and its strange vibrations, were probably mounting a desperate search for earplugs. The strange thing was, that this time, faint as it was, Sam could also hear something coming from the scroll.

"It's a huge and intricate labyrinth in here," Professor Hawthorne suddenly called out. "Luckily, there are a few excellent hiding places, too."

Sam wished that the professor would find one of those hiding places now. For a man of his age, the old fellow was remarkably fit. He didn't appear to be in the least bit tired. As they raced along together, however, it became apparent that the unexpected arrival of Avery Mandrake had rattled Professor Hawthorne. He staggered occasionally as he ran, stopping once altogether. He rubbed his hands together, looked about nervously and muttered.

"Now, where was that hiding spot again?"

Sam heard Mr. Goodfellow whisper from his pocket.

"What's happening, my boy?"

"I'm not sure," Sam whispered back. "I think he might be getting confused or something."

"Just what I was afraid of! He's losing focus again. It's his weakness in times of stress. Sam, perhaps you might be able to get me just a little closer. A few words of encouragement, whispered into his ear right now, might be beneficial."

"I can't seem to reach him, Mr. Goodfellow!" panted Sam, as he ran behind.

Some of the dust-covered rocks were starting to look familiar. Sam began to wonder if Professor Hawthorne had run back into the passages they had already been through. He was on the verge of politely pointing out this possibility when the professor suddenly stopped, spun around and put his fingers to his lips.

"Shhh! Did you hear that?"

As they both stood listening, the sound of footsteps drew closer. Clutching the scroll tightly, Professor Hawthorne leapt forward, sprinting down another rock-strewn, dust-encrusted passageway to elude their pursuer. Mr. Goodfellow whispered frantically from the inner lining of Sam's vest.

"Just a little closer, if you can, my boy! If I can transfer myself into the professor's pocket, I may be able to offer some calming thoughts."

With every ounce of strength he could muster, Sam tried to overtake Professor Hawthorne, but it was no use. Sam's magnet-laden fishing vest was weighing him down. The professor turned around just then and, realizing Sam's plight, reached out to take the heavy vest. Sam didn't like the idea of separating himself from his friends, but it would finally give Mr. Goodfellow the opportunity to impart his much-needed words of inspiration. Sam struggled out of the vest and handed it to the professor, who draped it over his shoulder. Suddenly freed from his burden, Sam was able to keep up again. He watched the fishing vest with concern as it bounced up and down on the professor's shoulder. He hoped that the four passengers inside were not experiencing too much discomfort, especially Edgar, who suffered from motion sickness.

Suddenly, the professor stopped in mid-track. Sam, unable to brake in time, stumbled into the back of him.

"Of course, my boy! That's it!" he exclaimed, slapping his forehead with the palm of his hand. His voice had taken on a new air of confidence. "I can't explain why, but that inexplicable collection of dots and swirls on the scroll is suddenly becoming much clearer to me. I've just been thinking too hard about it, if you can imagine!" He pointed excitedly at the shimmering, silver scroll. "This part, right here. See, Sam? It's not a section of script to decipher, after all. It's a map!"

Professor Hawthorne spun around in a circle, balancing the scroll in one hand.

"This larger dot is that big boulder over there, if I'm not mistaken. Look, Sam. It's the same odd shape, isn't it? And the two smaller ones in the corner correspond with these," the professor declared, tapping his finger lightly on the surface of the scroll.

"It's so simple! The swirling lines that crisscross back and forth are all the passageways, and..." Squinting his eyes, Professor Hawthorne lifted the scroll up as one of the strange floating lights passed by. "I can barely make it out, but there's another line here, as thin as a strand of hair, running through the rest of them, finally spiraling into the center, right..."—the professor dropped his finger on top of the scroll with conviction—"here!"

Pulling Sam along, Professor Hawthorne began running with a newfound purpose. The short rest had given Sam the opportunity to catch his breath. They ran on for the next few minutes—weaving between towering boulders and leaping across smaller rock formations—as Professor Hawthorne consulted the scroll map. He turned back to Sam only once during their journey, to tell him that they had almost reached their destination. Halfway through this announcement, just as they entered a circular crossroads of sorts, the professor's voice grew fainter and his words became garbled. Then, right before Sam's eyes, Professor Hawthorne vanished in a burst of blinding white light and a cloud of red dust.

151

Sam let out a cry of astonishment and froze. Not sure for a moment in which direction he should move, he decided at last to place his feet directly inside the last two eerie-looking footprints that the professor had left behind. A great flash of light momentarily blinded Sam. When his vision cleared, the professor was standing in front of him again, absently tapping the re-rolled scroll back into its case and staring with awe at the ceiling of a great cavernous chamber.

"I believe we have made a significant breakthrough," Professor Hawthorne whispered, slipping the scroll into his jacket pocket. "Noticeably colder, isn't it, my boy?"

Shivering, Sam nodded his head.

"Harder to breath, too," the professor commented, panting. "It reminds me of an experience I had once at high altitude in the Himalayas. With a little perseverance, though, I adjusted to the rarified air. But do try to take care when moving about, my boy. There appears to be some sort of reduction in the gravitational influences in here. I took a step just before you arrived and found myself propelled halfway up to that ceiling."

Sam placed one foot very cautiously in front of the other, grabbing a large boulder as he felt himself lifting up off the ground.

"Are we in that core place?" asked Sam, looking up to where the professor was staring.

The professor nodded his head. "Fascinating, isn't it? It's like the dome of some great crystalline cathedral. Look at the cluster formations up there, Sam. Emeralds, diamonds, rubies, sapphires, every precious gem imaginable; it's magnificent!"

"There must be millions of dollars worth of minerals in this place, right, professor?" asked Sam, excitedly.

"Billions, I'd say."

"Wow!"

"If, of course," said the professor, carefully bending down to pick up a small rock, "they were real."

"Huh?"

Professor Hawthorne swung his arm back and hurled the rock at the ceiling with the grim determination of a major league pitcher. Instead of colliding with one of the hanging, gem-encrusted clusters, the professor's little missile sailed right through.

"The whole thing is a projection, my boy," the professor declared. "Or a hologram of some sort. Quite a good one, too. If you look *really* closely at those clusters, though, you can still make out the faint outline of the rocks behind them. See?"

The professor picked up another small rock and let it soar.

"Professor Hawthorne?" whispered Sam, as he tugged at the professor's sleeve. "Maybe we shouldn't be doing this."

"It's quite alright, Sam, I assure you. Holographic projections can't be damaged in this way. I was just demonstrating how..."

"But Professor!" interrupted Sam, tugging more vigorously. "Something weird is going on over there! Look!"

The professor turned his gaze away from the ceiling and directed it to where Sam was pointing. Dozens of small moving images, suspended in transparent balls, were floating up from the shadows and heading straight toward them, bobbing up and down in the air like a huge spray of soap bubbles. As the balls drew closer, Sam could see great cities of metal and glass, airships and flying machines, long arched bridges spanning deep red canyons, pyramidal arcades and rows of towering columns intricately carved from stone, graceful statues of bronze and gold, glistening fountains and lush hanging gardens.

"Fascinating," uttered the professor. "The collected accomplishments of the world's great civilizations... or so it would appear." He paused to peer directly into one of the transparent balls that was passing by his nose. "Though they're unlike anything I've encountered before. Curious, indeed."

"What are these things?" cried Sam nervously, as the balls floated closer to him.

"More holograms, I'd say," replied the professor. "Sound- or motion-activated, perhaps."

"I told you we shouldn't have been hurling those rocks!"

"Inconsequential, I suspect, my boy. Our very presence may have been all that was needed to set these things off."

Sam ducked as one of the small bubbles, holding the image of two long stone faces, like the ones on Easter Island, almost collided with his head.

"I don't believe their intent is to harm us," the professor said reassuringly, as Sam ducked another. "If this is indeed the inner core, then according to the scroll, it is a repository of information. I believe that the balls may simply be here to impart a message of some sort. I say, it really is terribly exciting, isn't it? Please, Sam, if we just try to stand still for a second perhaps they'll..."

"I can't move my feet anymore, anyway!" interrupted Sam, with a panicked cry.

"Indeed," proclaimed Professor Hawthorne, staring down at his own feet. "Nor I. Well, at least we won't be soaring to the ceiling for the moment. And you must admit, it is a rather interesting way to get one's attention."

The transparent balls finally came to rest, floating in the air directly above their heads.

"What should we do?" asked Sam, as the balls suddenly began to descend toward them.

"Not much we can do, I'm afraid," replied the professor. "I imagine these things have been pre-programmed in some way. I suggest we just..." The professor's voice suddenly faded.

"What?" cried Sam, turning his head sideways. "Professor! What did you say?"

Through the curtain of floating images that was slowly encasing him, Sam could just make out the figure of Professor Hawthorne beside him. Surrounded by his own collection of images, the professor was chattering away excitedly, oblivious to the fact that Sam could no longer hear him. The fishing vest that held Beatrice and the Goodfellows was still casually draped over his shoulder. Sam sighed and turned away, hoping that everyone inside was alright. He had never felt so alone.

Sam had little time to think about his own plight. The collection of suspended balls and fantastic images now extended all the way around him from his head to his feet. Mesmerized, he watched herds of animals thundering across verdant grasslands, pods of giant sea creatures plying the oceans and flocks of a thousand colorful birds flying across sunrises of fiery red and pink where not one, but two tiny moons twinkled in the sky. They were the most beautiful images that Sam had ever seen. It was as if paradise itself had been captured in each ball. As Sam stared at them, a sensation of peace and tranquility swept over him—a feeling so powerful that he wished it could last forever. But even as his enchantment with the floating balls continued, something inside them began to change.

The grasslands transformed into arid deserts and the herds of creatures dwindled to just a few. Oceans that only seconds before had brimmed with life were now empty and polluted. The magnificent cities of sparkling glass and metal seemed tarnished now, the skies above them no longer teeming with great inventions. The beautiful flocks of birds had also vanished, and the horizon they had once swept across was now colorless and barren.

As the images continued to float before him, strange words

began to fill Sam's ears. Incomprehensible at first, one word eventually became clear, then another and another. Sam turned his head sideways for one brief second. At that same moment, Professor Hawthorne had looked over at Sam, too. By the solemn expression on his face, Sam could tell that the professor had seen the same things transpire. The words, now clear and forceful, were speaking directly to them. When Sam felt compelled to close his eyes, the images remained with him, as if they had become part of his own thoughts.

11

SEEK AND
YE SHALL FIND

To all who might still remain, let this be our testament. As a humble servant of my people, I commit these words to the memory of a great world that once was. Let the message of the moving circles be heeded for all time so that we may not forget why we have journeyed here or the true purpose of our mission. Let the place you have entered provide solace, a sanctuary of peace and remembrance and the record of all we had hoped to preserve. To those who find their way here, and especially to the chosen one who will guard the great sacred scrolls, mark these words: Search all things, hold fast that which is true."

Sam eyes flew open in recognition. How many times had he heard that old proverb? Must be some kind of weird coincidence, he supposed. Sam looked over toward Professor Hawthorne. Head bowed, the professor was completely engrossed in the words. On his shoulder, the fishing vest rippled slightly. Beatrice and the Goodfellows, Sam imagined, must be as intrigued by the strange testament as he and the professor. As Sam continued to watch and listen, a remarkable story began to unfold.

"When our world, once a peaceful and benevolent land, fell prey to dark forces, those of us who wished to preserve its light came together. While avarice and greed filled the hearts of many of our brothers, we spoke our message of warning. But the seeds of corruption had already taken root, strangling the life from the great cities of our ancestors, polluting our waters, laying waste our beautiful crimson mountains and valleys, and poisoning the plants and animals that had flourished there. But no one would hear our words. Even the pleas of the oldest and wisest of our prophets fell upon deaf ears. His vision of a great watery deluge that would destroy us all was met with disbelief. Those who refused to hear, he warned, would be the makers of their own ruin and that of our world, too. Taking instruction from his visions, the great prophet prepared the two scrolls that would be the record of all that we had once cherished, and the blueprint for the new world that we were to build. The visions had decreed that we would set forth on a long journey to a strange land, in a great vessel of silver. Taking as many of our world's wild creatures as we could carry, we would travel a great distance to another land—a land that would be deluged like our own world, but was destined to thrive once more. It would be a vast place of blue oceans and green valleys, far bigger than the home we had left behind, and populated with many kinds of animals. Here we would see the star of day fill the sky with a great warmth and light. In the time of darkness there would be one great moon. Only in a place such as this, the visions foretold—where the land and the creatures upon it were pure and uncorrupted—could the two sacred scrolls be joined together by one worthy of the task. Only then would the prophecy of our new world be fulfilled.

"Many days into our voyage, we watched with despair as the prophet's vision came to pass. The world that we had left behind was destroyed in a great flood. We were powerless to help, unable to do any more than mourn its passing and look ahead to a new and better life.

"None of us could have imagined then that our voyage was doomed. Soon after this, a sinister presence made itself known to us. Conscious that an element of evil had managed to slip aboard our ship, our leader did everything in his power to find and contain it, but his efforts proved to be in vain. By the time we reached our destination, some of our weaker members had turned against us. Influenced by this evil force, they enacted a plot to take control. Many of our number were killed in the horrific crash that followed. The sacred scrolls were lost, and our leader himself was mortally wounded. The visions, he then explained, had warned that such a thing might come to pass. In the event of disaster, the visions proclaimed, he was to document all that had transpired, as a warning to those who might follow. He lived long enough to perform one final act: to set the circles in motion.

"And so ends the story of our voyage. We can do no more than commit the future of our people into the hands of the Fates. Those of us who survive are few, marooned now in a strange land, uncertain if evil stalks us still. Soon we will be scattered to the four winds. But we must try to survive. We can only hope, as the prophet did, that one day the scrolls will be found by one worthy of their protection and guarded until the world is ready to receive them again. If this comes to pass, it must be only as decreed. Joined together, the scrolls contain power, knowledge and the promise of a just and peaceful world. But if they fall into lesser hands, and are united by one who is unworthy and in a world that is unprepared, a great force will be unleashed that will commit this planet to evil as surely as our own beloved world."

A strange silence filled the air as the words stopped. The transparent balls and the images inside were beginning to fade. Sam gingerly lifted one foot and stepped forward, trying not to bounce off the ground. A few feet away, Professor

Hawthorne was attempting the same procedure. When they managed to come together, they clung to each other for support. Neither could speak at first, still enthralled by everything they had heard and seen.

"Do you know what all of this means, my boy?" Professor Hawthorne finally blurted out, as he shook Sam by the shoulders.

Sam wasn't sure. He was still trying very hard to digest everything he had just witnessed.

"I don't know, Professor. I..."

"All of these years, Sam! All this time we've been scouring the heavens, searching for signs of intelligent life in the universe! It's been right here all along!"

"Huh?"

"Don't you see, Sam? It's us! You! Me! We're—we're extraterrestrials!"

"We are?" replied Sam nervously.

Professor Hawthorne nodded vigorously. "Our ancestors were, at any rate. From Mars, if I'm not mistaken! It was all in the images, Sam. The distance to the sun, the two moons! And look around you, my boy. The red dust, the gravitational influences. It's a place of remembrance!" Professor Hawthorne looked toward the holographic ceiling. "I imagine there must have been a treasure trove of precious minerals there, too. Precious to an Earth dweller, at least. On Mars, they may have been as plentiful as common rocks. And the unique metallic composition of our scroll, too. Impossible to be found on Earth, because it wasn't mined here!"

The more he thought of the possibilities, the less Professor Hawthorne could contain his exuberance. He began to giggle with excitement as he paced, forcing him to grab Sam's shoulder again to stop from soaring too high into the air.

"It's the most important discovery in the history of humankind! It's going to change everything, Sam—the way we have written our own history and how we have perceived the advancement of every civilization on Earth. It may even fill in some gaps in the evolutionary development of many of the Earth's creatures. It's like finally finding the missing link."

The professor paused for a second as if he were listening to a little voice in his head. He suddenly slapped his forehead.

"What am I thinking, my boy! It *is* the missing link! It explains everything, doesn't it? So many of the world's great mysteries, at least. How did the ancients draw their maps of the world from space, or carve giant animal forms into the Peruvian plateaus of Nazca, thousands of years before the invention of flight? Where did they receive the intricate knowledge of mathematics and engineering required to construct the great pyramids of Egypt, or the astronomical expertise to build Stonehenge?"

Sam shrugged his shoulders.

"They weren't from here, Sam! Just imagine it! A band of people, survivors of a great tragedy, are forced to wander the Earth and live by its wits," said Professor Hawthorne as he combed his fingers through his long, thick hair. "They are from a highly advanced world, with the ability to harness and utilize a host of energy sources, but living now in what amounts to little more than a primitive jungle. They eventually become separated from each other, surviving by intermingling with the scattered groups of Earthlings they begin to encounter. Many thousands of years pass. They have settled wherever they can, eventually assimilating into their new world, becoming true dwellers of this planet, living and dying amongst the many creatures who have been here since life first developed in Earth's primordial ooze. The newcomers and their offspring forget most, but not quite all, of what they had once known, including the existence of their sacred scrolls and the message left for them in the circles. Forgetting, that is, until one day, tens of thousands of years later, one of their descendants, by the name of Elijah Hawthorne, with, by now, only an infinitesimal drop of Martian blood still coursing through his veins, makes a remarkable discovery. And the rest, as they say, is history. A whole new history! Just waiting to be written, my boy!"

With this final declaration, Professor Hawthorne threw all caution to the wind and leapt high into the air with an impassioned whoop. When he alighted, he reached forward and grabbed hold of Sam's arm.

"I can't begin to imagine what my great-grandfather Elijah would have made of this! To think that his research would lead us here. It's incredible!" The professor's eyes were alive with wonder. "The world must know, dear boy! I must tell them the truth! I can't help but feel it is my duty, especially after all that great-grandfather sacrificed."

"But professor!" cried Sam. "What about the warnings? About the wrong people joining the scrolls at the wrong time and everything..."

"Of course we'll protect our scroll, Sam," Professor Hawthorne replied in a more solemn tone. "But this kind of knowledge—why, think of the incredible good that could come from it. The opportunity to examine the decline of one great world to save our own!" He placed his hand on Sam's shoulder. "I'm going to take a bit more of a look around here, if you don't mind," the professor announced. He peered into the shadows at the far end of the chamber. "For one, I'd love to know how that crop of floating holograms was formed, before we find our way out of here." He turned back to Sam. "And you, my boy, you look like you could use another rest. It's been quite a lot to take in all at once, hasn't it? If it wasn't for my prolonged exposure to the rejuvenating aspects of this place, I imagine I would have collapsed long ago. All of this does inspire one to reflect on the original Martian environment, doesn't it? At one time, its inhabitants must have enjoyed considerably longer and more energetic lives than we do now."

Professor Hawthorne carefully led Sam to the nearest boulder and sat him down, then pulled the fishing vest off his shoulder and laid it over Sam's knees.

"I'll be back in a flash," he said with a wink. "I think I've finally managed to master this gravity business. If you feel the need to move around, Sam, I think you'll find that, even with their reduced weight, the magnets will act as a bit of a stabilizer."

As Professor Hawthorne disappeared into the shadows, Sam breathed a sigh of relief. He flipped his vest open and hastily unzipped the inside pocket.

"Mr. Goodfellow? Edgar?" he whispered. "Hello...anybody?"

"Sam? Is that you, dear?" he heard Beatrice's voice reply.

"Yes, it's me. Are you alright?"

"Much better now, thank you, Sam," said Filbert, popping his head out of the pocket. "It's been a bit of a cliff-hanger, as you can imagine. The professor does bounce around quite a bit for an old fellow, doesn't he? Nevertheless, we have all managed to survive the ordeal, although Edgar, I believe, is still feeling a tad queasy."

Sam could hear Edgar's pitiful groans from the bottom of the pocket.

"I was afraid of that," said Sam.

"Jolly, of course, has remained with Professor Hawthorne for the time being," explained Beatrice.

"The recent developments here have been quite a revelation for us all," explained Filbert solemnly. "I'm sure you understand that we are all standing at a great crossroads. Professor Hawthorne will need the guidance of an experienced Sage, like Jolly, more than ever."

Sam looked at Filbert and Beatrice and nodded his head. Edgar, recovered from his bout of nausea, joined them. He had just started to comment on something that was puzzling him when a sudden and very bright flash of light turned everyone's attention to another part of the chamber. Through a thick cloud of billowing red dust, a green—and very tall—image was beginning to materialize.

"It's Mandrake! He's broken through!" cried Sam, grabbing his vest as Beatrice, Filbert and Edgar clung to the edge of the pocket.

Sam slipped himself behind the boulder as quickly as he could. He crouched down low to the ground while Professor Mandrake, admiring the richness of his new surroundings, attempted to master the odd gravitational conditions.

"Sam, what's happening?" Beatrice whispered from inside the fishing vest.

"He's getting closer!" Sam whispered back frantically. "No, wait—he's stopped. I think his feet are stuck!" He held his breath for a moment. "Yep, here come the balls again. This is terrible! Mandrake's about to find out everything." Sam turned his back to the boulder and slid himself down to the ground.

Beatrice and Filbert pulled themselves up to the edge of the pocket.

"Unavoidable, I imagine," said Filbert. "The holographic images, it would appear, are not terribly discriminating. Whoever enters this place, good or bad, becomes privy to their message."

"Well, there's *one* good thing about him being stuck," announced Edgar, pushing his head between Beatrice and his father as he climbed out of the vest pocket. "I need to stretch my legs and get some fresh air."

"Not too far, Edgar," warned Filbert. "Mandrake won't be trapped for long. In fact, I suggest that Sam locate Professor Hawthorne as soon as possible and inform him of the situation." He looked back over to Edgar just then, who was bouncing up and down on the ground rather uncontrollably. "If you insist on moving about, Edgar, perhaps it would be prudent if you accompany Sam. Beatrice and I will keep an eye on Mandrake until you return."

Confident that Professor Mandrake was now completely absorbed in the message, Sam put on his fishing vest and slipped away from the boulder. With Edgar springing about as if he were mounted on an invisible pogo stick, Sam made his way toward the dark corner of the chamber. As they navigated their way across the ground, Edgar suddenly ceased his erratic jumping, pointed his mouse mask into the air and took a great sniff.

"Do you smell something, Sam?" he asked, a little nervously.

"Um, I don't think so," Sam replied, stopping to crunch up his nose as he took a big breath of his own.

Edgar's eyes darted left, then right.

"Just for a second there, I could have sworn that I—" Edgar froze. "What was *that*?"

Sam had heard it, too. A rustle, then a long scraping sound, then a rustle again.

"Come on, Edgar," whispered Sam. "Let's get out of here."

"Oh, please don't leave on my account," said a slow, slippery voice from the shadows. "I've been waiting such a long time to get you two alone again. You wouldn't want to disappoint me now, would you?"

Sam felt sick to his stomach. The sound of that voice was

167

already evoking painful memories. He held his hands up to his temples as they began to throb.

There was another rustle and a scrape as a small, cloaked figure slithered out from the shadows.

"Shrike Fen!" gasped Edgar.

12

A BAD PENNY ALWAYS

COMES BACK

Edgar's mind was reeling and his throat felt painfully dry when he tried to speak again. "But...I thought you were..."

"DOG FOOD?" shrieked The Fen, gathering his black cloak around him. "Hardly, Sage! But you'll soon wish that I had been! That stupid beast was no match for me. I do, however, have a bit of a score to settle with her. WITH ALL OF YOU!" He flung one side of his cloak open just wide enough to reveal the sore and tattered remains of what had been his left leg. The sickly maggot-white kneecap was strapped to a thin stump of pale yellow wood.

It was not a pleasant sight. Edgar grimaced while Sam recoiled in horror. The overpowering stench of something rotting wafted toward them.

"Lovely, isn't it, boys?" sniggered Shrike, as he folded the cloak around him again. "I'm usually such a shy fellow, but this time I just had to make an exception. Now perhaps you will understand when I show you no mercy. I only regret that my young nephew Bogg is otherwise occupied with his own little assignment. I'm sure he would have been delighted to see you again. He did so enjoy the fun he had with you the last time."

Shrike started to move toward them.

"Marvelous place, isn't it?" he crowed. "With the reduced pull in here, I'm finding it so much easier to get around. I'll be sorry to leave, I suppose, but my human charge and I have rather a full schedule now. We really must be getting back. There's so much to do! I just don't know what to tackle first," he snickered. "Should I dispose of you first or take the other scroll, reunite it with its twin and snatch control of the world right away?"

Sam gulped.

"Oh, don't look so surprised, human! I know all about it, already. Once you and that Professor Hawthorne of yours found the way in, any idiot could have followed your dusty footsteps. I decided to slip in ahead of my associate. I had quite a good time watching you get all choked up over that sad little tale. Humans are such an emotional, sniveling lot. If some of you weren't occasionally useful, I think I would lobby for the extinction of the entire species," he sneered.

Shrike suddenly looked up toward the frozen figure of Professor Mandrake, still surrounded by the wall of floating balls.

"Speaking of humans, there's a particularly fine example right over there. I give you," said Shrike, as he pointed a long jagged nail toward Mandrake, "my distinguished associate. Such an agreeable fellow when it comes to my wicked suggestions. He hardly needs convincing at all; he's so deliciously greedy! I can't wait to get on with it."

"You'll never win, Fen! Never! Never! Never!" Edgar shouted.

Shrike clamped his white bony fingers on either side of his black hood. "Spare me your tiresome phrases, Sage! I can't

170

abide that 'never, never' nonsense. It makes me sick! Those incessant words sent a particularly brilliant human of mine into such uncontrollable rages that he went quite mad. He'd have had all of the free world on its knees, too, if it hadn't been for that stupid old Churchill character and his victory signs and his speeches and his blasted 'never, never's."

Shrike had worked himself up into a tirade. He clenched his long fingers into two tight fists, then thrust them above his hooded head and screamed. The throbbing at Sam's temples reached an unbearable level, forcing him to the ground. Edgar rushed to his side and began tugging at his pant leg.

"Sam! Look at me! Look into my eyes! Remember the last time when we joined our thoughts? We can defeat him together, if we try! I know we can! Look at me, please!"

Sam tried to speak, but the pain inside his head was excruciating. As during his first encounter with Shrike, Sam began to feel the control of his own thoughts slowly slipping away.

"Let him go, Fen!" Edgar cried in anger.

"You don't think that you or this weak-minded friend of yours can get away from me a second time, do you, Sage? I'm not about to let you use any of your ridiculous mind tricks, either," he croaked. "I'm ready for you this time, fool!"

Shrike bent over then, gathering up a bony white handful of red dust. With another great rattle of his black cloak he hurled it straight into Edgar's eyes, causing him to reel backward in pain. Edgar lifted his paws to his face, trying desperately to wipe his eyes free of the stinging dust. Seconds later, he could feel The Fen's sharp nails clawing through his mouse suit and piercing his skin.

"How do you like that, Sage?" Shrike screamed. "AND THIS! AND THIS!" He screamed even louder, poking again and again through Edgar's suit.

Receiving a deep gash in his side with Shrike's last thrust, Edgar fell to his knees. Struggling to stay conscious, he suddenly heard another voice.

"AND HOW DO YOU LIKE THIS, SHRIKE FEN!"

There was a splintering crack, followed by a great shriek of terror, and then a loud, echoing thud. Edgar managed to open one eye. Through a misty red film of dust he could see the figure of Beatrice, standing in battle stance, wielding her Scandinavian Sea Mouse Knife over her head like a broadsword. Shrike Fen lay in a crumpled black heap on the ground, cradling his stumpy knee and glaring up at her with a look of pure evil. His pale yellow wooden leg, dislodged by the blow from Beatrice's knife, bounced up and down a few times before coming to rest some distance away. Edgar felt the strong arms of his father lifting him up from the ground.

"Are you alright, Edgar?"

Edgar managed a slow nod, then wiped the rest of the dust from his eyes with the back of his furry arm.

"Sam?" Edgar cried, looking over at the slumped figure of his friend.

The stranglehold of Shrike's evil thoughts was gradually beginning to loosen, and Sam managed a slow nod of his own.

"It's a good job we came by when we did," exclaimed Filbert. "Beatrice and I couldn't understand what was keeping you boys. I'm sorry to insist on rushing you after your ordeal, but it's imperative that we get a move on. It looks as if Professor Mandrake will be coming to the end of his little show at any second now. We've got to find Jolly and Professor Hawthorne immediately!"

No one noticed Shrike slithering across the floor to retrieve his wooden appendage. Distracted by the urgency of the

situation, they had all turned their backs for just a second, presuming that the shock of being upended, and short a leg, had rendered him more or less harmless.

"WE'LL HAVE NONE OF THAT, FEN!" The voice of Jolly Goodfellow rang out in the chamber.

Shrike Fen, clutching the jagged end of the wooden leg in his bony fist, was poised to strike the back of Filbert. He screeched as Mr. Goodfellow trapped the edge of his black cloak under the heel of one mouse foot, while kicking the wooden leg out of his grasp with the other.

"You again, Goodfellow!" Shrike screamed, struggling to free himself.

"I must say, Jolly," said Filbert thankfully, "you've always possessed the most amazing sense of timing."

"I hope that continues, dear brother," replied Mr. Goodfellow. "I'm afraid that timing could turn out to be either friend or foe now. Professor Hawthorne has almost completed his examination of the chamber. I came ahead to alert the rest of you, never imagining that I would find you in such— Great heavens!" he suddenly exclaimed, "is that Mandrake over there?"

"I'm afraid it is, Jolly," replied Filbert. "The scoundrel followed us in. So has this Fen here."

"So he knows, then?" asked Mr. Goodfellow, staring into Shrike's steely eyes. The hood of The Fen's cloak had slipped from the top of his shiny, bone-white head. He gurgled and hissed repeatedly as he continued to twist back and forth to free himself.

"What are we going to do with you now, Fen?" Mr. Goodfellow exclaimed.

"It's too late, Jolly Goodfellow," Shrike sneered with satisfaction. "I know everything! All of the delicious little secrets of this place. And I know just how to use them, too! You'll never defeat me!"

The sound of Professor Hawthorne returning suddenly echoed through the chamber.

"Sam! Sam! Where are you?" the professor cried. "It's Mandrake! He's followed us through!"

The rapid approach of Professor Hawthorne startled the group. Beatrice dropped her Sea Mouse Knife to the floor with a clatter. Mr. Goodfellow's mouse foot slipped a mere fraction, but it was enough to loosen the hold on Shrike Fen's cloak. With one great tug, Shrike pulled free and began to slither toward the shadows.

With an impassioned cry, Mr. Goodfellow lunged forward, grabbed the edge of the cloak with both of his mouse paws and began pulling it toward him. In his urgency to escape, Shrike pulled even harder in the opposite direction until the cloak suddenly tore from his body. Exposed now, an unimaginable indignity in the Fen world, Shrike shrieked with rage and horror, but it was nothing compared to the loud gasps coming from Sam and The Sage. They had imagined that seeing an uncloaked Fen would be horrifying. They had, after all, already stared into his cold eyes, and seen the thin layer of sickly white, translucent skin that stretched across his pointed nose and chin. The rest of him—the same translucent white flesh stretched tight and shiny over a gray, skeletal form—didn't surprise them; but the unexpected sight of two bony knobs jutting out from Shrike Fen's back sent shockwaves of revulsion and disbelief through them all.

Beatrice and the Goodfellows stood frozen as Shrike retreated into the shadows. Mr. Goodfellow shook himself and made another lunge at the escaping Fen.

"You won't get away this time, Shrike!" he shouted.

"No!" whispered Sam, struggling to open the pocket that lined his vest. "There's no time! I can see Professor Hawthorne coming around that boulder over there!" He bent down and motioned The Sage over to him. "Get in! Quick!"

"The boy's right!" cried Filbert, as he helped Beatrice retrieve her knife, then gave her a leg up into Sam's vest pocket. Edgar was next.

"Jolly!" Filbert pleaded again. "Please! We'll have to deal with Shrike another time!"

Shrike Fen had already disappeared into the shadows. Reluctantly, Mr. Goodfellow made his way to the vest pocket and, with Sam's assistance, climbed inside.

Sam quickly zipped the pocket closed and stood up just in time to greet the returning professor.

"Sam! Why did you leave your spot?" the professor exclaimed in a panicked voice. "I've been beside myself looking for you."

"I saw Mandrake come through, Professor. I thought I should find you and tell you. I'm really sorry..."

"Well, never mind that now. The important thing, my boy, is that we leave this place before he's free again."

The unfurled scroll was back in the Professor's hands.

"I've been doing some further study of the scroll map. It seems to coincide with an interesting collection of anterooms that I have located over there," the professor explained, pointing across the chamber. "There's one in particular that..."

"Professor!" cried Sam. "The balls around Mandrake! They're starting to float away!"

"We've no time to lose then!" Professor Hawthorne shouted. "Our only hope now is to keep ahead of him!"

He grabbed Sam by the arm and started bounding across the chamber floor. As the two passed the figure of Avery

Mandrake, they noticed that the balls had almost dispersed completely.

Sam looked over just as Mandrake was lifting his head. There was a look of surprise when he spotted Sam, then his eyes flashed with delight as a sly, snaky smile slid across his face.

13

WE NEVER KNOW HOW
MUCH WE LOVE TILL WHAT
WE LOVE IS LOST

A few moments later, Sam was standing in a strange little room, as the professor pored over the open scroll. Like the larger chamber, it, too, was domed and crystal-encrusted.

"Now if I'm reading this thing correctly...no...no—wait, this isn't the right one at all!"

Professor Hawthorne fled into the next room with Sam close behind. They bounced in and out of three more small chambers before the professor vanished with a flash of bright light and a puff of red dust. As the faint smell of mothballs floated into his nostrils, Sam shuddered and jumped into the professor's last footprints.

They found themselves back in the maze of rock and stone again, and Sam could make out a faint humming sound in the distance. Professor Hawthorne had heard it, too.

"How convenient, Sam! I believe we are about to take a little trip," the professor announced. He fumbled around in his coat pocket. "Drat! Where's that blasted timetable? There's no time now for me to make even a quick calculation. That sound always starts up just before another circle forms and I'm jettisoned off someplace. Heaven knows where to this time." He pointed his nose in the air. "There's that odious mothball smell again, too."

"Mandrake's about to come back through!" cried Sam.

"Oh, dear!" wailed Professor Hawthorne, a look of horror on his face. He quickly rolled up the ancient scroll, popped it inside the cylindrical tube and clutched it to his chest.

"We have to get the scroll out of here and away from him, Sam!" the professor cried. "We need a plan; yes, that's it, my boy! We must have a proper plan of some sort!"

Professor Hawthorne was beginning to babble. If he knew about the existence of the Fen, thought Sam, he would collapse completely. The little lights that floated continually through the air in this strange crop circle world had begun to shimmer and dance again, and the humming sound was growing louder by the second.

"Professor, listen to me! I have an idea," Sam shouted.

He grabbed Professor Hawthorne by his trembling arms and looked straight into his eyes.

"You could try your re-entry theory now. A new circle is starting to form somewhere, right? If I can give you that push of energy that you talked about at just the right time, then you and the scroll are out of here!"

The professor's eyes widened.

"Yes...yes, of course."

Professor Hawthorne slowly pulled himself together as he considered the possibilities.

"A brilliant and timely plan, Sam, but I fear that you wouldn't have the strength to propel a man of my bulk." He rubbed his chin in thought. "*You*, on the other hand, would make the ideal subject!"

The professor reached forward to open Sam's fishing vest, shoved the scroll back into its pocket and pulled the zipper across.

"Hey! Wait a minute! What are you doing?" cried Sam, fiddling with his zipper. "I shouldn't have this anymore. It belongs to you, Professor. You haven't finished deciphering it all yet."

"Think about it, my boy. It's all that Mandrake really wants, isn't it? If I stay here and lead him astray, it will give you the time to get away and hide it. Take it back home with you and wait for me there. I'll get out another time."

"But how?" Sam protested. "How are you going to get out of here?"

The professor waved his hands impatiently. "I'll have to worry about the details later." He patted the side of the vest that held the scroll. "Take her home, Sam."

"But will you be alright, Professor?"

"Of course. No matter how long Mandrake is in here, I've been here longer. I'll always be able to keep one step ahead of him."

The humming had reached a deafening level. Sam shivered as a cold blast of air passed through him. There was little time to lose. Sam unloaded the magnets from his vest pocket and began to arrange them, in reverse order, at his feet. He was so engrossed in this whole procedure and distracted by the escalating activity around him that he failed to notice the frantic pushing and nudging from inside his vest. Mr. Goodfellow was trying desperately to get Sam's attention. If Sam didn't act soon, Professor Hawthorne would be left behind without the benefit of Sagely counsel.

"Ready, Sam?" shouted Professor Hawthorne over the noise.

"Yeah. I guess so," Sam replied, standing inside the circle of magnets.

He could feel a steady rumbling as the magnets started to spin around his feet.

Faster and faster they spun, until the white circle of light and heat slowly moved up from the ground and began to surround him.

Sam took one last look at Professor Hawthorne before the blinding light reached his face. The professor's eyes were twinkling. He gave Sam a quick wink and walked around him.

"You never know, Sam," he shouted. "Maybe one day I can get that scoundrel Avery Mandrake to give me a great big push, too!"

Just at that moment, Sam felt two hands on his back, then the full force of the professor's weight. A tingling sensation stretched from his head to his toes as he was hurled back into the field of wheat, out of the warm mist and into the damp night air.

Sam lay still for a moment before opening his eyes. He staggered to his feet, trying to shake off the lingering dizziness before stooping down again to retrieve his magnets. Slowly, he made his way toward the road and the lonely clump of bushes where he had left Fletcher. He placed a hand on the left side of his vest and felt for the shape of the scroll tube. It was still there. He opened the other side of his vest and was about to unzip the inner pocket when he heard rustling in the bushes up ahead.

"Fletch! Fletcher!" Sam called. "Are you there?" He heard more rustling. Fletcher's head poked out from the middle of a rhododendron bush.

"Sam! Where have you been? I stayed right here, just like you told me to, thinking you'd be back any second!" Fletcher exclaimed in exasperation. "I've been freezing to death, you know! You've done this to me before! 'Wait right here, Fletch,' you always say, and then four hours later..."

"Four hours! Ahh, come on Fletcher! Stop exaggerating already! It's been like maybe forty-five minutes!"

"What?" Fletcher cried, holding his wrist out toward Sam. "How come my watch says almost 3:00 in the morning, then?"

"Huh?" Sam muttered, looking over at the lighted dial of Fletcher's wristwatch, then down at his own. "Wow," he exclaimed. "I just thought my watch was busted again or something. It's really weird in there."

"In where?"

"In the...hey, wait a minute! You *must* have seen the crop circle forming, right?" asked Sam.

"Crop circle! No! Honest! The wind just started blowing around a bit. Then my flashlight quit working. I thought I heard some humming and I saw a few lights in the air, but I just figured it was you messing around with your flashlight. Then everything went dark and I was kinda stuck here. I didn't want to leave, anyway. I kept thinking you'd be back any minute."

Sam reached over the bush and pulled out a huge handful of wheat strands that were embedded in Fletcher's hair.

"Any idea how these things got stuck in here so deep, Fletcher?"

"Um..." Fletcher hesitated.

"An energy vortex, Fletch!" Sam exclaimed impatiently. "And by the way, your flashlight seems to be working again. Mine, too."

Fletcher picked up his glowing flashlight and trained it on the field, where three gigantic circles of swirled wheat now lay pressed against the ground.

"Wow! That's unbelievable, Sam! How did it get there? What happened?"

"The magnet thing, Fletcher! It worked! I've been inside the circle. Professor Hawthorne's there, too. He's been there all this time. You didn't see anyone else near the field while I was out there, did you?"

"No. Why?" asked Fletcher, nervously.

Sam shone his own flashlight at the opposite side of the crop field, then slowly dragged the light beam across the clumps of bushes that framed the edge.

"I guess he came in from over there somewhere."

"Who?" asked Fletcher. "What are you talking about?"

"Mandrake! He's in the circle now, too. We figure he found the professor's notes after all."

The thought of Avery Mandrake creeping past him in the dark made Fletcher feel faint. He slumped back down into the rhododendron bush.

"There's a second scroll, too, Fletcher, and Professor Hawthorne's pretty sure that Mandrake has it," Sam continued. "The two scrolls were going to be joined together a really long time ago, but something went wrong. The whole crop circle thing is a kind of warning message. And you're not going to believe this either, but Professor Hawthorne had a tiny piece of his scroll analyzed and dated before he disappeared. It's thousands and thousands of years old and made of some kind of stuff that you can't find on Earth! And it was your dad who did the tests!"

"Sam," said Fletcher, his voice rising with excitement. "I think that must be what his Commonwealth Science Conference paper is about. I saw him working on it, I just didn't know what it meant. It was all about the chemical properties of some newly discovered compound or something!"

"It was the scroll, Fletch."

Fletcher fell silent as he digested the importance of what Sam had revealed, but Sam continued to talk.

"I haven't even told you the best part of all. Get a load of this."

Fletcher looked up blankly, still trying to digest what Sam had already told him.

"You're a Martian, Fletch."

"Yeah, sure, Sam," Fletcher laughed nervously. "And you're from Pluto, right?"

"Pluto! What are you, crazy?" Sam grinned. "I'm a Martian, too. Well, kind of. I'll explain it all later."

Fletcher slowly shook his head back and forth.

"Wherever you were, Sam, I think you were there *too* long."

"Look, Fletcher, the important thing is that both of the scrolls need to be kept safe," Sam continued. "Professor Hawthorne wants me to take *his* scroll back home and wait for him there. If Mandrake really does have the other one, then we're gonna have to figure out how to..."

"Wait a minute! You brought Hawthorne's scroll with you?!" cried Fletcher. "We've been carting it around with us this whole time and you never told me?"

"I'm sorry, Fletch. I didn't want anyone to..."

Thoroughly engrossed in his explanation, Sam had turned his head toward Fletcher while he continued to wave his flashlight at the crop circle. A high-pitched yelp and a look of absolute terror on Fletcher's face spun Sam's head back around. The thin beam of the flashlight had settled on the equally startled face of another figure, crouched in the bushes at the other side of the field.

"That's—that's..." Fletcher stammered. "Basil Mandrake!" He finally blurted out the name, in unison with Sam.

For a moment, Basil froze like an animal caught in the glare of a headlight. Then he stood up, lurched out of the bushes and headed straight toward them.

"He's coming!" Fletcher yelled, struggling to break free of the rhododendron branches that seemed to be suddenly holding him in their grip.

"Get up, Fletcher! We've gotta get out of here!"

Sam, also caught up in a wrestling match with the rhododendron, managed to pull himself free first. There was a loud ripping noise. He grabbed Fletcher by his jacket sleeve and started to run.

Holding tight to Fletcher's arm, Sam raced through farmers' fields—stumbling down gullies and sliding across streams filled with round, slippery pebbles—until it felt as if all of the air had been sucked out of his lungs.

"Stop looking back, Fletch!" he cried. "It'll slow you down!"

"Sam—I have—to stop. Can't run—anymore," Fletcher panted.

"Over there," Sam could only whisper. "That stone wall—we'll get behind it and rest for a while, okay?"

"But, what about..."

"He'll be just as tired as us by now, Fletch. We'll be able to see him coming and we need time to think, anyway."

Sam took his friend by the arm and dragged him the last few feet to the base of the wall. He searched along the edges of the rough stones with the tip of his sneaker and found a toehold. He hoisted himself onto the top, then reached for Fletcher's hand and pulled. Grunting with exhaustion, the boys rested for a moment on the top ledge of stone before heaving themselves over its edge and sliding down to the ground below. Bracing their backs against the wall of cold, hard rocks, Sam and Fletcher fought to catch their breaths.

"Do—do you think—we lost him, Sam?"

"Maybe—I—I don't know," answered Sam, gently patting his hands down each side of his fishing vest.

In his haste to escape from Basil, Sam had forgotten all about his little passengers. Now his face suddenly turned pale with fear. Sam leaned forward and began to grab frantically at his inside pockets. Jumping up, he quickly struggled out of the vest and turned it inside out. One of the two larger silk pockets, its zipper flapping open, had been gashed across its bottom seam. A sharp rhododendron twig clung to the strands of ripped material and tangled threads. Sam let out a plaintive cry.

"What is it?" whispered Fletcher. "It's not the scroll, is it?"

"Fletcher! I've lost them!"

"The notes?"

"No! Not the..."

"It's okay, Sam." Fletcher reached for the vest and opened the undamaged pocket.

"Look, they're still here—the scroll and the professor's notes. Relax." Fletcher zipped up the pocket again and gave it a little pat. "It's a good thing you didn't have them in that other one, though."

Sam felt sick. The most horrible thing he could possibly imagine had just happened, and there was nothing he could say about it. They could be anywhere now, anywhere between the crop circle field and the old stone wall. Sam's imagination ran wild as he thought of the scene that must have unfolded inside the tearing pocket. He saw each of them falling through the widening hole, clinging to a shred of silk or a sliver of rhododendron twig as the others tried to save them. Mr. Goodfellow would have held onto Beatrice until every ounce of his strength was gone. And Filbert and Edgar, a father and

187

son finally reunited after 120 years, would have each watched helplessly as the other slipped away again. It would have been heartbreaking. One by one they would have tumbled onto the hard ground of a farmer's field, or down a deep rock-strewn gully or into a cold, pebbly stream. Sam held his head in his hands as he thought of the magnitude of such a tragic loss: the lives of four Sage, three of them close to a thousand years old, and the fourth just a boy who had not even reached his 200th birthday. Even if they had survived the fall, they could have been crushed beneath Basil Mandrake's big black boots. And Sam, panting and grunting as he and Fletcher took flight, would never have heard their cries for help.

"Sam, you don't look so good. Maybe you'd better sit down again."

Sam nodded his head mechanically, sliding himself all the way down the stone wall until he was resting on the ground. He wished he could share his fears with Fletcher, but he knew that this was a tragedy he would have to face alone.

"I really think we should get out of here, Fletch," Sam said after a few minutes, slowly lifting himself up from the ground. "Basil may be tired or lost, but he'll get his second wind pretty soon."

Sam put the professor's notes in with the scroll for safe-keeping, making certain that the tube was well secured before they set off again. With no idea how far or in what direction they had traveled in their attempt to elude Basil, the pair decided to follow the line of the old stone wall. After a fifteen-minute walk they came upon a dirt road, its surface littered with potholes and oversized wheel treads. They waited in the shadows for a long time until they realized that it was far too early for any farm wagons to be making the rounds. They curled down together in the roadside ditch, covering their bodies with a few stray tree branches and making themselves as comfortable as possible. Fletcher wanted to know everything about the crop circle world, and Professor Hawthorne, and Mars and all the other weird things that Sam had seen. Unable to rest, his mind a turmoil of distressing thoughts and worries, Sam obliged—leaving out any mention, of course, of the Goodfellows or Beatrice Elderberry. Not speaking of them, however, did not remove them from his thoughts. Even as he told Fletcher about Elijah Hawthorne and the scrolls, the murderous mind of Hugo Trenchmount, the shady dealings of the Mandrake family and the strange testament from another world, his heart ached for his friends. He hoped that by some miracle they had found their way to safety.

At first light, a few hay wagons began ambling down the country road. After catching a ride back to Auntie Nellie's, Sam and Fletcher, bleary-eyed and exhausted, pulled on their pajamas and crawled into their beds. About ten minutes later, Auntie Nellie's perpetually cheery voice called them down for breakfast. They struggled back into their clothes and stumbled down to the kitchen. A few moments later they were joined by a yawning India. They were too tired to notice that her hair was a little more askew than normal and spiked with tiny sprigs of wheat.

14

THE GREATEST BLESSING
IS A TRUE FRIEND

The last few days at Auntie Nellie's were uneventful, and both Sam and Fletcher were happy enough to rest for a while after their all-nighter in the farmer's field and their race with Basil Mandrake.

Sam was torn between a sense of duty (to return home with the scroll and wait for Professor Hawthorne) and an overwhelming desire to find out what had befallen Beatrice and the Goodfellows. He would not allow himself to think that he might never find out. That was just too painful to consider. It was sad enough to see Jemima pacing back and forth on the bunk bed, or mewing fretfully in the garden, as if she had misplaced something of great value.

Bright and early on their last morning in Wiltshire, Auntie Nellie saw them off at the train station for their trip back to London. India managed to polish off another epic in the time it took to return to Paddington Station. Fletcher was beginning to wonder why she had even come. She could have stayed at home and read just as easily, he complained to Sam. She probably hadn't even realized she'd been in England all this time, he said, imagining instead (with the aid of her novels) that she was in Tuscany or Capri or on the French Riviera. Sam, however, had begun to suspect otherwise. He couldn't help but feel that there was a lot more to India than romantic novels and an overactive imagination.

Sam was right. India was never as completely engrossed in her reading as Fletcher believed. She was quite capable, in fact, of doing more than one thing at a time—and quite well, too. For the time being, she had decided to keep her own counsel and a watchful eye on her younger companions.

Sam's parents had thoroughly enjoyed their time in London. They had wined and dined as never before, taken in a new gallery opening, attended a sale of rare British watercolors at one of the larger auction houses and seen two West End musicals. The only unpleasant ripple in their visit, they complained, had occurred on their last day, when they went to the Science Conference to deliver Sanjid Jaffrey's research paper to an assembly of prominent academics. As soon as Sam's parents arrived at the hall they were descended upon by none other than Professor Avery Mandrake. He was friendly enough at the outset, but his unrelenting insistence on acquiring the Jaffrey paper for himself unnerved the Middletons enough to send them back to their hotel without making the delivery at all. This news of Mandrake and his reappearance outside the crop circle was enough to send shivers of terror and disbelief through both Sam and Fletcher. How had *he* managed to get out, anyway? And what had befallen Professor Hawthorne? Sam, knowing the whereabouts of neither Professor Hawthorne nor his Sage friends, took the weight of these new worries as courageously as he could.

When it came time to leave London, Sam fretted over the best way to transport the scroll. He transferred it back and forth between his fishing vest and his knapsack several times, wondering where it might be safer. He finally decided on the sack. Keeping it with him at all times seemed to make sense, until he arrived at the airline's walk-in security check. Sam passed through it without a peep, but he must have appeared nervous enough to warrant a second look. In an officious tone, the security officer asked him to open his knapsack. The scroll tube was removed and one of the stoppers pulled off. The officer peered into it for a second or two, then looked up at Sam.

"It's from the British Museum gift shop," Sam offered, then quickly added. "A reproduction of an ancient Babylonian manuscript. I'm going to hang it in my room."

The official grunted as he popped the stopper back onto the end of the tube. He poked for a second or two among the other items in Sam's knapsack, then quickly replaced the scroll and zipped up the bag.

Sam breathed a sigh of relief. Then the man leaned forward and whispered.

"Off you go, then. But if you'll take a bit of friendly advice, young man, it's about time you gave the stuffed animals away. You're getting a bit old for them, aren't you?"

Utterly confused, Sam smiled politely, then followed everyone else down the corridor toward the departure gate. What had he meant? Sam sat down on a seat next to Fletcher in the departure lounge, holding his knapsack tightly and pondering what the security man had said. It was slow to dawn, and when the realization finally came it was like a bolt out of the blue. After boarding the aircraft, Sam made a beeline for the toilet. He darted through the narrow bathroom door and quickly locked it behind him.

Sam's mother, her eyes fixed on the toilet's occupied sign, fretted.

"I told him not to order the steak and kidney pie for breakfast, Trev."

Sam laid his knapsack on the floor, sat down on the closed toilet seat and leaned forward. He took a firm hold of the zipper and pulled on it very, very slowly. Carefully moving the scroll to one side, Sam stared into a well of blackness. Three pairs of dark, twinkling eyes stared back. Goodfellow eyes!

"Mr. Goodfellow! Edgar! Filbert!" Sam cried, his voice trembling with relief. "What are you doing in there? Where have you been? I've been so worried about you!"

"Sorry to frighten you like that," said Mr. Goodfellow, as he climbed a little closer to the top of the knapsack. "I'm afraid there just wasn't time to do it any other way. We did try to locate you in the crop field, after we were all dislodged from the top of your pocket by the good professor's push. We were actually able to roll out quite easily. Beatrice sustained a slight sprain to her ankle, forcing us to slow down. We didn't anticipate any problems catching up to you eventually, but by the time we had followed your flashlight beam to the edge of the field, you had dashed off as if the very devil was after you."

"Basil Mandrake was there."

"He saw you then, at the crop circle?" asked Filbert, who had just joined his brother at the edge of the knapsack.

"He came after us. Me and Fletcher."

"Well, that certainly explains your haste, doesn't it?" Mr. Goodfellow rubbed his furry chin with his paw. "We must tell you something now, Sam. Try not to be too alarmed. It's the reason, in fact, that we have all decided to return home with you. Mandrake, it would appear, has somehow managed to exit the circle. He'll be after our scroll, of course, and you, too, I imagine, now that he's linked you to the circle phenomenon.

We have requested that the London mouse network be put on high alert. Apparently, they sighted Mandrake at—"

"The Science Conference!" interrupted Sam. "I know! My parents saw him there. They'd gone to deliver a paper that Fletcher's dad had written."

"Really? How extraordinary. A paper on what, my boy?"

"The chemical properties of..." Sam began excitedly.

"A previously undiscovered metallic substance, I'll bet!" panted Edgar, who'd had a little more trouble scrambling to the top of the bag than the others.

"The sliver of scroll that Professor Hawthorne gave to Fletcher's father? Of course!" Mr. Goodfellow proclaimed. "Not knowing what had befallen Professor Hawthorne and in possession of such a significant substance, Jaffrey would have been in professional turmoil. He must have agonized about what to do; not only in the best interests of his friend and associate, but for the rest of the world. And if he was concerned about Mandrake, he probably felt the most prudent thing to do was to reveal what he knew to the scientific community at large. Take some of the wind out of Mandrake's sails, as it were. Until, that is, he began to suspect just how dangerous Mandrake might be."

Edgar nodded his head.

"This sliver, Sam. Do you know where it is now?" asked Filbert.

"With Fletcher's dad, I guess. I'm not sure, really. My mum and dad said Mandrake was acting creepier than usual at the conference. He was only interested in getting his hands on the paper. He was so pushy about it that my dad called the Jaffrey place from our hotel last night. Fletcher's dad asked him to bring the paper back home right away."

"Well, this certainly complicates things, doesn't it, my

boy?" Mr. Goodfellow observed. "Mandrake with one scroll, us with the other and a stray sliver floating around somewhere else."

Deep in thought, Mr. Goodfellow clasped his two paws in front of him and absently tapped his claws together. Another fur-clad head suddenly popped up beside his.

"I thought I heard your voice just now, Sam." It was Beatrice, straining to keep her head up. "It's wonderful to see you safe again, dear."

"Good heavens! We have been rather remiss, haven't we?" Mr. Goodfellow rushed to apologize, taking Beatrice gently under the arms and hoisting her into a more comfortable position at the edge of the canvas sack.

"I'm afraid this silly ankle of mine has caused us no end of trouble," Beatrice fretted. "I can't help but feel that I have been a burden to everyone at the most inconvenient of times."

"Nonsense, my dear," Mr. Goodfellow interjected. "It gave us all a much-needed opportunity to rest and regroup. Filbert and Edgar were able to return home and enjoy a long-awaited reunion with Hazel, and we were still able to find Sam in short order and get on with our mission."

Beatrice sighed. "When we couldn't find you that night in the field, Sam, Jolly insisted on taking me home. We had tried to get him out of your pocket before we exited the crop circle, but everything happened so quickly. Naturally, Jolly was heartsick over leaving Professor Hawthorne alone. And then this ridiculous ankle business! Our one consoling thought was that the scroll was safe with you, Sam. Jolly, Filbert and Edgar were even planning to re-enter the circle to help the professor. That was until we learned that Mandrake had escaped, and that you and the scroll were in jeopardy."

"What's happened to Professor Hawthorne?" asked Sam.

"I'm afraid we're not entirely sure," replied Mr. Goodfellow. "But the answer to that will have to wait. The security of the scroll must take precedence. When we decided to intercept you on your way home, we journeyed to London and have been guests of the Heathrow airport mice ever since. There's something else we really should tell you—"

His words were suddenly interrupted by a knock on the bathroom door.

"Excuse me," said a flight attendant, from the other side. "You'll have to take your seat now. We're preparing for takeoff."

"I'll see you later, okay?" Sam whispered.

"Yes, of course, my boy. I suppose it can wait..."

The Sage slid down into the darkness of Sam's knapsack. Before they had completely disappeared from view, Sam called one last time.

"Can I get you guys anything—some snacks or something to drink?" he asked.

All four turned pale and shook their heads in unison, Edgar even more enthusiastically than the others.

"I believe I speak for all of us, Sam," answered Filbert, "when I say thank you, but no. We have had enough airline food for the time being. The Heathrow mice don't seem to possess the same sophisticated palates as the rest of their kin."

A series of short little raps sounded at the bathroom door. Sam closed the knapsack, jumped to his feet and slid open the lock. He squeezed himself and his sack through the narrow door, under the icy glare of the irritated flight attendant.

As he walked down the aisle, Sam's mother leaned out and touched his arm.

"Tummy alright, dear?" she whispered.

"Yes, Mum." He rolled his eyes at Fletcher. "Boy! A person can't even go to the bathroom these days without a big deal!"

When he flopped down into his seat, a loud and rather rude noise erupted, followed by a stifled giggle from the next seat. Lifting himself up on one arm, Sam pulled an object out from underneath him and turned to his companion.

"A whoopee cushion, Fletch? Really hilarious," he said dryly.

"Aaww, come on, Sam!" said Fletcher, between peals of laughter. "It's just a joke!" He could sense, however, that Sam did not appreciate this brand of humor. "Okay, okay. I'm sorry. Look, why don't we shake on it?"

Sam looked at his friend suspiciously for a moment, then reluctantly agreed. As Fletcher took Sam's hand, a hidden buzzer sent an electrical charge tingling across Sam's palm.

"Fletcher!" Startled, Sam pulled his hand away. "What's with you?"

"I got them in the airport gift shop, while you were look-ing at the comics. Aren't they neat?"

"Yeah, they're really great," Sam grunted sarcastically. "And my stomach's *okay*, Mum," he said, without even look-ing up.

Peggy Middleton, who had been leaning over the back of her seat, clutching a travel-sized bottle of Pepto-Bismol and a white plastic spoon in her hand, slowly slunk back down.

Annoying as it was, Sam didn't ponder his friend's odd behavior for very long. The knapsack that he had laid care-fully at his feet (next to Fletcher's gift-shop bag) was too much of a distraction. His small companions had managed to elude detection on their first pass through security, but there was no guarantee that they'd be able to pull it off again. Mr. Goodfellow had wanted to tell him something else, too. What was it? Sam drummed his fingers impatiently on the arm-rests until the "fasten seatbelt" light had finally clicked off.

Fletcher, rattling through the thick paper bag at his feet, pulled something out and offered it to Sam.

"Piece of gum?"

"No, *thanks*, Fletch." Sam grimaced as he considered the possibility of having his fingers caught in a miniature mousetrap or his tongue set ablaze with Tabasco coating.

Quietly picking up his knapsack, Sam slipped out of his seat and into the aisle.

"Suit yourself," Fletcher called after him, as he popped the gum into his own mouth. Sam hurried back to the bathroom. He was unprepared for the scene that greeted him when he unzipped his knapsack and peered in. It was dark inside, but with several miniature flashlight beams darting about, Sam had no trouble counting the heads that sat together chatting. There was quite a party going on—and a few more heads than there should have been. Edgar, struggling to perfect the trunk on his elephant shadow puppet, looked up as Sam looked down.

"There's *seven* of you!" cried Sam.

"Seven and a worm, actually," offered Edgar.

"What?"

Mr. Goodfellow stood up.

"I wanted to tell you this before, my boy. Unbeknownst to us, the rest of our family took it upon themselves to follow us to the airport. They managed to stow themselves away in another compartment of your bag."

"You're kidding! Who else is in there?" Sam cried.

"Let's see now," he said, looking around the group. "There's Hazel, of course. It *had* been 120 years since she'd seen her husband, after all, and she's determined not to let Filbert *or* Edgar slip away again. Isn't that right, my dear?"

A lady with auburn hair, swirled up in a topknot, smiled

199

and nodded. Sam noticed Edgar watching happily as his mother nestled her head against his father's shoulder.

The boy had daydreamed all of his life about reuniting his family and, now, here they were.

Mr. Goodfellow continued with his introductions. He turned to the figure sitting next to Edgar. Strands of long dark hair, adorned with silver barrettes and colored bows, trailed out from under a beautifully groomed mouse cap.

"As you may know, Sam, Beatrice contacted young Charlotte in America when Edgar first returned to us. It was while Charlotte was on her way to meet with him again that she received news of our disappearance. She continued on her journey to Beatrice's to provide whatever assistance and comfort she could."

Next, Mr. Goodfellow threw his furry arm around a sturdy little boy.

"And this young lad here is Charlotte's brother, Porter—a mere infant, you may recall, during our summer adventures in northern California sixty-odd years ago. With their parents on another lengthy assignment in South America and their grandparents busy running the Sparrow Ranch, spa and vineyard, Charlotte was to deliver Porter into Beatrice's care for the summer holidays." Mr. Goodfellow took a deep breath and looked around once more. "I think that covers everyone."

Porter suddenly tugged at Mr. Goodfellow's suit. When Jolly bent down, the boy whispered something into his ear.

"Of course. I beg your pardon, Porter." Mr. Goodfellow looked up. "There is another of us, apparently. A worm, is it Porter? Yes...well...he seems to be unaccounted for at the moment. Probably wandered off for a bit of peace and quiet. Worms are like that sometimes. We'll give him a call, Porter, alright? What's his name?"

"It's Duncan," Porter whispered shyly.

"Really? Filbert and I have an Uncle Duncan, you know. Funny old soul actually. I wonder what he would think if he knew you had a worm of the same name."

"It means 'brown warrior,'" said Porter, with a little more confidence, "in Celtic."

"Really? Well then, I am sure our Duncan would be most honored to share such a distinguished moniker."

Sam sat in silence, mesmerized by this bizarre conversation. He was just beginning to digest all of the unusual information when the flight attendant resumed her tapping on the door.

"Excuse me. Are you alright in there?"

"Yeah, fine," Sam replied. "I was just feeling kinda sick. I'll be right out!"

Sam had no idea how long he had been in the bathroom. Before he could zip up the knapsack, Mr. Goodfellow popped his head over the top edge and whispered to him.

"I'm sorry about all of this, my boy. It's become a bit of a circus, hasn't it? It's not my usual method of operation, as you well know, but they are *so* determined to help. I can assure you that I will do everything I can to keep them all in line."

Mr. Goodfellow gave Sam a wink before he disappeared into the sack. Sam zipped the knapsack closed, heaved it over his shoulder and scrambled to his feet. He unlocked the door and squeezed through. A long line of very uncomfortable-looking people had gathered on the other side. Sam scuttled past, excusing himself several times. He averted his eyes from the glare of the flight attendant and rushed down the aisle. To his relief, both of his parents had fallen asleep. He tiptoed past and took his seat, laying the knapsack very gently on the carpeted floor. He patted it several times over the next few minutes, just to make sure it was still there. In a matter of minutes, his level of responsibility had climbed from guarding one priceless relic, a set of invaluable research notes and four Sage to guarding one priceless relic, a set of invaluable research notes, seven Sage and a missing worm.

India, as usual, was glued to the pages of a romance novel that she had picked up in the airport gift shop, along with the only bag of gingerbread biscuits she could find. She absently munched away as she read, not in the least bit embarrassed that her snacks were in the shapes of bunnies and kittens. In the cloth book bag at her feet, peeping out from the middle of her other reading selections, was the abandoned anthology of crossword puzzles from Auntie Nellie's bookshelf.

Fletcher had dozed off, too, an empty drink box of Tang on his pull-down tray. He was clutching a small paperback in his hands. Sam twisted his head to read its title, expecting to see something by Carl Sagan, or the latest work on the meaning of the universe by Stephen Hawking. *One Thousand REALLY Funny Jokes*, Sam read on the front cover. Definitely a change from Fletcher's usual reading material, he thought. Maybe it would be good for him to unwind with something silly. Feeling tired himself, Sam laid his head against the back of his seat and closed his eyes, falling into a gentle slumber as the airplane's engines droned in the background.

15

A Man Is Known by the Company He Keeps

S am awoke to the sound of distant voices and the rattling of paper. He focused his eyes on his wristwatch to
see how many hours he'd been sleeping, but only ten
minutes had passed. Something brushed against his leg. When
he leaned over to take a look, he discovered that a small section
of his knapsack's zipper had been pulled open, and voices were
coming from the direction of Fletcher's now fluttering paper
bag. With another rustle, Fletcher's bag suddenly tilted toward
the floor. The voices grew louder, as if they were engaged in an
argument of some sort. If the noise continued for much longer,
Sam feared, it would attract the attention of everyone on the
plane. Hoping that it was just another one of Fletcher's noisy
gag gifts, Sam opened the top of the bag and looked inside.

"Mr. Goodfellow!" he whispered. "Why aren't you in my
knapsack? And who's that?"

"We're having a spot of trouble here, my boy. I know I
promised you that I would keep everything quiet and under
wraps, but..."

"I'll thank you kindly not to refer to me as a spot of
trouble, Jolly," another figure interrupted. "Really, it's not

professional at all!" He lifted his head just then, smiled and offered his paw. "You must be the famous Sam," he shouted up.

"Shh!" whispered Sam. "You have to keep it down! Somebody will hear you!"

"You're quite right, of course." Mr. Goodfellow looked annoyed as he addressed his companion. "The boy has more sense than the two of us put together. Come on, Redwood. We'll have to take this discussion outside...er...rather, inside, if you will. I suggest the knapsack next door."

Sam watched as Mr. Goodfellow climbed to the top of Fletcher's bag. He grasped one of the bag's handles with both paws. Like an experienced gymnast, he spun himself through the middle of the handle, over its top and back through three times, gaining enough momentum to propel himself through the air. After a midair somersault, he made a perfect landing—arms outstretched and knees bent—right on top of Sam's knapsack. He turned around and called over to the bag, where the other figure was having a little more difficulty negotiating the climb.

"Require some assistance, Redwood?"

"Always the competitor, aren't we, Jolly? If I wasn't loaded down with this stuff, I'd be able to show you a gold-medal performance you wouldn't soon forget."

Sam moved his hand forward to offer assistance, but it was brushed aside.

"No need, young fella. I'll be okay, thanks," he grunted.

Struggling to the top of Fletcher's bag, Mr. Goodfellow's companion grabbed a rope handle and cautiously dangled one leg over the edge. Pointing a toe claw as far as he could toward the knapsack, he tried in vain to establish a foothold. The brown flight bag that was strung across one of his shoulders suddenly swung forward, pulling him further over the edge of the bag and down toward the floor. The thick paper of the bag slowly began to tear along one side. With the reflexes of a special-forces commando, Mr. Goodfellow dropped on all fours, then crawled on his stomach to the edge of the knapsack. He stretched out one arm and grabbed the strap of the dangling flight bag. With a mighty tug, Mr.Goodfellow pulled the bag onto Sam's knapsack, leaning out with his other arm to capture the outstretched leg. It was not an elegant operation, but it was successful. His companion was now able to swing the rest of his body onto the knapsack and to safety.

"Show-off," he declared between labored breaths, as he lay with his furry arms and legs outstretched.

"Not at all, Redwood," said Mr. Goodfellow. "It's simply a matter of keeping in tip-top shape. Always be prepared for any eventuality."

"Well, it was a lot easier to get into that bag than out, I can tell you that."

"My point precisely," Mr. Goodfellow continued. "If you had planned ahead a little better, you would have realized how difficult it was going to be to get that ridiculous flight bag out of there. Your choice of transport was..."

"The only one available to me at the time, Jolly! The kid was in the gift shop and his flight had been called twice already! I was about to lose him!"

They had started to raise their voices again.

"Shh!" Sam whispered frantically.

"It's no use, my boy," Mr. Goodfellow called back. "We've got to sort this mess out. Please take us back to the toilet facilities, if you will."

"What? I can't go back again! I was just there ten minutes..."

Suddenly feeling as if he was being watched, Sam stopped

talking and looked up. The man sitting across the aisle was giving him a very funny look. Sam smiled nervously.

"Okay, okay! I'll go!" he whispered toward his feet.

Shoving a stray mouse tail through the opening, Sam picked up his knapsack. He rose from his seat and started back along the aisle, trying his best to be inconspicuous.

He slipped back into the bathroom unnoticed and re-established his position on the toilet seat lid. By the time he reached down to open his knapsack, Mr. Goodfellow had jimmied the zipper from the inside and was squeezing himself through the opening. Sam leaned forward and gave the zipper a few extra tugs.

"Thank you, my boy! Most considerate," said Mr. Goodfellow, popping out of the top. He turned and called behind, rather brusquely. "Are you there, Redwood?"

"Right behind you, chief!"

By the time his companion had struggled to the top, his brown flight bag still slung across his shoulder, Mr. Goodfellow was shimmying down the outside of the knapsack to the floor.

"I've asked everyone else to join us, Redwood," he called up. "They'll be here presently to discuss the matter."

"You're just making a big deal about things, as usual, Jolly. We're not in the debating club anymore, you know. That *was* over 600 years ago, remember? This *matter*, as you call it, has already been decided by the Governing Council. There's nothing to talk about." He looked up at Sam. "And speaking of the Governing Council, this young buck has been quite the topic of conversation there for the last few months. A page in the history books, for sure!"

He extended his paw toward Sam again. "We never did have the chance to get acquainted, did we? The name's Redwood, Winchester Redwood of..."

"The California Redwoods," Mr. Goodfellow finished. There was a pause. "Well, you were going to say that, weren't you, Redwood?"

"I always say that."

"I know."

There was a pause as the two of them stared at each other. The light caught the tip of Redwood's ears as he moved a little closer to Sam. He pulled his mouse mask off and smiled. He was tall by Sage standards, at least an inch taller than Mr. Goodfellow. A shock of wavy, graying hair had been swept casually to one side of his forehead, just below his mouse cap. His features were ruggedly handsome: a chiseled chin, deep green eyes and a tan that could have been attained only on a southern Californian beach.

"Great state, California! There are tall trees, mighty rivers and ocean surf, vast forests as far as your eye can see..."

"Not to mention your enormous ego," Mr. Goodfellow interjected.

Redwood turned around and started to chuckle.

"You always were a big kidder, weren't you, Jolly?" He leaned over and slapped the back of Mr. Goodfellow's suit with a big open paw.

"If you *really* search your memory bank, Redwood," said Mr. Goodfellow, "you may recall that it was *you* who was the 'big kidder.'"

For a second or two, Winchester Redwood was at a loss for words. "Ahhh, I get it now!" he suddenly blurted out. "That's what this is all about! You're still holding a grudge after all these years. Come on now! It was just a joke!"

"And entirely at my expense, Redwood! You may have thought it was just a silly prank, but I was the laughing stock of the whole school that semester. Do you remember all of this, Filbert?" Mr. Goodfellow called over to the knapsack, from which his brother had just emerged. "I could have ignored the clothes-meddling incidents, Redwood, and even, perhaps, the love-letter scandal. But that whoopee cushion episode at the graduation ceremony—in front of every member of the Governing Council—was...well, unforgivable!" Sam raised his eyebrows. Whoopee cushion? This was getting *very* interesting.

Winchester Redwood put a furry arm around Mr. Goodfellow's shoulders and gave him a big shake.

"Ahhh, come on, Jolly. I said I was sorry, didn't I? How about a truce?"

Mr. Goodfellow wriggled out from under Winchester Redwood's firm grip and gave him a glare.

"As unpleasant as the thought may be, I must agree with you in this case. In the interests of our respective missions, I think it would be most prudent to put our personal feelings aside."

"That's my buddy!" Redwood reached over to give him another shake, but Mr. Goodfellow managed to jump out of the way. Redwood glanced across the floor. "Is that really you, Filbert? Don't recall the beard."

"Indeed it is, Redwood. Nice to see you again."

"I'll say! Last I heard, everyone was saying you were Fen food!"

"Only a rumor. I've been trapped elsewhere for quite some time, though. I have Jolly and my son Edgar here to thank for my rescue."

"Edgar Goodfellow, of course!" As Edgar slid down from the bag, Redwood rushed forward to greet him with an outstretched paw. "I want to shake the hand of the young buck who stood up to Shrike Fen. You're a bit of a legend, you know."

"I am?" asked Edgar in astonishment.

"Yep. You *and* Sam. You showed real courage that night."

Edgar started to blush.

Mr. Goodfellow noticed his nephew's embarrassment and decided to take control of the conversation. His attempts were in vain.

"Redwood, it's time we sat down and sorted out this problem—"

"You know, Jolly," said Redwood, "it's been really terrific seeing you again, remembering the good old days and all that. In fact, speaking of those occasions when I tampered with your togs back in school, I've got to ask you: What's with the suit? New fashion statement or something?"

Mr. Goodfellow looked down at himself. He had forgotten all about the odd condition of his attire. There was a long section of his argyle socks showing between his mouse feet and the rest of his suit now, making him appear as if he were wearing baggy, old-fashioned golf trousers. And furry ones, at that. Although Beatrice had done the best she could under the circumstances, he really wished that Redwood hadn't been there to revel in his misfortune.

"The suit was the victim of a minor accident, that's all. Had to do a bit of mending on the run. Now let's get back to..."

"Well, I gotta say it. I'm impressed. It may be unconventional, but the workmanship is first rate, Jolly. Didn't know you were so talented."

"Beatrice is really good at that sort of thing, isn't she Uncle Jolly?" piped Edgar.

"Beatrice?" asked Redwood with sudden interest. "Hey, it *really* must be our day for walking down memory lane. We knew a Beatrice back in school, didn't we, Jolly? I think we both had a bit of a thing for her, too. She was quite a dish, as I remember. I thought I might have had a chance, you know, but she always had her nose stuck in a book. Yep," he sighed "Beatrice Elderberry."

"She's here with us!" Edgar cried.

"No kidding!" said Redwood with a huge grin on his face. He turned to Mr. Goodfellow. "Trying to hide her from me, are you, chief?" He started walking toward Sam's knapsack. "Well, I'd love to see her again."

Edgar ran ahead of him.

"I'll go and get her for you, Mr. Redwood."

Mr. Goodfellow grimaced. "Isn't she *very* busy with something right now, Edgar? Perhaps you shouldn't disturb her."

"I don't think she'd mind that much, Uncle Jolly," said Edgar innocently. "She and my mum and Charlotte were just helping Porter look for Duncan, remember?"

"Yes, Edgar," Mr. Goodfellow sighed. "I remember."

"So that's why you suddenly dropped into my paper bag— when I was just minding my own business and getting on with my mission," Redwood complained. "Who in the world is this Duncan you were searching for, anyway? A lost kid?"

"A worm," Mr. Goodfellow mumbled.

"A what?"

"A *worm*, Redwood! Young Porter's beloved pet, if you must know."

Winchester Redwood guffawed loudly and slapped one of his knees. A minute or so later, Edgar popped out of the top of the knapsack with another figure close behind.

"Beatrice Elderberry! I can't believe it!" cried Redwood, looking up.

Leaning over the edge of Sam's sack, Beatrice lifted her mouse mask from her face and placed it on top of her head. Her eyes widened.

"Winnie? Winnie Redwood? Is that really you?"

"It sure is, doll!"

As Beatrice started down the outside of the sack, and before Mr. Goodfellow had a chance to react, Redwood rushed forward to help, enveloping her tiny mouse paw in his much bigger one. She jumped down to the ground with a short, ladylike hop.

"Isn't this something?" Redwood remarked. "To finally run into you on an airplane. Of all the crazy things! What are the odds, Bea?"

"It's remarkable, Winnie! It really is!" Beatrice exclaimed. "Isn't it, Jolly? Filbert? All of us together again, just like old times!"

Filbert smiled at her and nodded. Mr. Goodfellow stood to one side, looking like thunder.

"Didn't I hear you'd retired early, Bea?" Redwood asked. "A spread on the ocean or something?"

"Well, I *had* actually, Winnie. And it's really just a little cottage. I've come out of retirement for a while to help Jolly. I do like to keep my hand in from time to time."

Mr. Goodfellow cringed. Redwood grinned at him.

"Need a hand, do you, chief? You know, Bea," said Redwood blissfully as he turned back to her again, "I can't tell you how great it feels to be called Winnie again."

"Redwood!" Mr. Goodfellow interrupted. "We have to talk!"

Once again, Winchester Redwood thwarted Mr. Goodfellow's attempt to discuss his concerns.

"Oh, great! What's this stuff I've got on my suit?" Redwood pulled his paw away from his side. As he did, a long strand of sticky white goo followed. "Wait a minute. It's all over my flight bag here!"

He lifted his paw and took a sniff. "Chewing gum," he remarked glumly. "Peppermint, if I'm not mistaken, and *used*." He shuddered. "Can you believe it? There's a perfectly good trash bag on the back of everyone's seat."

The harder Redwood tried to remove the strands of gum from his fur, the more entangled he became. "Jeepers!" he declared, looking down. "I feel like a spider's lunch!" he cried. "I better get out of this thing."

Redwood unclipped the sides of his flight bag, unfolded it flat on the ground, then pulled at the zipper that ran around its edge.

"Let me see. I have a real nice palomino-colored suit in here somewhere," he said, as he started sorting through his clothes.

"I say!" Mr. Goodfellow cried, leaning over his shoulder. "That looks just like my best houndstooth jacket there!" He bent down to get a closer look. "That *is* my best houndstooth jacket! I'd recognize that chutney stain on the lapel anywhere! It was in my trunk. What are you doing with it, Redwood? Hand it over!"

"Hey, now, wait just a minute, chief," Redwood said calmly. "Cool your jets. Apart from the fact that the sleeves are up to my elbows, how was I supposed to know it was *your* jacket? The whole thing was going to have to be altered, but I took a liking to it, anyway. And I traded fair and square for it, too. Four Cheerios and a sugared almond, if memory serves. Highly prized commodities, they tell me, for those who appreciate them."

Edgar, who had been silently watching the proceedings, suddenly piped up.

"The almond, Mr. Redwood? Was it the kind with a smooth candy shell?" he asked, with a wistful look in his eye.

"No, it was the kind that they roast in that clear sugary stuff..."

"Redwood!" interrupted Mr. Goodfellow. "*Where* did you get the jacket?"

"Relax! I'm trying to tell you. It was while I was visiting my second cousin, Clayton. He has a hobby farm in Surrey that he works when he's not on assignment. Last week, while I was staying with him, he hired a family of migrant moles to do some digging. They had a bunch of things with them for barter. Told me they had found them on their travels. Somebody's old throwaways, I figured. One of them was the jacket here."

"Moles!" Mr. Goodfellow cried. "Not moles! Oh, why couldn't it have been mice? Moles are such unpredictable creatures. I can't begin to imagine what has befallen my other possessions," he fretted. "My beloved trunk! It's been vandalized! A lifetime of memories gone forever! Probably all bartered away for more breakfast cereal and a few candy-coated nuts!" He put his head in his hands.

Beatrice, a look of sympathy on her face, glided over and touched his shoulder.

"I'm so sorry, Jolly. Perhaps there is something we can do. Make some inquiries..."

"Thank you, my dear," he sighed sadly, "but I hardly think it will help now. The contents of my trunk have been scattered all over the English countryside, it would appear. And here we are, hurtling 500 miles per hour in the opposite direction."

"It's rotten luck, old man," said Filbert, "but maybe Beatrice has the right idea. If we can get the mouse network working on this..."

"Yeah," interrupted Redwood, "and I'll get in touch with Clayton, too, as soon as we land. See if he can track the moles and the rest of your things down. In the meantime, you can have your jacket back, if you want, chief."

Mr. Goodfellow glanced over at his best houndstooth jacket—the one that he had worn to countless cocktail parties, every family gathering since 1850 and, of course, all of his anxiety-ridden visits to Great-Uncle Cyrus's—and sighed again. After being pulled onto Redwood's massive frame a couple of times, there was little hope for it. It had been twisted completely out of shape.

"No, that's okay. You keep it, Redwood."

"Really? Hey, thanks pal!"

"Mr. Redwood, sir?" Edgar called over to him. "You wouldn't happen to have any more of that breakfast cereal on you, by any chance? It's really delicious sliced in half with a little butter and cream cheese."

"Maybe, Edgar." Redwood knelt over his flight bag and started to search. "Hey! Whaddya know. Looks like I got a couple of them left. Can't help you with the other stuff though, kid."

Edgar looked up hopefully at Sam, who was already vigorously shaking his head. If he were caught rummaging through the airplane's galley for butter and cream cheese now, he thought, that flight attendant would have him locked up.

16

SOMETHING IS
LEARNED EVERY TIME A
BOOK IS OPENED

A commotion suddenly emanated from the inside of Sam's knapsack. Charlotte popped her head out.

"We've found the worm," she announced with breathless relief.

"Thank goodness," proclaimed Mr. Goodfellow. "Porter?" he called up to the top of the bag. "Where are you, my boy?"

Hazel appeared beside Charlotte. Then came Porter, smiling from ear to ear. Duncan, brownish pink and plump, was draped around his neck.

"Please try and keep him tethered, if possible, Porter," Mr. Goodfellow cautioned. "We can't have him wandering all over the aircraft. I dread to think what fate might befall him if he were discovered exploring someone's dinner tray."

Porter nodded solemnly. Duncan, languishing happily on Porter's shoulders, seemed oblivious to the trouble he had caused.

"Good hunting, Charlotte!" Edgar called to her. "Where did you finally find him, anyway?"

"Crawling through a bag of those gummy candies," she shouted back. "The worm ones, naturally. Must have been looking for some of his own kind, I expect."

"I could have— Aahh! Yuck!" Sam sputtered, covering his mouth with his hand.

"Well, let's be thankful it didn't come to that, Sam," said Mr. Goodfellow. "Young Porter, I suspect, would have been inconsolable. Losing a pet that way is never easy. Anyway, it's all's well that ends well, isn't it? Now that we're all here, I insist that we address the issue at hand."

"There's no issue, Jolly," Redwood declared firmly. "I've already told you. It's settled. I am to be the boy's Sage."

"What boy?" asked Sam. "Whose Sage?"

"I don't know what you're talking about, Redwood," Mr. Goodfellow said impatiently. "The last time I spoke to the Governing Council, they assured me that the proper plans had been in place for some time. I understood that the assignment papers had been filed and one of the best Sage available was being briefed."

"Well, there have been some changes," said Redwood.

"But what of Cornelius?" asked Mr. Goodfellow, puzzled.

"Indisposed. I think that's what they're calling it, anyway. I'm surprised you haven't heard, Jolly. It's been the big talk lately."

"I've been out of touch for the last little while," explained Mr. Goodfellow, a look of concern on his face. "What on earth could have happened? Cornelius Mango's record is impeccable. He's guided some remarkable people in what has been, throughout, a most illustrious career. There was Étienne Montgolfier, the French balloonist, at least one of the Mercury astronauts, if memory serves, and, of course, a Wright brother. I think it was Orville. I, myself, was particularly fortunate to obtain his advice while I was working on my Earhart and Lindbergh assignments. He's one of the most capable and experienced Sage around, Redwood!"

"*Was*, Jolly. They've forced him into retirement."

"Retirement! That impossible! He can't be more than seventy-five years older than the two of us! How could this happen?"

"Well...it all started with the flying-squirrel accident on Veteran's Day," Redwood began, in the hushed tones of someone who really likes telling a tale. "A whole bunch of us had gathered out on the flats that morning," he said, sweeping his furry arm out in front of him in a huge arc. "You could see for miles around. The desert air was clear and still. There wasn't a single cloud above us. And the sky was as deep and as blue as... as...Beatrice's lovely eyes." He looked over at her and winked.

"They're *brown*, Redwood," said Mr. Goodfellow, rolling his own eyes.

"Oh, well, anyway, you know what Cornelius is like—into those daredevil hobbies of his and always up for something new. It was crazy, I know, but he talked one of the squirrels into taking him up for a ride. It seemed to be going well at first. Everybody was whoopin' and hollerin' and having a great time. But on their final pass over the crowd, as the squirrels swooped low to the ground, one of Mango's claws snagged on a tumbleweed. He was thrown from his harness and landed about twenty feet away, right in a big clump of cacti."

Beatrice covered her eyes. "Oh, how terrifying!" she exclaimed.

"He seemed to survive the fall okay, even though he did land pretty hard on his head," Redwood continued. "I hear they were more concerned about the forty or so cactus needles stuck in him, but Cornelius *seemed* fine."

"Lucky to be alive, I'd say, after that kind of experience," observed Filbert.

"No kidding! Anyway, he went about his regular business after that, preparing for his next mission—this very one, in fact. No one suspected that anything was 'off,' until he turned up at his farewell with...well...his jockeys on the outside of his suit."

"His what, Redwood?" asked Mr. Goodfellow.

"You know—his skivvies. His boxers." Redwood threw his paws up in frustration. "His *underwear!*"

"Ohhhhh," said all the others in lengthy unison.

"How dreadful for him," said Beatrice.

"Yep, I was there," said Redwood. "Saw the whole thing. They had little zoo animals all over them, too. Poor guy had no idea."

"My word," said Mr. Goodfellow quietly, obviously shaken by this news of a fallen hero. "What happened then?"

"Well, it kind of sent everyone into a panic. Mango was all set to go on his mission, see. Since he didn't have any close relatives to pass The Sacred Seal to, the Governing Council started looking for another candidate. As you know, I've done a fair bit of work in the field of..."

"Ahhh," said Mr. Goodfellow, nodding his head knowingly. "They were desperate and you were the last-minute replacement, right, Redwood?"

"I think I resent that, Jolly," Redwood exclaimed. "I'm hardly inexperienced. I was probably their best choice, well... after Mango, anyway. Have you forgotten that I've been to the moon? With Neil Armstrong, no less?"

"Wow," said Sam. "Really?"

"I certainly haven't forgotten, Redwood," continued Mr. Goodfellow. "As I recall you were a last-minute stand-in on that job, too. Mango was out with the bends from that Cousteau mission. It was sloppy work, Redwood! You almost ruined the whole thing!"

"I *know* I resent *that*, Jolly."

"As is usually the case with you, Redwood, you were unprepared. Or too busy taking in the sights."

"Well, it *was* the moon, pal."

"You're preposterous!"

"Now, now, boys." Filbert finally intervened. "No point quarreling…"

"Don't you remember, Filbert?" Mr. Goodfellow continued. "He fluffed his lines. During the career opportunity of a lifetime! Those first words should have been 'One small step for *a* man, one giant leap for mankind' not 'One small step for man…' It changes the whole meaning!"

"I've explained that a million times!" Redwood lamented, throwing his paws in the air. "The acoustics were terrible. We were on the moon, and I was crushed in the back of a sweaty helmet. He couldn't hear me properly. It's not my fault that an inspirational word or two was lost in space."

"Well I, for one, am not about to sit around and risk it happening again," Mr. Goodfellow spoke firmly. "I'm sorry to be so blunt, Redwood, or be the cause of your certain embarrassment in front of the Governing Council, but I can't let you do it. I know this boy. He needs a special kind of encouragement. If he's going to go to Mars one day, then he must have the very best guidance. That is why I intend to contact the Governing Council as soon as possible and offer myself as Sage."

"Mars?" Sam cried. "Wow! It's Fletcher you're talking about, isn't it? Fletcher really *is* going to Mars!"

"If it is his destiny to do so, Sam, then indeed he will. But

219

not, if I have anything to say about it, with Winchester Redwood as his Sage."

"Hey! Thanks a *lot*, pal! There's nothing like a little appreciation," Redwood huffed. "I'm not sure you can do anything about it now, anyway, Jolly. The Sacred Seal..."

"Will just have to be transferred once again, Redwood," said Mr. Goodfellow, with conviction.

"But that's never happened..."

"If you took the time to look around, Redwood, you'd soon discover that there are a lot of things that have never happened before. There is a greater plan at work here than we can comprehend just yet. I've been saying this for some time now. It's a convergence of some sort, Redwood. Sam has been drawn into it and I'm beginning to believe that the same fate awaits young Fletcher as well. The key to it all is in the scrolls!"

"Scrolls?" Redwood raised his eyebrows. "As in the Hawthorne scroll?"

"That and...well, it really is time we filled you in. We owe you that much, at least."

"Allow me the honors, everyone," Filbert announced, arching his back and stretching his arms above his head. "Come on, Redwood, I've got a *really* interesting story to tell you, and it all starts, you'll be intrigued to hear, on Mars..."

There was sudden knocking on the bathroom door.

"Sam? Sam, are you in there? It's me, Fletcher. Your mum sent me to look for you. She's freaking out that you're really sick or something. Are you okay?"

"I'm fine, Fletch. I'll be right there!"

There was little time for pleasantries. Sam picked up as many of The Sage as he could and gently unloaded them at the top of the knapsack. They quickly descended, one by one, into the interior.

"Hold on!" Sam whispered, as he fell on his knees to apprehend a wiggling Duncan, already halfway under the door and inching his way to freedom. Sam draped him around Porter's neck just before everyone disappeared from view. Only Mr. Goodfellow remained. Sam lifted him up and deposited him beside the sack's open zipper.

"I think it might be best if we stayed put until our arrival," Mr. Goodfellow advised. "Take care until then, my boy." He hesitated as he looked down into Sam's knapsack and made an unpleasant face.

"I fear it's going to be far too crowded in there for my liking, Sam. I can't imagine what the Governing Council could have been thinking, giving an oaf like Winchester Redwood an important assignment again."

Sam looked toward the closed door. "Is it true about Fletcher? And Mars?"

Mr. Goodfellow nodded his head. "I feel it must be, Sam. He is a gifted one—like yourself."

"Like I *was*, you mean."

"No, Sam, like you *are*. Being a gifted one can mean many things. Remember what I say now. You will be called upon to make many choices throughout your life. It may not be clear at the time where destiny will take you, but if you make those choices with a pure heart, my boy, then you can't help but find yourself on the right path."

Sam nodded, then smiled.

"Fletcher would be so excited..."

"But you can't..."

"Tell him. I know," said Sam with a sigh.

"Until we meet again, then?" Mr. Goodfellow gave Sam a nod before he slipped down through the opening.

When he opened the door to let Fletcher in, Sam

221

couldn't help but imagine his friend fully space-suited and helmeted. But the bottle of Pepto-Bismol and the plastic spoon that Fletcher was clutching in his hand spoiled the illusion a little.

"Here," he said, pushing them at Sam. "These are from your mum."

Sam sauntered back down the aisle. When he reached his mother's row, he returned the bottle and spoon to her.

"Thanks, Mum. You were right. I'm feeling better already."

Sam was about to flop down into his own seat when he noticed that a book had been left in his place. It was Auntie Nellie's cryptic crossword puzzle anthology. A pen was laid across its front cover.

India looked over from her seat by the window.

"Thought I'd help you out a bit," she called sweetly. "If you study the answers, the clues will start to make sense. I've made a few notes for you, too."

"Thanks," said Sam, picking up the pen and book.

He took his seat and started flipping through the pages. India had completed each and every crossword. Along the way, she'd left little messages for Sam, explaining how she had solved certain clues. It was, he concluded, extremely nice of her to have gone to all that trouble.

Fletcher threw himself into his seat with a force strong enough to jostle Sam's elbow and dislodge the crossword puzzle book from his hands, sending it tumbling to the floor below.

"Sorry, pal."

"It's...okay," Sam replied slowly, giving Fletcher an extra long stare.

Sam reached down to retrieve the book. In its fall, it had opened to the very back page. Sam had forgotten all about the word game he'd invented on that rainy afternoon in Wiltshire. India had written something here, too, in a tiny space that he had left in one corner.

"Interesting game. Something to do with anagrams, right? Not clear about the rules. Maybe you can tell me sometime. I got the last one. See?"

Sam looked down to where he had written the word SAGE, then AGES, then the letters L and N, the ones his hand had guided him to when he had closed his eyes and thought of Mr. Goodfellow. Underneath, in India's handwriting, the letters had been rearranged.

Sam stared at the word and slowly closed the puzzle book. He laid it on his knee and stared out the airplane window, his mind still frozen on the book's inside back cover and the word that India had written there: ANGELS.

17

BAD NEWS
TRAVELS FAST

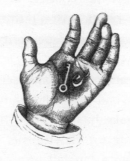

onsidering all the strange and confusing things that had happened to Sam in the past two weeks, he was relieved to be home. If he was destined to confront Professor Mandrake and The Fen again, he would rather do it here than anywhere else.

Sam's reunion with Figgy was boisterous. There were some protests from the house mice, especially after one of their elder members was rear-ended in a baseboard collision. Two weeks of running wild with Luciano, Placido and José had taken its toll on Figgy's behavior, but after a day or two, Sam managed to regain some measure of control.

Rollo, the ever-faithful gypsy mouse, once again agreed to provide assistance in keeping the Hawthorne scroll safe. He directed the rest of the house mice to spirit the scroll back into the maze of tunnels behind Sam's bedroom wall, where a detachment could provide around-the-clock surveillance. And now that eight Sage had taken up residence in his sock drawer, Sam felt a new surge of confidence. But sadly, this was to be short-lived. Four days after their return home, Fletcher rushed over to Sam's house with an urgent bulletin.

"Mandrake's back!" he announced breathlessly. "I heard my mum and dad talking just now. He came into my dad's office at the university today, acting real friendly at first. Then he started asking a whole bunch of questions about the Science Conference paper. I don't think my dad was very pleased. And Mandrake had some pretty weird things to say about Professor Hawthorne, too."

Sam had been dreading Mandrake's return, and after Fletcher revealed what else he had overheard, Sam was beside himself.

Professor Mandrake had returned home with a disturbing story about Professor Hawthorne. In next to no time, Mandrake had woven a tangled web of lies to discredit the good professor and gain the support of the university community. According to the story that was now spreading rapidly across the campus, the whole business had started while they were away in England.

After an investigation that had taken several months, a large sum of money was now being reported missing from the university's pension fund. Although it was believed to have been an inside job, there were no suspects at first. None, that is, until Professor Mandrake stepped forward to help, divulging the details of a rather unusual encounter he had had with his dear friend, Professor Cedric Hawthorne, just a week or so earlier.

Professing himself terribly concerned about what he described as Professor Hawthorne's "emotional breakdown," Mandrake explained how he had canceled a long-awaited trip to Central America in order to locate and help his colleague. It had taken some time, said Mandrake, but he had finally tracked Hawthorne down in England, where he was found to be in a most disturbed frame of mind. The poor, confused old soul had apparently lost all touch with reality and Mandrake had been forced—after much soul-searching and anguish, of course—to place his dear friend in a sanitarium somewhere in Scotland. He was, in Professor Mandrake's esteemed opinion, a danger to himself and possibly the rest of society, too.

As far as the missing pension funds were concerned, Mandrake didn't want to point any fingers, but he felt obliged to mention (frequently) that he had discovered Professor Hawthorne tearing around the English countryside in a brand-new Rolls-Royce, sporting an impressive collection of expensive clothes.

After planting these little seeds of suspicion, Professor Mandrake must have watched with satisfaction as a great rumor tree sprang forth. The current story circulating had Professor Hawthorne growing tired of his threadbare academic existence, absconding with a trunkload of cash, then going to extraordinary lengths to fake his own disappearance.

For a while, even Abigail Spender, administrative head of the Fine Arts Department (and lovesick colleague of Professor Mandrake's), seemed a willing dupe. Caught up in Hawthorne fever, she suddenly rushed forward to claim that a large chunk of the proceeds from her art auction the September before last had never been deposited into the university account. It all seemed to fit with Professor Hawthorne's despicable behavior, she openly speculated, but she was forced to retract her accusations a few days later when the missing auction receipts were actually discovered at the bottom of her pink purse.

Refusing to be derailed by Ms. Spender's annoying interference, Mandrake continued to spread his own cleverly concocted story, collecting an ever-growing number of believers along the way.

All of this gave Sam a great deal to feel nervous about, especially when Professor Mandrake suggested that the authorities, with *his* assistance, of course, should mount a search of Professor Hawthorne's former residence in order to obtain clues about the missing money. Sam's parents resisted such an invasion into their home, claiming that not enough concrete evidence against Professor Hawthorne had come forth.

Throughout this whole affair, it seemed to have escaped everyone's attention (apart from Sam's and Fletcher's) that young Basil Mandrake had suddenly taken to wearing designer clothes and boasting about his expensive new toys and electronic equipment. How Mandrake might be managing all of this on a professor's modest salary didn't appear to have aroused any suspicions about *him* at all.

Not content to leave this intriguing story alone for too long, Mandrake was busy inventing the next few chapters. After a few more days had passed, a visibly shaken Professor Mandrake announced to colleagues that he had received a most upsetting message from the Scottish sanitarium. Professor Hawthorne, it appeared, had managed to escape and was now "on the loose." The doctors had concluded that his dear friend might never be found. All the more reason, he pressed again, to search the Hawthorne house for clues.

Over at the Jaffrey house, things had grown uncharacteristically somber. Even the dogs, sensing that something was wrong, were much more subdued. Mandrake's revelations about their old friend Cedric Hawthorne had left the entire family in a state of stunned disbelief, especially Fletcher's father. For hours at a time now, Sanjid Jaffrey would sit in the chair in his study, staring out of the window and idly toying with something in his hand.

Like Sam and the Jaffreys, The Sage were also grappling with a number of troubling concerns. The startling testimony they had heard in the crop circle made it all the more imperative that the Hawthorne scroll be protected, especially if Mandrake held the second scroll in his possession. Not knowing whether Professor Hawthorne was in or out of the circle, dead or alive, was also a constant worry. The matter of the missing sliver of the Hawthorne scroll had been passed along to Sam. He had elicited Fletcher's help, but after a preliminary sweep of the Jaffrey house, they had been unable to locate either the sliver or the paper that Fletcher's father had written about it.

All of these problems had been discussed at length among Sam and The Sage. There was one topic that hadn't come up for conversation. Though he desperately wanted to, Sam couldn't bring himself to ask about the knobs on Shrike Fen's back, and The Sage had not broached the subject either. But Sam could sense that, for them, this may have been the most mysterious and troubling discovery of all.

Every night since his return home, Sam would find himself jolted awake by a disturbance in his sock drawer. This particular night was no exception. He sat up and rested himself on his elbows while the sounds of a heated discussion, featuring (as it usually did) the voices of Mr. Goodfellow and Winchester Redwood, drifted across to his bed.

"It just won't do, Redwood!" Mr. Goodfellow exclaimed adamantly. "In light of what's happened now, surely you must agree that the boy's progress needs to be carefully monitored. His Sage must be someone sensitive, someone who understands him, someone..."

"Like you, I suppose?" Redwood interrupted, impatiently. "Let it go, Jolly! The Governing Council's already decided that I've got the job, right? So, if you don't mind, pal, I could really use some shut-eye."

"But everything's changed, Redwood!" Mr. Goodfellow insisted. "Young Jaffrey's potential endeavors have taken on a new significance now. Think of where he is destined to go! Anyway, I think I should inform you that the Council has agreed to consider the transfer of the boy's Seal to me. They have promised that a decision will be brought down shortly, so you might as well start getting used to the idea! Redwood? I say, Redwood!"

Winchester Redwood, humming loudly, had stuck the tips of his fingers into his ears to drown out Mr. Goodfellow's last few words. He took them out briefly to announce that he was going to bed, then dramatically pulled one of Sam's socks over his head, turned his back and walked away.

"Well, don't say I didn't warn you!" Mr. Goodfellow called after him.

With a loud rattle, answered by protests from the rest of The Sage who were still trying to fall asleep, Mr. Goodfellow clambered up to the top of the half-opened drawer, then shimmied down the outside. He marched across the floor to the end of the bed and hoisted himself up the edge of Sam's comforter. Figgy, curled in his usual spot at Sam's feet, yawned and blinked his eyes. Mr. Goodfellow absently patted the dog's wet nose as he passed by. When he reached Sam's head, Mr. Goodfellow plunked himself down with a great sigh.

"I've almost reached the end of my tether with that— that—buffoon!" he exclaimed. "If he would only see sense and accept the inevitable, then the Council would be able to make their decision without these lengthy deliberations."

Sam nodded his head in agreement. Mr. Goodfellow wasn't the only one who was hoping that this thing could be settled soon. Elements of The Sacred Seal that was to exist between Fletcher and Winchester Redwood were already starting to develop. Sam wasn't sure how much longer he could put up with Fletcher's little jokes. Even after two invigorating showers and a good long soak in the tub, Sam was still trying to remove the last vestiges of the black ring marks from around his eyes. He really should have seen that binocular prank coming.

Mr. Goodfellow looked down for a moment and wiggled his feet. The tip of one toe was peeping through a big hole in his argyle sock. He hung his head and sighed again.

"What I wouldn't give to rummage through my trunk right now," he lamented. "Just one pair of fresh footwear, that's all I ask! I feel quite grubby like this. Dear Beatrice did her best with the suit repairs, too, of course, but it's not the same..." Mr. Goodfellow suddenly stopped speaking. An odd scraping sound was coming from the direction of Sam's window.

"What was that?" Sam whispered.

Figgy, instantly alert, lifted his head and cocked it to one side.

"The wind, perhaps?" Mr. Goodfellow suggested. "It has picked up a bit in the last hour. I seem to recall a forecast for rain, too, my boy. A stray branch from the tree outside the window may have..."

The scraping sound repeated, much louder this time. A black, hulking shape suddenly swept in front of the window, throwing dark, eerie shadows across Sam's room.

"That's not a branch!" Sam whispered nervously. He jumped out of his bed and tiptoed across to the window frame. Trembling, he stood beside it with his back to the wall. Figgy began to growl. Heavy drops of rain flew against the windowpane. Mr. Goodfellow leapt from the edge of Sam's comforter to the floor below, and scurried toward the chest of drawers to retrieve his mouse suit and alert the others.

Figgy's ears flattened against the side of his head. There was a flash of white as the dog bared his teeth and started to slink slowly down Sam's bed. The hulking shape that had swept across the window was looming right in front of it now. As something pushed hard against the window frame, the latch rattled. Sam stared in horror, realizing just then that he had forgotten to lock it.

He tried to swallow, but his mouth was too dry. He shuffled a few feet along the wall to retrieve the Chilean rainstick that was leaning against his closet door. Whoever, or whatever, was out there was desperate enough to have climbed to the second story to gain entrance to his room. Only one person came to mind. As the window slowly inched its way up, Sam sniffed the rain-soaked air, fully expecting the smell of mothballs to come drifting through as well.

When a dripping hand slipped through the opening and grasped the inside window ledge, Sam raised the rainstick high above his head. Hundreds of tiny pebbles began tumbling through the hollow tube of dried cactus. With Figgy at the edge of his bed poised to leap, Sam closed his eyes and swung with all his might. The rainstick cracked against the window frame with enough force to split it down the middle, spilling pebbles across the length of Sam's bedroom floor. There was a startled scream as the wet hand grasped the ledge even tighter, its knuckles scraped and bleeding.

With a ferocious snarl, Figgy leapt from the end of the bed and snapped at the still-clinging fingers. Sam, confident that he and Figgy had just gained the upper hand, jumped in front of the window to face the intruder.

"Professor Hawthorne!" he gasped.

Sam rushed forward, straining to push the rest of the window up and out of the way.

"It's okay Figgy!" he called behind him. "It's a friend. Calm down!"

Figgy, backing away on his master's command, continued to emit a low growl as Sam grabbed hold of the professor's arms and pulled as much of him as he could into the room. Shivering, Professor Hawthorne slid across the wet window ledge and down onto the floor with a thud.

"Are you alright, Professor?" Sam cried. "You scared the living daylights out of me!"

"I believe we may have done a rather magnificent job of scaring each other!" Professor Hawthorne panted as he struggled to his feet.

"What are you doing here? Where have you been?" Sam blurted out.

Still trying to catch his breath, the professor hunched over for a second and held his hand up. "So many questions, Sam! A moment please, dear boy. My lumbago's killing me."

The professor took two or three deep breaths before he straightened up and began to speak again. "I had no idea you had taken my study over for your bedroom, Sam. Since it's rather late and I didn't want to alarm you, I thought I would just shimmy up the old oak tree out there and quietly make myself at home until the morning. It never occurred to me that I would encounter a welcoming committee."

Professor Hawthorne winced as he rubbed his sore knuckles.

"You have quite a swing," he observed, nodding toward the rainstick that Sam was still holding. "I can assure you that it's quite safe to let go of it now."

"Oh...right...sorry, Professor," said Sam, loosening his grip and letting what was left of the stick fall to the floor. "I thought you were Professor Mandrake and..."

"Mandrake!" Professor Hawthorne cried out. "The scoundrel's back here, then?"

Sam nodded as the professor started to pace across the floor. Little rainstick pebbles crunched under his feet, but he was too engrossed in thoughts of Mandrake to notice. Sam, trying hard to dodge the rolling pebbles, tiptoed over to his bedside table and switched on the soft light.

"After I helped you exit the circle, Sam, I led that villain on quite a chase for a while," the professor started to explain, "always keeping just far enough ahead of him. When the lights and humming started up again, just like they do before the energy peaks and we're hurled off somewhere else, I stopped, surrounded myself with my magnets and waited for Mandrake to find me. Sure enough, he appeared before too long, playing right into my plan. I knew that if we could create the right amount of kinetic energy together, the door to escape would be opened. Believing that I was still carrying the scroll he so desperately wanted, Mandrake made his move. We struggled quite violently and, just as I had predicted, we were thrown back into the crop field. He's a crafty devil that one, my boy. Surprisingly craftier than I've given him credit for over the years, I'm afraid," the professor brooded, rubbing his chin. "I must have let my guard down for just a moment after we returned, because before I knew what was happening, he was upon me again! And this time, he was armed and dangerous!"

The professor suddenly pulled the flowing hair back from his forehead to reveal a large purplish bruise just above one temple. A deep red, crusted dent marked its center.

"The blackguard bludgeoned me on the head with a rock! Then he dragged me into some bushes and left me for dead, just the way Hugo Trenchmount left my great-grandfather

Elijah all those years ago. It's funny, isn't it, how history has a way of repeating itself?"

Sam shuddered. "What happened next?"

"Well," the professor continued, "by the torn and tattered condition of my clothes, I concluded that Mandrake had conducted a thorough search for the scroll. Finding nothing, he must have left the scene in a foul temper. When I finally came to, I managed to make my way to town, where I was able to clean up and attend to my wound. Not wanting Mandrake to discover that I had survived his attack, I hid for several days until I felt it was safe to return home. I imagined that Mandrake was well gone by then. Since I didn't have possession of the scroll, he would have assumed that someone else did."

Professor Hawthorne gave Sam a long look.

"He knows I have it, doesn't he?" Sam asked nervously.

"Quite possibly, my boy," replied the professor. "Though exactly where it is may have eluded him so far. We can only hope, can't we? That's why I wanted to return here as soon as I felt able. When I tell everyone about our amazing discovery and Mandrake's dastardly deeds..."

Professor Hawthorne suddenly stopped speaking.

"What is it, Sam? You look simply dreadful."

"Professor...you...you can't."

"Can't what?" asked the professor, looking perplexed. "Whatever do you mean, my boy?"

"It's Mandrake. He's been spreading lies about you ever since he got back. He said he took the summer off to track you down and when he finally found you, you were acting so strange that he had to put you in a hospital. He's got everybody thinking that you stole a whole bunch of money from the university and ran away to England with it and that you've been spending it on all kinds of stuff and..."

"And no one's going to believe a crazy old man like me, right, Sam?" said Professor Hawthorne, finishing the thought that he was certain Sam was thinking. "Or a young boy with a big imagination, either."

The professor slumped down on Sam's bed. Resting his aching head in his hands, he let out a tired sigh. Thin streams of rainwater trickled down his pants and onto his shoes, finally collecting in little puddles at his feet.

"What am I to do, now?" Professor Hawthorne lamented sadly. He grasped some locks of thick, white hair in his hands and absently tugged at them. When he took his hand away to examine the swollen knuckle, a big clump of hair came away with it.

"Well that's a fine 'how do you do,' isn't it?" he remarked sarcastically, staring into his palm. "Not only am I to be unjustly branded as a thieving lunatic, but it would appear that I am to be an aging one again, too. Ah well, nothing lasts forever, I suppose. Not here anyway."

Sam could see that Professor Hawthorne needed a boost. Even Figgy was trying to help, pushing his soft muzzle into the side of Hawthorne's knee, but the professor remained oblivious to the dog's friendly advances.

"I'll be back in a minute, Professor," Sam suddenly announced. "Just stay right here."

The professor nodded his head in resignation as Sam slipped out of the bedroom door. "I hardly think there's anywhere else I dare go now anyway, my boy," he whispered after him.

Sam returned a couple of minutes later clutching a large blue bath towel in one hand, and a roll of gauze and a bottle of antiseptic in the other.

"Here you go, Professor," said Sam, as he draped the bath towel around the old man's shoulders.

"That's very kind of you, indeed, my boy," said the professor, holding out his bruised and bleeding hand so that Sam could dab at his knuckle with the antiseptic.

When he looked up just then and saw the edge of the pillowcase move behind Professor Hawthorne's back, Sam stared straight ahead without so much as a blink. Even when he spied the little brown mouse slowly edging its way down the comforter toward them, Sam never let his face change. But when the mouse gave him a quick wink before it disappeared into the soft folds of the towel, Sam couldn't help but smile. Professor Hawthorne suddenly looked up.

"You know, my boy, I believe I am beginning to feel better already."

18

GREAT MINDS THINK ALIKE

It took Sam a few minutes to orient himself the next morning. He woke up to the sound of snoring, and found himself zipped up in his sleeping bag on the floor of his room. None of it made sense until he suddenly spied the pair of mud-encrusted loafers under the windowsill and two sock-clad feet dangling over the edge of his bed.

"Professor?" he whispered. "Professor Hawthorne?"

Sounds of yawning and several muffled snorts erupted, and the dangling feet began to stir. Professor Hawthorne slowly lifted his head from Sam's pillow, leaving behind a chunk of long white hair. His eyes cautiously scanned the room.

"Where am...oh, yes, I remember now! There you are, Sam!" he exclaimed. "I've had the most extraordinary dream!"

Professor Hawthorne got out of bed and walked to the window. He turned the latch and pushed the window up. One of the Middleton's neighbors had just mowed his lawn, and the sweet summer smell of freshly cut grass blew inside. Professor Hawthorne took a deep, cleansing breath.

"It's amazing how just a couple of hours of deep sleep can rejuvenate a weary mind. I've been attacking this whole

Mandrake mess the wrong way, you see. I don't know why I didn't think of it right off. If the academic community won't believe *me*, then we must find someone whom they will. I can't think of anyone who commands more respect in our little community than my dear friend Professor Sanjid Jaffrey. He already knows about the strange properties of the scroll." The professor rubbed his hands together in gleeful anticipation. "Just wait until we tell him the rest, my boy!" he chuckled. "He'll be fit to burst!"

Professor Hawthorne walked away from the window and sat down on the edge of Sam's bed again. Lost in thought, he scratched at the side of his nose.

"There's only one small problem, Sam. I don't quite know how, but you must get me to the Jaffrey house as soon as possible."

Sam nodded his head. Without another word, he slipped out of his room and down to the kitchen where his parents were already on their second cup of tea.

"Hungry again this morning, Sam?" his father called across the kitchen. "Four waffles, as usual?"

"Well, actually Dad, I was thinking more like eight. I'm *really* hungry."

Sam's mother popped the last two waffles onto the stack that she'd been keeping warm in the oven and handed them to Sam with a look of wonderment. After he had applied liberal amounts of butter and maple syrup, he grabbed a knife and fork and the white wicker tray that his mother kept on top of the fridge.

"Is it okay if I eat these upstairs? I already started a game on the computer. Thanks! Got any of those strawberries left, Mum?"

"Well, thank goodness for that, at least," said his mother, as she handed him the small glass bowl of berries from the table. "If it wasn't for all the fruit you eat, Sam, I think I'd worry myself silly about you."

Sam ducked into the laundry room on his way back to the stairs. He took an old tracksuit of his father's off the freshly folded pile and shoved it under his arm.

Professor Hawthorne, still staring out the window and deep in his own thoughts, hadn't budged from the edge of Sam's bed. Sam discreetly backed over to his chest of drawers. He fumbled around for the knob of the second drawer, opened it a little, and began to push the fruit bowl inside. On the way up the stairs Sam had somehow managed, while artfully balancing the tray and the tracksuit, to tear half of the top waffle into bite-sized, syrup-drenched chunks, which he had then sprinkled on top of the fruit. When it appeared as if the bowl had become stuck at one edge of the *Queen Mary* toffee box (now doubling as a private dressing room for the ladies), Sam turned his head just enough to see several pairs of tiny hands guiding the bowl over it and through a narrow opening. From the muffled "oohs" and "aahs" that were floating up from the drawer, Sam could tell that this morning's offering was a big hit.

"How wonderful, Sam!" the professor exclaimed when he saw the tray. "I'm absolutely starving!"

Sam had intended that he and Professor Hawthorne share the breakfast tray, but after the professor had wolfed down the first seven waffles in a matter of seconds, Sam was able to claim only the remaining half of the one that had gone into the Sage drawer.

After Sam indicated to the professor that he had brought some drier clothes for him to put on, he returned the wicker tray to the kitchen. To the utter astonishment of his parents, the waffle plate had been licked clean.

241

"The berry bowl, Sam?"

"Still working on it, Mum."

"Well, please bring it down and pop it in the sink when you're done, especially if you don't finish everything. Every now and then, I find a few old bits of food in your room and in the oddest places, too. If you're not careful, you'll start attracting rodents. And we don't want that sort of thing happening *again*, do we, Sam?"

Peggy Middleton shuddered just then, still trying, it would appear, to banish the hideous memory of a small black mouse's mad dash through the middle of her dinner party the year before.

Sam hovered in the kitchen for a few more minutes until his parents finally brewed their third pot of tea and retired, as they always did, to the sanctuary of the backyard patio. As soon as the door shut behind them, Sam lunged for the telephone.

"Fletcher? Get over here right away! You're never going to believe who's been eating waffles in my room!"

After the excitement of meeting the legendary Professor Hawthorne, Fletcher finally settled down enough to assist Sam and the professor in the next phase of their plan.

While Sam's parents were happily sipping tea beyond the back door, Sam, Figgy, Fletcher and Professor Hawthorne (squeezed very tightly into a purple and gold tracksuit) slipped out the front door and headed for the Jaffreys'. It was easy going for most of the way, except for an encounter with one nosy neighbor who felt compelled to comment on Trevor Middleton's expanding girth.

"Well, that's actually why we're out walking, Mrs. Brody," explained Sam. "Right, Dad?"

With his head bundled deep inside the tracksuit's hood, Professor Hawthorne offered a muffled grunt. Figgy, conveniently picking just that moment to jump up and place two muddy paws and a muzzle full of drool on Mrs. Brody's knees, soon sent her packing. Sam and Fletcher, holding onto the professor's arms at either side, rushed him down the street and around the corner.

When they arrived at Fletcher's, they were greeted by the usual canine contingent, and soon after that, the downcast figure of Sanjid Jaffrey as he shuffled into the front hallway and shooed the dogs away. As soon as Sam let him off his leash, Figgy dashed after the rest of the pack like a shot.

"Forgotten your key again, son?" Fletcher's father asked, hardly looking up. "How's it going, Trev?" he commented, spying the purple and gold of Trevor Middleton's tracksuit from the corner of his eye.

"From this moment on, I sincerely hope much better, Sanjid."

Sanjid Jaffrey slowly looked up and stared long and hard into the overhanging hood and the face that was staring back at him from inside.

"Cedric! I don't believe it!" he finally cried, grabbing his friend by the shoulders and pulling him inside. "We heard that you had—well, you know..."

"Lost my marbles? Gone on a crime spree?"

"Ah...well...something like that," Fletcher's father replied awkwardly.

"A figment of Avery Mandrake's twisted imagination, I'm afraid," explained Professor Hawthorne.

"I knew it! I just knew it! Both of us! Leonora, too! Wait until she gets home from her tour! She won't believe it!"

Sanjid cried. "But what for, Cedric? What on earth could have driven that man to..."

"Ah...you see, that's rather the point, Sanjid," interrupted Professor Hawthorne. "It's nothing on *Earth* at all."

Fletcher's father looked puzzled for a moment.

"The metal sliver?" he suddenly murmured.

Professor Hawthorne slipped his arm through Sanjid Jaffrey's and led him toward the study.

"I think it's time to brew that giant pot of tea I've been dreaming about, Sanjid. It's a very long story," said Professor Hawthorne. "But before I start, there's one thing that we really must attend to, isn't there, Sam?"

Sam, not quite sure what the professor meant, looked a little confused.

"The reunion, of course, my boy!" the professor declared, slapping him affectionately on the back. "I assume, Sanjid, that you have been keeping our little piece of another world in a safe place."

"As you asked me to, Cedric," said Fletcher's father. "But, I'm afraid that with the strain of your disappearance and not knowing how best to handle the unexpected results of my tests, I may have set the cat amongst the pigeons. I prepared a short paper of my findings for the recent Science Conference. When Mandrake began his sniffing around, I withdrew it, of course, but..."

"That's really of no consequence, Sanjid, as you will soon discover," interrupted Professor Hawthorne. "The world must know the whole truth, and you, the eminent Professor Jaffrey, should be the one to tell them. For the time being though, as we rethink what we are going to say in light of everything else that has surfaced, I think it may be prudent to keep all of this between ourselves. Mandrake is a force to be reckoned with, as

244

Sam and I have discovered. There is no need to endanger anyone else unnecessarily. It will be just you, Sanjid, and myself, Sam and young Fletcher here."

"And me," said a softer voice from the top of the stairs.

"India!" cried her father, looking up. "How long have you been listening?"

"Oh, just a few months or so," India replied casually as she made her way down the stairs, a pink paperback in her hand.

Sam's eyes flashed across at Fletcher.

"Lost in her books, right, Fletch?" Sam whispered. "Not interested in anything but her romance novels. That's what you told me! But I knew different all along, didn't I?"

Fletcher, at a complete loss for words, shrugged his shoulders.

"Very well then," announced Professor Hawthorne. "India's with us, too."

"You know, Sam," said India, sidling up to him. "I've been doing a little research into the phenomenon of the plasma vortex to understand the complexities of the whole crop circle enigma." She pulled an old copy of *American Physicist* out from between the pages of her romance novel and began to flip through it. "Now, considering the atmospheric conditions that were in play on the night you entered the wheat field and disappeared for four hours..."

"You were *there*?" Sam's eyes flew open in surprise.

"Of course. You don't think I'd let the two of you go traipsing around a strange country in the middle of the night, do you? Well, not you anyway, Fletcher." India smiled at Sam just then with a look that made his knees feel funny. "Ever wonder why Basil Mandrake didn't catch up with you that night?" she asked.

"Well, not right away, I guess," said Fletcher. "But when he came back from England with that broken toe, we just figured

we'd gotten lucky and he'd fallen over a rock or something..."
Fletcher's voice suddenly trailed off. He turned and looked
straight at Sam. Sam raised his eyebrows as India demurely followed her father and Professor Hawthorne into the study.

Straining to reach the top of his bookshelf, Sanjid Jaffrey
shifted one book aside and retrieved a small wooden box that
had been hidden behind it. Taking a gold key from his pocket,
he unlocked the box and passed the tiny object inside to
Professor Hawthorne. The professor turned it over in his
hands once or twice, as if he were stroking it for good luck,
before he pressed it firmly into Sam's palm.

"I think it's time we put this back in its rightful place, my
boy," said Professor Hawthorne. He pulled the little wad of scroll
notes from his shirt pocket and added them to Sam's hand. "I
think these will be safer there, too. When the time comes to sub-
mit our paper, we'll know where to find our proof."

Leaving everyone else behind, Sam returned home. As Sam
and The Sage looked on, Rollo carried the shimmering sliver
and the wad of notes deep into the maze of mouse tunnels.
When the stopper at one end of the scroll tube was pulled off,
the high-pitched whine of the scroll's energy field floated
along the passageways toward them. When it reached The
Sage, they all lifted their paws and covered their ears.

Filbert, noticing that Sam was wincing, gave Edgar a quick
nudge.

"Are you alright, Sam?" Edgar called out, shuffling closer to
his friend.

Sam gave his head a few shakes.

"I don't know. I feel kinda funny. There's this ringing in
my ears. It happened once before when I was with Professor
Hawthorne in the crop circle, but it's much louder this
time and..."

"It's the power of the scroll, Sam," interrupted Filbert.

"But I could never hear it like that before. Why now?" asked Sam with concern. "What's happening to me?"

"I'm afraid I'm not entirely sure," answered Filbert, scratching the top of his balding head. "Much of what is now happening is beyond our understanding. Perhaps it has something to do with the unique Sacred Seal that now exists between you and Edgar."

"Things were altered a little when you made your choice to remain with us, dear," offered Beatrice. "That's never happened before. You may be becoming, as a result, more attuned to the same metaphysical murmurings that we are."

"Well...actually," Edgar piped up, "Uncle Jolly thinks everything that's been happening has something to do with the scrolls directly and..." Edgar looked straight into Sam's eyes, "with you, too."

"With me? He does?" said Sam nervously. "Like how?"

"Like in the Martian testament, remember?" asked Edgar. "You know, that thing about the scrolls being found by one chosen to be worthy of their protection and guarded until the world is ready to receive them again. Or something like that."

"What? You don't mean *me*?" Sam asked, feeling a little queasy.

"Edgar, I really think..." interrupted Filbert.

"Well, that *was* kind of an important part, Dad."

"I *know* that Edgar, but look at the poor lad now!" admonished Filbert. "He's turned white. And it was only a bit of musing on Jolly's part, I believe," he added. "We really shouldn't be jumping to any conclusions until we know for sure. There's no sense frightening Sam just yet, is there?"

"Just *yet!*" blurted Sam.

"I'm sorry, Sam," offered Edgar, sadly. "I was only trying to help. Honestly."

Sam sat silently for the next few minutes. Filbert and Edgar remained at his side while Beatrice and Hazel busied themselves shepherding Charlotte, Porter and Duncan back toward the chest of drawers. Winchester Redwood, who would have normally exploited a reflective moment like this to tell a joke or relate one of his many grandiose stories, was crouching in a corner, quietly sorting through his flight bag instead.

"Is Mr. Redwood going away, Edgar?" Sam asked.

Edgar nodded his head. "He got word by mouse courier this morning. He's being sent on another important assignment. Immediately."

"What about Fletcher?" Sam asked.

"The Council has finally agreed with Jolly," Filbert replied. "Fletcher's Sacred Seal will be transferred over to him now."

"Uncle Jolly hasn't even heard yet," added Edgar.

"You know what," remarked Sam, as he watched Redwood buckle the straps of his bag, "I think I'm really going to miss him."

"He's only going three blocks away," Edgar piped up.

"Huh?"

"His new assignment is Sanjid Jaffrey," explained Filbert. "That's why Redwood's leaving right away. Now that Professor Jaffrey has become an important part of this whole thing, the Council has declared him a high priority. They really weren't prepared for this at all."

"Uh-oh," said Sam, as Filbert's words began to sink in. "But that means..."

"That Uncle Jolly and Mr. Redwood will be working side by side," Edgar finished.

"I don't have to be the one to tell him that, do I?" asked Sam with a grimace.

"No. Maybe it would be best if we just let Jolly find out for himself," Filbert suggested with a nervous smile.

19

EVERY DOG MUST HAVE
HIS DAY

For almost the entire month of August, Professors Hawthorne and Jaffrey worked diligently on their joint paper to the scientific community, while Sam, Fletcher and India kept as close a watch as they could on Avery Mandrake's movements. Following Professor Hawthorne's advice, they all promised to keep what they knew to themselves for the time being. It was critical that Professor Hawthorne's whereabouts remain unknown to everyone else, especially Mandrake. As far as he was concerned, Cedric Hawthorne—or his remains, at least—were still lying in a remote part of the Wiltshire countryside. There was no telling what Mandrake might do if he were to discover that his arch rival was not dead at all, but quite well and hiding out at the Jaffreys'.

It was easy keeping all of this troubling information from Fletcher's mother. Another set of rave reviews for her June performance in *Aida* had led to a summer-long contract with another critically acclaimed experimental theater group. Leonora was now touring up and down the East Coast, appearing at small town art fairs and festivals with the rest of her troupe.

Sam's parents were another issue, though one that, for the moment, presented only minor concern. Professor Mandrake was beginning to make quite a nuisance of himself, turning up with growing frequency at the Middletons' art gallery, often accompanied by Tippy Stanwyck. The flamboyant real estate agent (and town fashion plate) had sold the Middletons their home. Her failure to inform them of its rodent infestation had resulted in the near emotional collapse of Peggy Middleton on the occasion of her first dinner party. The mere sight of the woman now was enough to make Sam's mother break out in hives. Undaunted by Peggy's obvious discomfort, Professor Mandrake continued to show up, hovering at the gallery for hours at a time, explaining that he was finally pursuing an interest he had had for years in collecting American folk art. Since returning from England, however, Trevor and Peggy Middleton had become swept up in the production of another major art exhibition: *A Stroke of Genius—Folk Painting in the Civil War Years*. Once again they were rushing to get all the pieces framed and hung and were too distracted to attach much significance to Mandrake's visits. They remained unaware that he had about as much interest in folk art as he did in the raising and training of pedigree miniature poodles, a life-long passion of the meddlesome Ms. Spender. Informing his parents of the more maniacal intentions of Professor Mandrake was something Sam couldn't worry about just yet.

Sam juggled his time as evenly as he could between his house and the Jaffreys'. Whether he should stay at home (where the scroll was hidden and where Professor Mandrake kept popping up) or at Fletcher's (where toiling Professor Hawthorne was now installed in the basement guestroom) was a hard call. This decision was made all the more difficult by the sudden reappearance of Basil Mandrake. Broken toe now healed, it appeared that Basil had decided to spend the rest of his summer holidays patrolling the streets around Sam's house on his skateboard.

One afternoon, while Sam was on his way to rendezvous with Fletcher and India, a little yellow car zoomed past him and screeched to a stop in the Jaffreys' driveway. Recognizing the car instantly, Sam pulled his scooter into the bushes at the side of the garage, crouched down and listened.

Fletcher's father opened the front door to find Abigail Spender standing rather nervously on the porch, clutching a miniature poodle in her arms.

"Why, Ms. Spender, what brings you here?" he inquired politely.

He turned to calm the barking pack of boxers that had gathered behind him, all craning their necks to get a good look at the visitors.

"Come on now, boys! Manners, if you please!" Sanjid Jaffrey remarked.

When he turned back to Ms. Spender, she was clutching the trembling dog even tighter, and its little brown eyes were as big as saucers. Sanjid Jaffrey slipped out of the front door and joined Ms. Spender on the porch. There was a loud thump as several boxer paws made contact with the back of the door. "They're really quite friendly," Sanjid Jaffrey assured her. "Just a bit exuberant."

Ms. Spender could only manage a small, strained smile.

"I'm terribly sorry to appear unannounced like this, Professor Jaffrey. Especially when you have a guest," Ms. Spender apologized.

"A guest? No, Ms. Spender. It's just me and the dogs."

"Oh, I see," said Ms. Spender, seeming a bit confused. "It's just that I thought I saw someone else as I was coming up the steps. An older gentlemen, I believe. Behind you."

Sanjid Jaffrey tried very hard to conceal his concern. "Really? How odd," he replied, as casually as he could. "Those boxer faces can be incredibly lifelike you know. Just like wizened old men! And in the glare of this bright sunlight..."

"Of course, Professor; how silly of me," Ms. Spender suddenly declared. "I must have been mistaken."

There was a moment of awkwardness before Abigail Spender spoke again. "I did try to reach you by telephone, Professor Jaffrey, but your line seems to be busy all the time..."

"Oh, that would be Leonora!" he announced with relief, sounding thankful that they were off the other topic. "She calls us three or four times a day, just to check up! You see, she's away touring at the moment, doing a turn in summer theater at all the art festivals and..."

"Yes, I did know," interrupted Ms. Spender. "That's why I'm here. The festivals, I mean. In fact, it's to do with the big one they're planning for the Labor Day weekend: the New England Balloon Festival. Perhaps you've heard of it?"

"Indeed, Ms. Spender. The children and I are planning to meet up with Leonora there. It's her final performance of the season. We've even planned a little family camping expedition..."

"How delightful!" trilled Ms. Spender, feeling confident enough finally to loosen her vice-like grip on the poodle. "I don't know if you've heard, but this year's festival will be expanded beyond its usual scope. The theater and musical performances have been added, of course, and an amusement park, plus that delightful traveling gypsy troupe that entertained us all at the art auction the year before last."

Sam, still crouching in the bushes, swallowed hard at this

last bit of news. He recalled his own close encounter with Madame Zorah, the old gypsy fortune-teller and matriarch of the troupe.

It was in Madame Zorah's tent that Edgar had been reunited with Mr. Goodfellow and introduced to Sam. Taking refuge for many years with Rollo and the other gypsy mice that followed the troupe, Edgar had been drawn to the fortune that the old gypsy had been reading. She had been a mere whisper away from discovering The Sage before Sam took flight with them.

Sam imagined that Madame Zorah would jump at the chance to ask him a few more pointed questions. He shuddered and vowed to avoid her at all costs. As Sam pondered these troubling thoughts, Ms. Spender's voice suddenly intruded.

"Best of all, Professor Jaffrey, I'm thrilled to announce the first annual Valley Dog Show. The admittance proceeds will go to the Animal Welfare Society. Ms. Olympia Plumtree, our local director, has asked me to encourage dog owners in our little community to enter."

"Well, I don't know, Ms. Spender. It's rather short notice..."

"Yes, I do apologize for that, Professor, but it's for such a worthy cause and since you'll be attending the festival anyway, you really can't refuse us, can you?" Ms. Spender implored. "There'll be some wonderful prizes and ribbons for best of breed and best of show, plus an obedience trial." Ms. Spender looked up just then at the squirming row of paws and slobbering jowls that were pressing against the front door glass. "You might want to consider giving that last one a miss," she suggested, trying to sound tactful. "But now, François and I must be off! We have a lot of work to do!"

She shook Sanjid's hand before she turned around and

trotted down the front steps toward her car. The pink bow at the back of her swept-up hair bobbed up and down in concert with the little blue one clipped to the back of François's curly head. From his vantage point, Sam could have sworn that the boxers were grinning. Sanjid Jaffrey turned around and opened the front door again, struggling to squeeze past them.

Ms. Spender was just about to turn the key in the ignition when she glanced over at the passenger seat. She sighed loudly when she spied the stack of Valley Dog Show application forms. Grabbing one off the top of the pile with one hand and the confused François with the other, she slipped out of her car and crept up the steps again. Sam, who had repositioned himself behind another bush, right next to the front door, crouched down again and watched.

Ducking her head below the glass door panels, Ms. Spender folded the form in half, carefully lifted the swinging metal strip that covered the mail slot and pushed the form through. The paper floated silently from her hand. Ms. Spender breathed a sigh of relief. When she lifted the mail slot a second time to make sure, Sam surmised, that her paper had landed in a conspicuous spot, there was a sudden movement inside. Sam strained to see. Ms. Spender froze as one of the boxers trotted through the hallway, then pushed the door to another room open with a toss of its powerful head. Sanjid Jaffrey, with his back to her, appeared to be having a conversation. When the door swung open a little further and the face of his companion was suddenly revealed, Ms. Spender let out a gasp. By the time the boxer had jumped up at the front door and cocked his ear, Ms. Spender was already racing down the steps and back into her car. Tossing the startled François into the rear seat, she started the engine, flung the car into reverse and hit the gas.

Sam's heart was pounding. By the expression on Abigail Spender's face, he had no doubt that she had recognized Cedric Hawthorne. The gig was up! As she sped down the street at breakneck speed, Sam knew exactly where Ms. Spender was headed.

Dragging his scooter out of the bushes, Sam took the shortcut to the other side of town. Racing through the park and along the riverside bike path, he arrived in the alleyway at the side of Professor Mandrake's townhouse just as the little yellow car was tearing up the street.

"Ms. Spender, how absolutely charming to see you again."

Avery Mandrake had opened the door just enough to pop his head out.

"Oh, my!" he exclaimed. "And who is this delightful little creature?" He gave François a tweak on the end of his snout.

"François! Please!" whispered Ms. Spender, embarrassed by the poodle's growling. "I'm terribly sorry, Professor, but I just had to come by. I have some very interesting information."

It was obvious that poor Ms. Spender was still pining for Professor Mandrake's affections. To her great dismay, their relationship had never quite gotten off the ground. But she hadn't given up hope. One day, she dreamed, with the right kind of persuasion, Avery Mandrake would suddenly sweep her into his arms and declare his undying love.

"And what interesting information would that be, Ms. Spender?" he asked dryly, backing his head away from the snarling poodle's reach.

Trembling, Abigail Spender leaned forward with anticipation. "I've seen Professor Hawthorne," she whispered into his ear.

Avery Mandrake suddenly began to choke. With her one free arm, Ms. Spender reached around the door and began to pound her fist between the professor's shoulder blades. Sam was certain this wasn't the reaction she'd been hoping for.

"I beg your pardon, Ms. Spender," Professor Mandrake finally sputtered out. "I'm afraid I may have accidentally swallowed a crumb the wrong way. I was just having some cheese and crackers." He tried to regain his composure. "Did I hear you mention Cedric Hawthorne's name just now?"

"Yes, Professor. I thought you might be interested," Ms. Spender exclaimed with excitement. Considering the condition you left him in, his recent escape from the sanitarium in Scotland and all that missing money..."

"Yes, of course, Ms. Spender. How very kind of you to pass the news along. This is indeed most interesting. And you saw him where?"

"Well, that's the odd thing, Professor," replied Ms. Spender. "He was at Sanjid Jaffrey's house. I can't imagine why he'd come back and what he would want with Professor Jaffrey. But, come to think of it," Ms. Spender began to babble, as her vivid imagination suddenly kicked in, "Professor Jaffrey was acting very guarded, as if he were in some sort of terrible danger." She suddenly grabbed Professor Mandrake's arm. "You don't suppose that Professor Hawthorne was threatening him, do you? Or the children?"

Avery Mandrake's eyes flashed and his nostrils began to flare.

"Possibly, Ms. Spender. Perhaps the crazed old fellow's run out of cash and he's come back..."

Ms. Spender gasped and clutched her cheek. "Oh, no!" she cried. "He must have heard about the funds we're hoping to raise at the festival! How dreadful! We should inform the authorities immediately!"

"Actually, Ms. Spender," Professor Mandrake began, slowly taking her by the hand, "or may I call you Abigail? If it's not being too forward, of course."

"Of course not...um...Avery," she stammered.

"I think we should hold off for the time being. We don't want to scare him away now, do we? If he's really up to something, it will be much better if we catch him in the act. Are you with me, Abigail?" he purred, caressing her hand.

Speechless with bliss, Ms. Spender nodded her head.

"Let's keep in touch, then, shall we? Be sure to let me know if you hear or see anything else unusual, my dear. It will be our little secret." Professor Mandrake gave Ms. Spender's hand a final squeeze and François a little pat on the head, pulling his hand away just in time to avoid a nasty nip.

"Of course, Avery," Ms. Spender whispered, as she floated back to her car.

Temporarily blinded by passion, Ms. Spender hadn't noticed the fiery red sports car, crammed with real estate signs, parked down the street. While Avery Mandrake waved cheerily from his front door, another woman's voice called to him from inside the house.

"Who was *that*, Avery?"

"Just that insufferable Spender woman, Tippy, my love," he snarled through the side of his mouth. "Some nonsense about the university." He walked back inside, clenching his fists and grinding his teeth.

As she backed down the driveway, Abigail Spender began to hum. François stood on hind legs, his beautifully manicured poodle paws firmly planted on the back of the rear seat and his blue hair bow quivering with anger. He refused to take his eyes off Mandrake's front door or to stop his incessant growling until they had turned the corner for home.

His heart heavy with worry, Sam returned home to tell the others about these unsettling developments.

20

EVEN A WORM

WILL TURN

By the time Labor Day weekend rolled around, the paper that Sanjid Jaffrey and Cedric Hawthorne were preparing was almost complete. Early that Saturday morning, the Jaffrey family minivan, overflowing with dogs and camping equipment, could be seen motoring along the State Turnpike on its way to the New England Balloon Festival. Sanjid was in the driver's seat with India beside him, while Fletcher, Sam and Figgy sat behind. Though not registered in the dog show, Figgy was happy to be along for the ride.

Protected behind dark, tinted windows, Professor Hawthorne shared the back seat with the six other dogs. Leaving Professor Hawthorne alone in the house, while Mandrake might be prowling about, wasn't an option that any of them wanted to consider.

Sam's duffel bag had been called into service once again, providing much roomier accommodation for The Sage than his knapsack did. Sam was wearing his repaired fishing vest, with the scroll safely zipped inside. Leaving the Hawthorne scroll alone in his house while Mandrake might be prowling about was another option that Sam didn't want to consider.

When Rollo heard that Madame Zorah and her troupe were going to be entertaining at the festival, he had booked a spot in the duffel bag, too, anxious to visit with his family again. Since Rollo and the scroll were spending the weekend away, the Hawthorne house mice had also made vacation plans, preferring to travel inland to a new Vermont cheese factory that they had been hearing great things about.

The group arrived at the fairgrounds to a stunning blow: Professor Mandrake and Basil were getting out of a shiny, new car that had just pulled up beside them in the parking lot. What had started out as an end-of-summer camping trip had just taken a turn for the worse.

After setting up their campsite and securing the feverishly writing Professor Hawthorne in one of the tents, Fletcher's father set off for the dog show arena, struggling to maneuver the leashes of seven highly excited boxers through the maze of picnic tables.

For their part, Fletcher, India and Sam had expressed an interest in exploring the amusement park before the dog show started.

"Don't be too long!" Sanjid called after them, his voice growing steadily fainter as the dogs dragged him away. "I'm going to need some help later on..."

It was the perfect weekend for the event. The bright blue sky was dotted with hundreds of colorful hot-air balloons. As well as the standard balloons, there were those depicting cartoon animals and famous people and some sporting logos of companies promoting a wide range of products and services. There was a balloon in the shape of a race car, a truck with the insignia of a local moving company, and a house-shaped one with an advertisement for the real estate office where Tippy Stanwyck worked.

While India and Fletcher took a ride on the Ferris wheel, Sam opted to visit the fortune-teller's tent, where he had promised to drop Rollo off. Shuffling around to the back of the red-and-gold striped tent, Sam was relieved to slip the duffel bag from his shoulder. Despite their tiny size, a mouse, a worm and eight fully suited Sage were heavy. After a great deal of discussion, it had been decided among The Sage that it might boost everybody's morale to visit the festival and enjoy themselves for a while. Sam crouched down and unzipped the bag at one end. Rollo crawled out and, with a short squeak, leapt to the ground and scurried under the tent canvas. Sam was just about to zip the bag up when Mr. Goodfellow, holding a roll of paper in his paw, suddenly popped through the opening.

"We're all quite ravenous, my boy! Before we begin our little sojourn in the park, we were hoping that you might be able to apprehend some items for us. It would be much faster, and safer, of course, for you to obtain them. We've taken the liberty of preparing a short shopping list." Sam took the end of the roll between his fingers as Mr. Goodfellow waved at him and disappeared into the bag. Sam swung the magnifying glass he often carried out from around his neck.

"Cotton candy," Sam read. "Caramel corn, candy apple. What! A whole one?"

There was some whispering from inside the duffel bag. Sam put his ear to the opening and strained to hear.

"Well, okay. I'll see what I can do." Sam continued to read. "Sno-Kone! Sorry, that one's out of the question. Too messy," he stated emphatically. "Gummy worms. For Duncan, right?" He put his ear back down. "Well, I guess so, if he's lonely. I'll look for them."

Sam came to the last item on the list: gingerbread.

"This one's for Beatrice, isn't it?" said Sam. "I remember that from your stories, Mr. Goodfellow. What? Some for Charlotte, too? *That* much? Is it a family favorite or something? Okay, let me take a look. But I don't know how easy it's going to be to find a thing like gingerbread around here. I'll ask India. She has some kind of built-in radar for that stuff."

Sam was just about to stand up again when Rollo suddenly scurried out of the tent in a state of complete agitation.

"Um...something's up with Rollo," Sam whispered into the bag. "He's jumping all over the place. Somebody better come up and check it out!"

"What's wrong?" whispered Mr. Goodfellow, as he popped his head out of the opening. "Rollo?" he called below. "What is it, lad?"

Rollo, stretching his arms first to one side and then the other, was squeaking too quickly for Mr. Goodfellow to understand.

"Alright, alright, Rollo, I'll come down, if I must," Mr. Goodfellow exclaimed in frustration, as he began his descent. "Edgar!" he called behind him. "Could you give me a hand with Rollo here, please? He's quite beside himself over something."

Mr. Goodfellow and Rollo were already disappearing under the tent by the time Edgar surfaced. Sliding down the duffel bag on his bottom was the only way Edgar could catch up to them.

Sam heard a cry from inside.

"What's going on in there? Are you okay?" he whispered, as loudly as he dared.

The tent canvas quivered.

"Edgar! Mr. Goodfell—"

Mr. Goodfellow suddenly pushed the canvas to one side with the sweep of a paw. The smile on his face spread from mouse ear to mouse ear.

"By the will of the Fates, Sam, this tent has become the scene of yet another blessed reunion!" he announced. "First it was dear Edgar almost two years ago, and...well, you won't believe what Rollo's just found in the company of his family. I'm really quite overcome."

He gave a great tug and pulled something out of the tent behind him.

"It's your trunk!" exclaimed Sam.

"It's a miracle, my boy! It must have had quite an adventure, finding its way here! It's wonderful to have it back! I feel whole again!"

He pulled the trunk further out, then looked back for Edgar.

"In the interests of time, Sam, perhaps you would be kind enough to secure this in your bag. It would appear that Edgar has become entangled in a reunion of another sort with Rollo's family. I do hope he can extricate himself as quickly as possible. We really had hoped to avoid this, at least until it was time to leave for home."

Mr. Goodfellow lifted up the canvas and whispered for Edgar as Sam plucked the trunk off the ground and carefully slid it through the bag's opening. As soon as Edgar emerged, his mouse suit crushed and matted from the emotional welcome, Mr. Goodfellow grabbed him by the arm and pulled him back up the duffel bag and down through the hole.

As Sam refastened the zipper and hoisted the bag back onto his shoulder, Mr. Goodfellow's muffled cries floated through the canvas.

"Great heavens! What have they done to it! There's graffiti all over the mirror! And the map of my travels! The pins have all been moved around! I've never even been to Tierra del Fuego! This is mole's work, Edgar! Mark my words!"

Sam glanced around nervously, then pressed his face into the duffel bag.

"Could you guys hold it down in there!"

When Sam looked up he was staring straight into the face of Madame Zorah, the old gypsy.

"*You* again!" she cried, grabbing him by the shoulders with her sinewy fingers. "The strange boy with three souls! Do you know how long I searched for you that day! My husband Gregor thought I was crazy!"

Sam swallowed hard and tried to push the talking duffel bag around to his back.

"What is this? You are a ventriloquist now, too, strange boy?"

Sam gulped again as Madame Zorah took her hands off his shoulders and reached around to touch the bag. The old gypsy gasped and began to swoon.

"So it wasn't a crazy dream! More souls than I can count now! *What* are you, boy?"

Clutching her head, Madame Zorah staggered back. Sam slipped past her and began running toward the people that were streaming into the amusement park.

"No!" Madame Zorah screamed. "Come back! I must know more!"

Sam didn't turn around once until he was certain he was safely lost in the crowd. When he did look back, Madame Zorah, her hands still clutched to her head, was scanning the amusement park trying desperately to find him. Sam felt a hard blow to his chest just then, as he suddenly collided with something.

"Hey! Watch where you're..."

The voice was familiar. Sam looked up and gasped. It was Basil Mandrake.

"Well, well, well, if it isn't Middleton! Just the jerk I've been looking for!" Basil sneered.

"SAM! SAM!"

Sam and Basil both looked up. Fletcher and India, their Ferris wheel ride over, were hovering above them in a swinging seat, waiting to get off.

While Sam was still looking up, Basil suddenly lunged, tearing the duffel bag straps off his shoulder.

"Whadya got in here, Middleton?" Basil taunted, twirling the bag over his head. "The crown jewels or something?"

"No!" cried Sam. "Give it back!" He reached his arm out to grab it, but Basil kept spinning the bag out of his reach.

"Not so fast!" Basil chuckled. "Must be something pretty important for you to get all choked up about it! Maybe I'll just keep it for myself."

Basil shoved a big hand into Sam's chest and pushed him to the ground before turning on the heels of his big black boots and bolting through the crowd, the duffel bag dangling from his shoulder.

Spurred by a rush of adrenaline and the fear of what might befall his friends, Sam raced along behind. Basil seemed to know exactly where he was going, cutting through amusement ride service lanes and dodging down food stall alleys. He was heading all the way out to the campground. With everyone at the park enjoying the festival, Basil easily made his way between the deserted campsites and through to the woods beyond. Hot in pursuit, Sam flinched every time Basil lurched too close to a tree, slamming the duffel bag into its hard surface.

Basil suddenly stopped when they reached a clearing. He spun around to face Sam, took the duffel bag off his shoulder and began to twirl it above his head again. Sam, gasping for air, felt sick. The sweet scent of cedar trees filled his nostrils, but there was something else in the air, too. A putrid, moldy smell, like something rotting, and then another odor—this one unmistakably mothballs.

"That's quite *enough*, Basil!" a voice cried out angrily. "You've got him here now, there's no need to endanger the merchandise any further!"

Basil made an unpleasant face before he dropped the duffel bag on the ground and gave it a few kicks with the toe of his boot.

Avery Mandrake strolled out from behind a tree and into the center of the clearing. He was holding a steel briefcase in his hand and smiling at Sam like a snake that had just swallowed a mouse.

"Well, young Middleton. We meet again. The last time I saw you, you and Cedric Hawthorne were leading me on quite a dance in that circle, weren't you? Well, it's time to face the music, boy! I believe you have something that I want."

"I...I don't know what you're talking about," Sam stammered.

"Oh, please! Let's not play games!"

Mandrake knelt down and snapped the steel case open. He reached his hand inside and pulled out a shining silver tube. Sam gulped.

"Look familiar?" he hissed, holding it up for Sam to see. "I believe yours probably looks just like this one. And you *do* have it, don't you boy? In fact, I'll bet you've got it with you now, just like me. Wouldn't want to let a thing like that out of your sight for too long." He suddenly looked up and snapped at his son.

"Check the bag, Basil!"

Basil reached down and unzipped the duffel bag. He pulled the sides open and poked his arms inside.

"There's no tube in here, Dad!" he yelled at his father. "Just a bunch of creepy stuffed animals. Aww," Basil teased, "still can't leave home without your little toys, huh, Middleton?"

Basil stood up and kicked the bag behind a tree. Professor Mandrake look annoyed, then started to smile again as he stared at Sam.

"That fishing vest," he mused. "I've seen it before, haven't I? Lots of lovely pockets and things."

Mandrake had started to walk toward Sam when there was a rustling in the leaves beside them. India and Fletcher bolted out of the trees and into the middle of everything.

"Stand back children!" Mandrake warned with a steely glare. "This doesn't concern you. It's between young Middleton here and myself. He has taken something that's very precious to me and I intend to have it."

"Sam! Are you okay?" India cried.

Fletcher, puffing himself up with a big breath of air, started to walk forward.

"Basil!" Mandrake snapped. "Take care of them! I'm too busy to be bothered with these annoying distractions."

Basil grabbed Fletcher by the scruff of his neck and lifted him clean off his feet, then carried him back to India and dropped him with a hard thump on the rocky ground. Fletcher, wincing as he rubbed a deep cut on his temple, rose to his knees for a moment before slumping forward again and losing consciousness. India lunged at Basil, managing to give him a good kick in the shin before he grabbed her by the neck and hurled her down beside her brother. Basil placed himself in front of the two of them, thick arms folded, as unmovable as an army tank, while India struggled in vain to get past him again.

Sam, still fighting for air after his race through the woods, flailed his arms about helplessly as Mandrake took him in a rough headlock and spun him around. He tore into the lining of Sam's vest with one great rip and pulled the scroll tube out with a victorious cry. Still holding Sam tightly around the neck with one arm, Mandrake threw the tube into his briefcase and closed it with his foot. He reached into his pants pocket and pulled out a ball of thick nylon rope, tossing it across to Basil.

"Make sure they don't have a chance to spoil things any further!"

Basil tied the struggling India and a now semi-conscious Fletcher to the base of a nearby trunk with obvious enjoyment, while Mandrake kept Sam in a headlock. As soon as Basil was finished with them, Mandrake held Sam down so that Basil could finish the job.

Smoothing his hair and straightening his tie, Mandrake picked up the briefcase and smiled again.

"Well, I'm afraid I must be off! I have a pressing engagement." He looked up through the trees at the balloons floating high overhead. "Actually, I really must fly!" he chuckled with glee, before he turned and started to sprint away through the trees.

Basil, twirling the rope around Sam's wrists with a huge smirk on his face, suddenly started to twitch uncontrollably. The smirk melted away as Basil clutched frantically at his clothes.

Meanwhile, inside the overturned duffel bag, The Sage were trying to recover from their ordeal. While Beatrice nursed her reinjured ankle, Hazel tended to a large bump on Filbert's head. Winchester Redwood, wincing in pain from what he suspected to be a dislocated shoulder, was trying to help Mr. Goodfellow set things upright again so they could rest more comfortably. The most upset of all, though, was Porter. Pressing his face into Beatrice's shoulder, he sobbed inconsolably over the loss of Duncan, who had gone missing in action somewhere along the way.

Although he had sustained only minor cuts and bruises, Edgar was feeling terribly nauseated. He climbed to the top of the bag, and put his head outside for a breath of fresh air. When that seemed to help, he got out and slid down the side of the bag to stretch his legs.

"Edgar Goodfellow!" said a surprised voice behind him. "I remember you! Still following that stupid human of yours, are you?"

Edgar spun around. Bogg Fen, rubbing his bony white hands together in glee, was slithering toward him, his black cloak fluttering. Edgar shuddered as he stared at Bogg's long sharp nails, remembering the time they had torn all the way through his mouse suit and gashed him viciously.

"Uncle Shrike will be so pleased with me when I bring you back to him," hissed Bogg, as he circled slowly around Edgar. "We didn't get a chance to finish things off properly, did we, Sage?"

"Not so fast!" Mr. Goodfellow suddenly called from the top of the bag. "Can you handle both of us, young Fen!"

Bogg looked up and sneered.

"It's my first assignment, so Uncle Shrike's given me some helpers. It's a Fen tradition."

When Bogg clapped his long sharp nails together, two dark figures swooped in from the shadows and stood at either side of him.

"A pathetic display, if you ask me!" shouted Winchester Redwood. He stood beside Mr. Goodfellow, trying his best to conceal his wounded shoulder.

Filbert, sweeping the few strands of hair he had left over the huge bump on his forehead, came out of the bag next.

"Hardly a fair match is it, Fen?" he said, as lucidly as he could through the lingering effects of a concussion.

Bogg began to sway, then quickly caught himself.

"Foolish Sage!" he screamed, billowing his cloak around him.

Bogg moved closer, unaware that his companions were already scurrying back into the shadows. Suddenly noticing that he was alone, he turned and shrieked at them.

"Cowards! When I tell my uncle, he'll have you both flattened!"

"Excuse me," said Mr. Goodfellow, pointing across the clearing. "I wouldn't be as concerned about them as I would about your assignment over there, young Fen. You really should attend to him. He seems to be having a spot of trouble. I don't imagine Uncle Shrike will be very pleased with you now, will he?"

Growling with anger, Bogg turned around to see Basil Mandrake still in the throes of some sort of peculiar dance as he wiggled and twitched.

"I'll finish it with you one day, Sage!" screamed Bogg, shaking his fist at all of them before he swept his cloak around him and hurried back to Basil.

Filbert whispered into his brother's ear. "I say, that was a bit of a risky bluff, wasn't it Jolly? If they'd actually decided to challenge us in the state we're all in, I dread to think..."

"All's well that ends well, right Filbert?" Mr. Goodfellow interrupted, patting him gently on the shoulder before he turned to the figure at his other side.

"I say, Redwood, that was awfully decent of you."

"Ahh, don't mention it, pal," Redwood replied, as they all climbed back into the bag. "Couldn't have you gettin' all clawed up out there, could I? Beatrice would never forgive me." He gave Mr. Goodfellow a little wink.

While Basil was preoccupied, Sam wriggled out of his ropes, rushed behind the tree to retrieve his duffel bag, and returned to untie India and Fletcher, still groggy from Basil's assault.

"India," Sam whispered, "somebody's got to go and make sure Professor Hawthorne's alright. Fletcher, find your dad and tell him what's happened, okay?"

Sam threw the ropes on the ground and shoved his duffel bag into Fletcher's still somewhat shaky hand.

"Take care of this for me, Fletch. I'm going after Mandrake!"

Just then, Basil shrieked in horror as he pulled something out of his shirt with his hand and hurled it to the ground.

"EEYOOO!" he screeched. "It's a worm! I hate worms!" To everyone's surprise, Basil burst into tears. "I didn't know those stupid things could bite like that!"

With his nose streaming, Basil bent down to crush the worm, but it had disappeared. By the time he looked up again to check on his prisoners, he was alone.

21

To the Brave and Faithful Nothing Is Impossible

A very! You finally made it!" Tippy Stanwyck called out from the basket of the tethered real estate balloon as Professor Mandrake, clutching the steel briefcase under his arm, raced across the grass toward her.

"I'm so glad you got my little note! I'll pour the champagne, darling!" she cried.

"I don't care," snapped Professor Mandrake, as he tossed the case into the basket with a grim expression. "As long as it doesn't take all day!"

"Yoo-hoo! Captain Carew!" Tippy shouted, cupping her hands to her lips. "I believe we're ready to lift off for our little sightseeing tour now!"

A very large man in a scruffy pilot's uniform waved to her from the opposite end of the field, then pointed repeatedly at his wristwatch before he turned back to his companion to finish their conversation.

"Why isn't he coming?" snarled Professor Mandrake, as he struggled to pull himself into the basket.

"I'm sure he'll be along presently," said Tippy, offering Mandrake a glass. "We have the rest of the afternoon to enjoy ourselves. We don't have to rush, do we, dearest?"

"Perhaps you don't, Tippy," he barked into her ear, "but I'm a busy man and I hate to be kept waiting!"

Tippy backed as far away from him as she could and started to pout.

Ms. Spender had been watching the lovers' rendezvous unfold from a distance. Wracked with sobs of betrayal, she crept into one of the gypsy performer's tents, emerging seconds later with something that she had stuffed under her pink sweater. She inched her way toward the balloon basket until she was directly beside one of the tether ropes that secured it to the ground. Pretending to play with François, she withdrew from under her sweater the knife she had found and made short work of the first rope. Casually she sidled over to the next one.

Abigail Spender was still sobbing as she cut the last rope. Freed from its tethers, the balloon's large wicker basket lurched forward. Avery Mandrake, struggling to regain his balance, accidentally grabbed the gas lever on the burner above his head. A burst of bright orange flame rose through the neck of the open balloon, heating the air inside and pulling the basket and its startled occupants high above the crowd. The screams of surprise from Professor Mandrake and his ladylove were music to Ms. Spender's ears. It would have been a perfectly wonderful moment of triumph for her had it not been for François, who, distraught over his mistress's grief, had suddenly decided to defend her honor.

With all the strength in his spindly poodle legs, François had leapt at the side of the basket as it floated away, dug his manicured nails into the woven sides, then dragged himself up and over the edge. He lunged at Mandrake's face, sinking his sharp little teeth right into the end of Mandrake's long, pointed nose.

"Oh, Avery!" screamed Tippy Stanwyck, as a powerful gust of wind swept the basket further up into the sky. "We're going higher! Do something! Save us!"

"I don't know how to fly this blasted thing! And if you haven't noticed, I have a poodle on my face!" he screamed back. "Get this wretched little animal off me!"

The festival crowd realized that this was not a regularly scheduled flight and swarmed onto the field below. Captain Carew waddled over to the center of the crowd, shook his chubby fist in the air and called out some incomprehensible flight instructions. Tippy Stanwyck's screams grew fainter until she could barely be heard above the cries of anguish from Ms. Spender as she watched her beloved François sail away, too.

Following the cries from the runaway balloon, Sam came upon the strange scene as he emerged from the woods. He noticed a bright glint of sunlight reflecting off the steel brief-case wedged under Mandrake's arm. When the balloon passed directly overhead, Sam turned and started to run with it. It floated toward the fields of tall grass and on to the dunes that bordered the tidal river beyond. At the wide mouth where the river met the sea, the balloon showed no signs of slowing down. Another gust of offshore wind suddenly pushed it upward. Tippy Stanwyck screamed and grabbed hold of the basket's sides as Professor Mandrake, still trying to pry François off his nose, lost his footing completely and stumbled into her. The steel briefcase slipped from Mandrake's grasp and teetered on the edge of the basket for a second or two before plummeting into the deep water of the tidal river below. Shrieking with rage, Professor Mandrake broke free from François with one great pull and hurled the dog out of the basket, too. Legs flailing, the little poodle dropped through the air and hit the water with a huge splash.

By the time Sam reached the riverbank, another blast of wind had started to sweep the balloon back inland toward the crowd of people who were racing to catch it. Sam could see the briefcase begin to sink as the river, rushing out on an ebb tide, started to carry it toward the sea. Sam threw his shoes and socks onto the sand and waded through the water toward it, until he heard François' pitiful cries. The little dog was clinging to a piece of bobbing driftwood that kept pulling him under with the current. Sam turned and splashed toward the drowning poodle, stopping for only a second to look back at the case. It was disappearing under the water and heading out to sea.

"Decisions, decisions! What a dreadfully delicious dilemma!"

Sam spun around. The voice that was calling out to him from shore was unpleasantly familiar. His head began to throb.

"What are you going to do now, human?" Shrike Fen cackled, pulling his wet cloak around him. "What will you choose: a pair of priceless scrolls, with a power that could seal the fate of all humankind, or the life of a stupid dog? Really, Sam, it can't be all that hard, can it? Why, if you listened to me for a change, you wouldn't have to be making all these tiresome choices. Everything would be so much easier."

The words slithered out of Shrike's mouth and into Sam's thoughts as the Fen dragged himself down the sand.

"I bought myself a little present, see?" Shrike opened one side of his cloak to reveal a shiny metal leg. "So much more durable than the last one, I find. I was furious when I found myself tumbling out of that basket just now. It's not like me to go absent in mid-assignment, especially this one. That man

is a spineless simpleton without me! But it has turned out to be a most fortunate turn of events, after all," he hissed with delight. "Who would have thought that I would have you all to myself one day, with no annoying Sage about to help you, and in the middle of such a troubling decision? This is just too good to be true!"

"Get away from me, Shrike Fen!" Sam shouted.

"Go on, Sam," Shrike hissed again, creeping closer. "Save the scrolls, boy. You know what you have to do, don't you? Your future depends on it! Well, the future you and your kind envision, anyway. You couldn't possibly leave them floating around for someone like Mandrake to find again, could you? Let the animal drown. He's almost had it by the looks of him," Shrike sneered, then shuddered. "Oh, I do so despise those horrid things!"

"You're lying, Fen!" Sam cried through the pain that was tearing into his head. "You're trying to trick me! I can't let him drown, not even for the scrolls! I know what you're trying to do! Edgar Goodfellow warned me! When you have *me*, you will have everything else that you want, too!"

The sound of François' whimpering filled his ears, and Sam stumbled further out into the river. The current of the outgoing tide swirled around his legs and knocked him off his feet and he started to swim. The little poodle stopped crying, his strength gone. A few seconds more and he would slip beneath the waves for the last time. Sam reached him, grabbed him around the middle and started swimming back to shore.

"Have it your way then, human!" Shrike snarled. "Not really what I had in mind, but it will be entertaining enough, I suppose, to watch both of you drown."

As he struggled to swim through the swirling water, Sam could feel Shrike Fen poking through his thoughts again.

Exhausted and weak, he tried to block out the invasion, but it was futile.

"Oh, so that's the plan, is it?" Shrike suddenly howled. "Well, Cedric Hawthorne is a blind fool! Thinking he could show the world the scrolls and that everyone would see the light. Such a noble idiot! Why, our Fen network has thousands of devoted humans just waiting for an opportunity like that."

"No!" Sam yelled, trying desperately to keep François's head above the waves.

"Fool! Look at the world not as you would wish it, boy, but as it truly is! If you come to me now, I'll save you and the wretched animal. You won't regret it! I can promise you a position of great power in the new order of things."

"Never!" cried Sam, coughing as the seawater began to find its way into his throat. "If the scrolls are found again, neither you nor anyone who listens to your wicked promises will get their hands on them. Not as long as there is someone here to protect them!"

"What?" Shrike smirked. "Like you, boy?"

"I'd do it!" Sam shouted out. "And for as long as I live, too, Fen!" At that moment, as the words drifted from his mouth, Sam felt in his heart that his true destiny had been sealed.

"As long as you live, is it?" Shrike suddenly crowed. "Well then, we'll just have to do something about that, won't we?" He slithered further down the bank, closer to Sam and François. "I've just been getting myself warmed up, stupid boy! Now you're going to find out what it's really like to die by the will of a Fen!" He rattled his wet cloak, then threw the black hood back from his white, bony head and fixed his steel cold eyes on Sam.

Sam felt the final onslaught of Shrike's evil thoughts taking over as he battled to keep afloat. He tried to fight back, as he had once before, with the only thoughts that he knew could

defeat The Fen. But as soon as a vision of his mother and father, of Figgy, Fletcher, Beatrice, Mr. Goodfellow or even Edgar floated into his mind, Sam felt it slip away. All he wanted now was the sweet, painless refuge of sleep.

As his grip on François began to loosen, Sam felt something next to him in the water, moving through his legs and around his arms and pushing up against his chest. When he managed to open one eye, Sam was sure he could see little blobs of yellow, bobbing up and down with the waves. In his current state, he could make no sense of what was happening, but with relief, he rested his aching head on the flotilla of miniature yellow rafts that were now encircling him and François. The last thing Sam remembered was a great flurry of activity on the river shore and the hideous shrieks of surprise and horror from Shrike Fen. He lifted his head for just a moment and squinted his eyes to see a brown, bounding figure tearing up and down the sand.

"Figgy? Is that *you*?" Sam called, before he dropped his head again on the little, yellow cushions and fell into an exhausted sleep.

The next time Sam opened his eyes he was in his own room. His mother and father, both looking pale and worried, were sitting on the edge of the bed.

"Oh, thank goodness," his mother sighed, dabbing her eyes with a tissue.

Sam tried to lift himself up on his elbows.

"Take it slow now, Sam, okay?" he could hear his father saying. "The doctor wants you to rest a bit longer. You swallowed a lot of seawater out there."

Sam scanned his room nervously and was relieved to see the duffel bag in the corner. Fletcher had remembered to return it.

Everything else looked the same, except for an enormous flower arrangement that was perched on top of the old bookcase.

"They're from Ms. Spender," his mother explained.

"That little dog means the world to her," added his father. "I don't think she quite knows how to thank you."

"Is he okay?" Sam croaked.

"It didn't look good at first, but he's going to pull through," said Sam's father, just before he grabbed the tissue out of his wife's hand and let off a huge sneeze. "Anyway, why don't you ask Figgy?" he said. He turned around just then, as Sam's door slowly opened. "They've been roommates at the animal hospital for the last day and a half."

"Figgy! What happened?" Sam croaked again.

"He found you both lying on the shore," explained Sam's father. "They say that when that runaway balloon flew over him, he snapped his leash and set off like the dickens. He got a little banged up along the way, I'm afraid. It's really dreadful what some people leave lying around outside." Trevor winced. "Poor fellow got a steel rod right through his jaw. Haven't been able to figure out what the devil it is yet, either." He reached for something in his pocket and dangled it in front of Sam. "It's one of those funny little tools, I guess. Actually, I've been using it to tighten the screws in my glasses. Handy little gadget!"

Sam gulped as his father tossed Shrike Fen's artificial leg up in the air a few times before popping it back in his pocket.

"Fletcher's telephoned about a hundred times, too. If you're feeling up to it later, we may let you have a visitor."

Sam nodded his head, then reached down to touch the top of Figgy's bandaged muzzle.

"Try to get some more rest," suggested his mother, as she and Trevor headed out the door. "We'll be back in a while to check up on you."

Sam smiled as his father closed the door behind him. Figgy jumped onto the bed and curled up beside him. For the next few minutes, Sam lay in quiet reflection, still feeling a little groggy as he tried to remember everything that had happened. A gentle rustling from his chest of drawers drew his attention across the room.

Sam's sock drawer slowly opened. A long line of assorted footwear, tied together at the ends, suddenly pushed out the top and fell to the floor. A little group of Sage followed, each one carefully maneuvering his or her way down the sock rope in single file, then silently scurrying across the floor and up the edge of Sam's comforter.

Filbert and Hazel, hand in hand, greeted Sam first and asked how he was feeling. Then it was Charlotte and Porter. According to Porter's excited translation, Duncan's arduous trek back to the festival, slipping with his last ounce of strength into the fortune-teller's tent and the safety of Rollo's arms, almost rivaled his now-legendary assault on Basil. Too exhausted to travel any further, Duncan had been transported back to Sam's in a makeshift sling. Duncan, now a hero on the same level (at least in Porter's mind) as Figgy and Brunhilda, was draped around his master's shoulders, basking happily in the glow of instant celebrity. Edgar came next, still apologizing to Mr. Goodfellow for slipping on a sock and accidentally pushing a mouse claw up his uncle's nose on the way down the rope. Beatrice, carrying something in her hands, was last. As she drew closer, Sam could see that it was a Scandinavian Sea Mouse Knife. She made her way up the comforter and placed the knife in Sam's lap.

"This arrived last night by mouse courier, dear," Beatrice announced. "Extra Special Express."

"It's mine?" Sam asked in surprise.

"Indeed it is." Beatrice rummaged around in her mouse suit and pulled out a tiny piece of paper. "There was a lovely note attached. If you'll allow me, I will attempt to translate it. It's written in Sea Mouse, of course."

Beatrice wrinkled her nose as she attempted to decipher its odd scratches. *"While undergoing annual cold-water rescue trials off the coast of Maine,"* she began slowly, *"a band of operatives was summoned by the cries of a creature in peril some distance away. We would like to acknowledge that without the quick actions of Samuel Henry Middleton, the drowning creature would surely have perished before our arrival. We wish to honor Mr. Middleton with the customary gift of a Sea Mouse Knife in recognition of this unselfish act of bravery in the face of his own possible peril."*

Sam picked the knife up between his fingernails and stared at it.

"Wow," he exclaimed quietly.

"A great honor, my boy," remarked Mr. Goodfellow. "You must send a thank-you note as soon as possible."

"And a penny, too," whispered Sam.

"Indeed!" Mr. Goodfellow replied, smiling.

"There seems to be a postscript at the end of the note here," Beatrice suddenly announced. "Apparently, there was some minor damage to the inflatable raft while they were packing it. They promise to forward it separately, when the repairs are complete."

Beatrice put the note down and sighed. "I really think it's time they redesigned those things."

Sam turned the knife over a few more times, then looked up at The Sage that had gathered round him. One was missing.

"Where's Mr. Redwood?" he asked.

"With Fletcher's father," replied Mr. Goodfellow. "Professor Jaffrey's brilliant paper, 'Mars: The Cradle of Civilization,' was presented this morning at a Science Society news conference. He and Professor Hawthorne made the decision to come forward with it as scheduled. They were hoping that the scrolls might be found in the meantime. Actually, I should be heading back to the Jaffrey house as soon as possible. Professor Hawthorne is alone at the moment, and I imagine he may be in need of some encouraging words. Early reaction to the paper hasn't been quite what he'd hoped for, I understand."

"They're calling Fletcher's father a crackpot," Edgar commented.

"Poor Professor Jaffrey," sighed Sam.

"The burden of proof for the statements made in the paper will no doubt weigh quite heavily on Sanjid Jaffrey's shoulders," said Mr. Goodfellow. "It will be hard convincing anyone to believe him now, considering there is no physical evidence to back him up."

"No scrolls," Sam commented.

"Not even a scroll sliver," added Filbert.

"But it's not fair!" Sam suddenly cried. "The story in the crop circles! The voyage of the Martians to Earth! Professor Hawthorne was there; he heard everything!"

"But Avery Mandrake has made quite sure that his 'esteemed' colleague will never be believed if he comes forward, Sam," explained Mr. Goodfellow.

"But I was there, too!" Sam cried again. "I saw it with my own eyes and ... and ..."

"Will anyone believe that you were catapulted into a crop circle one night while on vacation in Wiltshire? Or that you met up with an eccentric old professor now generally considered to be unhinged? And that while inside the other-dimensional world of the crop circle, the origin of human civilization was revealed to you both by a message that was tens of thousands of years old?" asked Mr. Goodfellow. "And from Martians, no less?"

"No one's going to believe me either, are they?" sighed Sam, dropping his head back down on his pillow. "Hey, wait a minute!" he suddenly cried, as he sat up again. "What about Mandrake! He was in the crop circle, too! He knows that Professor Jaffrey's paper is true!"

"All Mandrake really cares about is getting his hands on the scrolls," explained Filbert. "His attempts to discredit Sanjid Jaffrey and those cruel lies he started about Cedric Hawthorne serve his own best interests. In fact, I believe it was Mandrake himself who uttered the 'crackpot' reference to the media this morning. He's calling the Jaffrey paper an outrageous piece of bunk."

Sam lay his head on the pillow again and closed his eyes. Avery Mandrake was *such* a conniving monster, he thought. He wished he could do something. Sam was lost in thought when he felt a gentle tapping on his arm. It was Edgar's parents. Sam quickly sat up again.

"We've decided to head back to England for a while, Sam," said Filbert.

"We've come to say good-bye, pet," added Hazel, squeezing her husband's hand.

"We were apart for such a long time. We need to spend some quiet moments at home together, just to get reacquainted."

"We'll be back before too long, though," said Filbert, giving Sam an affectionate pat on the arm.

Sam's eyes suddenly shot across the bed to Edgar. Hazel could sense his anxiety.

"Edgar will be staying on with you," she reassured him. "He'll have it no other way!"

"And I won't be far away either, my boy," said Mr. Goodfellow. "Professor Hawthorne will be needing me for a bit longer and then, of course, there's Fletcher. I expect I'll be spending quite a bit of time at the Jaffreys' in the future." He let out a long sigh. "It appears that Redwood and I are going to have to find a way to get on with each other, after all."

Mr. Goodfellow looked straight at Beatrice just then.

"Which brings me, my dear, to the question of young Porter. Someone is going to have to take the lad and his pet back to California and the Sparrows. I'm sure Hartland and Edwina would want a responsible person to deliver him home. Ever since my beloved trunk was returned to me, I've been feeling like taking a little trip."

Mr. Goodfellow cleared his throat nervously while Beatrice, with a puzzled expression on her face, looked on.

"Northern California is beautiful this time of year, isn't it? What do you say, Beatrice?" he finally blurted out. "Are you up for a few days in those lovely vineyards of Napa again?" Mr. Goodfellow cleared his throat again, took a great gulp of air and closed his eyes. "I've heard tell that it is the perfect place for a honeymoon."

There wasn't another sound in the room. Mr. Goodfellow was too frightened to open his eyes, until he suddenly felt Beatrice's paw in his.

"I'd be delighted, Jolly," she whispered.

"Well, it's about time!" cried Filbert, rushing forward to give his younger brother a hearty slap on the back. "Congratulations, old man!"

After a round of congratulatory kisses, Sam suddenly noticed that Charlotte was being particularly quiet.

"Is Charlotte okay, Edgar?" Sam whispered.

"I think she's just a little nervous. The Governing Council

sent her a letter yesterday, notifying her of her very first assignment. Actually, that's why she's not going home to California with Porter."

"Huh?" said Sam.

"Her assignment is India Jaffrey," said Edgar, grinning.

Sam raised his eyebrows.

When Fletcher came over to visit that evening, he and Sam stood by the window. Together, they gazed up at the moon, just as they had done almost two years ago. Fletcher looked across the sky at the bright light of Mars with a new intensity of purpose.

"I've really got to get there now," he sighed.

"For your dad?"

Fletcher nodded.

"He's right, you know," said Sam. "And when you go to Mars, everyone else will see it, too. You're going to find the proof, Fletcher, I know you are."

The next few days were very busy. School started again, although Sam missed the first two days; Trevor and Peggy Middleton's art exhibition was attracting sizable crowds; and Leonora Jaffrey, inspired by her exciting summer theater run, was once again doing the rounds of auditions as she searched for her next role.

Sanjid Jaffrey returned to the university to start the fall semester, proudly pointing out his first dog show blue ribbon for Most Promising Newcomer to whomever came into his office. The competition had ended in a three-way tie between Luciano, Placido and José, and the ribbon had been awarded just before the balloon fiasco. Some of his fellow faculty members also noticed his sudden and annoying preoccupation with practical joking. Although Professor Jaffrey had been considerably embarrassed by the scientific community's initial reaction to his paper, he was somewhat heartened to discover that there were some colleagues who were genuinely interested in his unusual theories. He continued to firmly believe that one day he (and his silent partner, Cedric Hawthorne) would be vindicated.

At the urging of Sanjid, Professor Hawthorne agreed to take a well-deserved rest at a secluded mountain retreat (actually a small, dilapidated cabin that had been in Leonora's family for years) just a few hours inland. It would be the safest place for him, Sanjid had suggested, until the whole stolen money issue was solved and he could return to town without being arrested. Cedric Hawthorne was happy enough to be left alone for a while, as it gave him time to document the amazing visions of the ancient Martian world he had witnessed in the crop circles and correlate them to Earth's civilization. With the loss of both the scrolls and his research notes, it was unlikely that the crop circle world could be entered again any time soon. Professor Hawthorne would have to work from memory alone.

Professor Mandrake, now fully recovered from the wild balloon ride, had also returned to his university post. Tippy Stanwyck was not quite as quick to forgive his outbursts of temper as he would have hoped and had decided to let their relationship cool for a while. This did afford him more time, though, to pursue something that had just recently piqued his interest. Much to the surprise of almost everyone in town, Mandrake traded his hobby of collecting American folk art for a new one; scuba diving. Every afternoon after classes, and on the weekends (accompanied by Basil), he would rent a small fishing boat and take it out into the bay. There, at the mouth of the same tidal river, he would spend hours mastering his craft.

On the night before Sam was to return to school, Mr. Goodfellow exited the sock drawer and made his way over to the bed where Sam and Figgy were just beginning to settle down.

"Beatrice, Porter and I will be off for California first thing in the morning, my boy. Beatrice is doing some last-minute packing but says she will be along to say her good-byes later. I believe Edgar and Charlotte are giving her a hand." Mr. Goodfellow scratched the top of his head. "Deciding what articles to take along to keep a five-year-old and a worm occupied has turned out to be quite a challenge. I suggested a selection of art supplies for Porter, but Duncan's got me stumped."

There was a loud scuffling noise just then, as Rollo came out of the baseboard mouse hole and raced across the floor toward Sam's bed. Squeaking with great excitement, he stopped every few inches or so and waved his arms above his head.

"Good heavens, Rollo! What is it?" Mr. Goodfellow called out, leaning over the edge of the bed to hear what the little black gypsy mouse was trying to tell him.

"For Sam, you say? Really?" he exclaimed. "Well, thank you, Rollo! Yes, I'll tell him."

Mr. Goodfellow hoisted himself back onto the bed.

"There's been rather a large delivery for you, Sam. In two parts, actually. It took a whole platoon of mouse couriers just to get it here," Mr. Goodfellow explained excitedly.

"What is it?" asked Sam, puzzled.

"Two shiny metal cylinders, Sam. No note this time, I'm told. Just an inflatable raft attached to one of them, with *your* name on the side."

"The scrolls!" shouted Sam. "The Sea Mice found them!"

Mr. Goodfellow nodded and smiled.

"But why did they send them *here*?" Sam asked. "To *me*?"

"Do you remember something I once told you?" Mr.

Goodfellow asked. "About animals being spirits many thousands of years old, much older than even The Sage? They are able to sense many things that we cannot fully comprehend." Mr. Goodfellow paused for a moment. "But if you search deep enough, Sam, I think you may find your answer."

"What?"

"Think about it, my boy. It's just as the message in the crop circles decreed, isn't it? One day, there would be someone chosen to protect the scrolls until the time for their unveiling was right; one who would defend them from all who follow a dark path. It is a prophecy that I've been puzzling about ever since we returned. But if you look deep inside yourself, Sam, I think you will discover what your role in all of this really is."

"I *think* I know," answered Sam quietly.

"And Edgar," Mr. Goodfellow continued. "It's with him, too. I'm sure of it. That's why The Sacred Seal that should have been dissolved between the two of you could not be broken. The bond remained intact so that you would not have to carry this burden alone."

"But what should I do?" asked Sam.

"Only you can decide," Mr. Goodfellow answered.

"But what about Fletcher's father and Professor Hawthorne?" he sighed. "The scrolls could prove everything..."

"Indeed, they could, Sam. But you must weigh the risks and choose wisely, however difficult the decision may seem. Follow your heart, my boy, and it will never steer you wrong. Remember?"

Feeling restless now, Sam got out of his bed and walked to the window. As he looked up at the moon, he couldn't stop his eyes from wandering back to that bright speck of Martian light just a few inches of sky away. Mr. Goodfellow, gently patting Figgy on the top of his head, suddenly called out.

"There's something else that you've been wanting to ask me, isn't there, Sam? I can feel it. It's something that's been preying on your mind."

Sam, still staring out the window, spoke in a whisper. "In the crop circle, when Shrike Fen was trying to escape..."

"It's those intriguing knobs of his, isn't it?" Mr. Goodfellow interrupted. "And why The Sage have them, too?"

Sam nodded.

"Another mystery for us to solve, Sam," Mr. Goodfellow remarked reflectively. "For now, just keep your eye on that spot of light in the sky, my boy. I have the strangest feeling that there are greater mysteries out there than we have even begun to imagine."